UNIVERSAL PICTURES PRESENTS
A GORDON COMPANY /
DAVIS ENTERTAINMENT COMPANY /
LICHT AND MUELLER PRODUCTION
A KEVIN REYNOLDS FILM

KEVIN COSTNER

"WATERWORLD"

DENNIS HOPPER
JEANNE TRIPPLEHORN
TINA MAJORINO

MUSIC BY MARK ISHAM   COSTUME DESIGNER JOHN BLOOMFIELD
LINE PRODUCER GENE LEVY   FILM EDITOR PETER BOYLE
PRODUCTION DESIGNER DENNIS GASSNER
DIRECTOR OF PHOTOGRAPHY DEAN SEMLER A.C.S.
EXECUTIVE PRODUCERS JEFFREY MUELLER
ANDREW LICHT AND ILONA HERZBERG
WRITTEN BY PETER RADER AND DAVID TWOHY
PRODUCED BY CHARLES GORDON · JOHN DAVIS
KEVIN COSTNER
DIRECTED BY KEVIN REYNOLDS

A UNIVERSAL RELEASE
© 1995 UNIVERSAL CITY STUDIOS, INC.

DIGITAL dts SOUND

DTS STEREO
IN SELECTED THEATERS

Original Soundtrack
on
MCA CDs & Cassettes

UNIVERSAL
AN MCA COMPANY

Waterworld *Titles from Boulevard Books*

WATERWORLD
WATERWORLD (Young Adult edition)
THE MAKING OF WATERWORLD

WATERWORLD

**A Novel
by Max Allan Collins**

**Based on the motion picture written by
Peter Rader and David Twohy**

BOULEVARD BOOKS, NEW YORK

WATERWORLD

A Boulevard Book / published by arrangement with
MCA Publishing Rights, a Division of MCA, Inc.

PRINTING HISTORY
Boulevard edition / July 1995

ISBN: 1-57297-001-4

BOULEVARD
Boulevard Books are published by The Berkley Publishing Group,
200 Madison Avenue, New York, New York 10016.
BOULEVARD and its logo are trademarks
belonging to Berkley Publishing Corporation.

PRINTED IN THE UNITED STATES OF AMERICA

10 9 8 7 6 5 4 3 2 1

For Rachel Lemieux—
the "best" in any language

"Swiftly, swiftly flew the ship,
  Yet she sailed softly, too:
  Sweetly, sweetly blew the breeze—
  On me alone it blew."

SAMUEL TAYLOR COLERIDGE
The Rime of the Ancient Mariner

PROLOGUE

They say before the polar ice caps melted, people dwelled in neither atolls nor villages, but in land-based "cities," living and working in towering structures called buildings, some of which stretched higher than a dozen windmills. Not all customs then would be foreign to us now: families did live together, in single dwellings, but the most modest of these would put our huts to shame; these lavish abodes of wood and/or brick could be found in the cities, yes, but also, here and there, along rolling green countryside where both animals and plant life were raised on "farms," to create food to nourish a population that spread across oceans of land. Ribbons of rock ran through the land oceans, connecting city and country, and land boats roamed these solid streams at will, with go-juice as plentiful as water. There were even, so it is said, "deserts"—vast stretches of ground so dry, so bereft of water that only spiny plants and spiny critters could grow; this was land that people avoided (imagine!). In those days, solid ground was not the exception but the rule for the feet of men and women, children, too. When was this? How long ago? Well, let me put it this way—it was before the world was thought to be covered with water.

That long.

But this tale, my children, is not of those ancient times, but of that more recent past, a past I can remember, firsthand, when these hands were not weathered and gnarled. It may be hard for you to imagine a time when my face was smooth and my brow unwrinkled, but even the eldest of Elders was once a child.

And once upon a time, when I was a smooth, unwrinkled child, I encountered the legendary figure whom some of you revere as "the Mariner," and whom others of you know by a name even more ancient than the time of buildings many windmills high.

But when I knew the Mariner, at least when I first met him, he didn't really have a name. Perhaps that's why Death could not find him. And he didn't have a home, not really, or people to care for. Is that sad? Yes and no. Having no one made him strong. He was not afraid of anything or anyone, but he could hear for a hundred miles—underwater. He could hide in the shadow of a noon sun—and he could be standing behind you and you wouldn't know it—not till right before he killed you.

Don't be frightened. He was a hero. Well, perhaps not at first; and, if he were here, he would deny the charge, perhaps even take offense at such a notion. But he was one. A hero. He was the bravest man in Waterworld, and he wasn't even a man at all. . . .

1

The water gliding under the bows of the trimaran was more amethyst than blue, as the three-hulled ragtag ship with its single eggbeater sail carved a trio of parallel paths in the smoothness of an endless ocean.

The wind, from the northeast, was so gentle, he was tempted to dive in for a pleasure swim. It was just hot enough to warrant so rash an action, and rash it would be: the Mariner knew the trimaran's seeming near-motionlessness was deceptive. Even as fast as he could swim (and no one was faster), he knew his ship—with the wheel lashed and close-hauled, as it was—could leave him behind in an instant, racing away into that vast sea, chasing the horizon, uncaptained.

Still, it was tempting. The glassy sea was so gently rippled you could forget the dangers beneath. Of course, there were dangers above, as well—some sharks were, after all, human—but the Mariner was well equipped to deal with both.

The gentle wind was perfect trawling weather. His ship—towing a dragline cable—was a cobbled-together collection of aluminum, plastic, and fiberglass, the fossils of an earlier time welded and stitched and glued and hammered together into a forty-foot, oddly fitted craft that was as weathered as its captain and, like him, unnamed. Its three hulls, of equal size, were interconnected with a netting that became a single deck for the ship, and made child's play of maneuvering from one hull to another. And yet for all of this, both captain and craft were oddly sleek, and whether this gray sleekness was an extension of him, or he of the ship, was a question as unanswerable as Waterworld itself.

He lived here, on his nameless ship. His clay-potted lime plant—its dark green fruit adding a rare splash of color to the drabness—was the only other life-form. Wind chimes fashioned from ancient computer boards and printed circuits tinkled and sang a melancholy tuneless tune; a prow-mounted harmonica played its own ghostly nonmelody; and cockpit controls shifted idly with the current. Clothing of his, washed in the salt water, twisted on a line in the breeze. A patchwork sunshade, an easily rocking hammock, a blood-encrusted harpoon gun—these were the company he kept.

A yellow-stained glass beaker at his feet was no

challenge for an aim long since perfected: his urine arced and its splash into the glass was as gentle as that of the lazy waves his ship cut through. Soon, he rebuttoned his pants—cut-off jeans, much older than he—and plucked the beaker of precious yellow fluid from the deck and proceeded to his homemade water recycling system. He poured the piss into the plastic funnel that began the process and stood tapping his foot while the liquid made its passage through the globes and filters and hoses and valves of a contraption whose design had been sold to him at an atoll by a wizened old trader who claimed the original inventor had been "a very great scientist in the Land Days, named Rube Goldberg."

By the time the liquid finished its tortuous journey, and a spigot was turned and the stuff allowed to puddle back into the original beaker, held beneath the contraption by the thirsty Mariner, the urine's yellow cast was but a pale memory.

He held the beaker to his lips, threw back his head, and returned the liquid to his body, saving and sloshing one last gulp, cleaning his teeth, then spitting the remainder with his usual accuracy at the dirt around his potted lime tree.

Weathered, with a wiry muscularity, the Mariner—wearing nothing, at the moment, but those cut-offs, a sheathed knife, and a shell earring—had features of a sort that in another time might have been considered handsome. But his eyes were slits under a brow furrowed by constant watch, and the face was hard and grooved and mostly obscured in a snarl of facial hair that at times mingled with the shoulder-length, sun-brightened brown mane that brushed his shoulders, and concealed a secret.

A sudden creaking lurch of the ship sent him nimbly racing to the stern, where he could see the dragline, attached to its winch, pulled taut over the fantail. An ancient rusty gauge attached to the winch indicated that at 402 feet his trawlnet had snagged something. . . .

With speed and grace, he plucked a zippered rubber salvage pouch from the deck, and grabbed his tool belt, too, snapped it on, and selected a metal weight—just the right one, not too heavy, nor too light—to fasten to the dragline's friction hand brake. Then he stood and flipped a plastic milk bottle hourglass, sending dried fish eggs dribbling through a hole into a tray attached to the winch.

He would have to swim down and transfer the contents of his trawlnet into the salvage bag before that timer ran out, tripping the lever engaging the gear that would automatically reel in the dragline.

This task would take longer, down under that shimmery amethyst surface, than even the most strong-lunged man could manage. But the mariner had not miscalculated: he was not foolish, nor was he worried.

He merely took a few moments to gather deep, hyperventilating breaths, standing on feet whose toes were webbed, flexing the gills behind his ears, beneath the flowing mane.

Then he dove over the side and was swallowed by a welcoming sea.

2

Just as the hourglass ran out of fish eggs, tripping the gear lever, pulling in the dragline, the salvage bag popped up on the surface, near the trimaran, and the Mariner's head bobbed up.

The bag was brimming with booty: the silver discs labeled "Compact DISC Digital Audio" (what had these been for? he wondered), a knobless square red plastic chunk with a gray screen (this was labeled "Etch-a-Sketch"), some empty glass bottles, some plastic bottles, too. And more. A good haul; too much, in fact, for all of it to make it into the salvage pouch. . . .

He pulled himself up and onto the deck, dripping wet, flush with success, depositing a few of the choicer items onto the deck of the central hull. Some of these were too large for the pouch, anyway: a bent ski pole, a broken ski, a discolored pair of ski boots joined by their laces (the first time, in all his treasure trawling, he'd ever snagged a *pair* of shoes!).

The rest of his bounty remained in the floating

bag—he'd have to tug that up on deck, too, or before long it would drift out of reach.

But he allowed himself a moment to focus on one tiny precious item; he'd run across these before, and had seen other traders with working examples, but had himself never found one that would work. A "Bic," it was labeled, but the Mariner had heard them called lighters, these round little sticks.

He flicked it.

A flame erupted from the Bic's tip, and a smile erupted on the Mariner's leathery face. Now wasn't *this* a prize. . . .

His attention snapped at the dual sound of the creak of a boat and the churning of the wake it was creating in these still waters. He flew to the harpoon gun, mounted on the bow, and swung it toward the sounds.

Was this boat approaching, or departing? *Departing*, the Mariner instantly knew. This patched-together, clumsy-looking sloop—smaller than his ship—must have glided up while he was below the surface. Had its one-man captain-and-crew—an Asian drifter in scroungy scraps of leather and cloth—taken the opportunity in the Mariner's absence to board the ship for some quick looting?

The Asian, at the tiller of the sloop, froze in the sights of the harpoon gun. His nervous smile was multicolored—running mostly to shades of yellow and green—but minitoothed. Cautiously, he raised his arms.

"I didn't board you," the Asian said in Hindi. "I wouldn't do such a thing."

The Mariner kept the gun trained on the drifter, but risked a glance around the trimaran. Nothing seemed missing. He lowered the gun slightly, but kept his gun-sight eyes trained on the man.

"You were down there a long time," the Asian said, still speaking Hindi. "Thought maybe something happened to you . . ."

"Or were you hoping?" the Mariner replied in the same tongue.

"No, Anglish," the Asian said, switching to a heavily accented English. "I wish bad luck on no man . . . except maybe Smokers."

Smokers were the worst breed of pirate in Waterworld, barbarians in the sway of a vicious madman called the Deacon.

The Mariner took a step away from his harpoon gun—a sign of good faith. "That depends on whether you consider Smokers 'men.'"

"More like beasts," the Asian said. Suspicion tightened his still-smiling face. "But tell me . . . how does a 'man' stay underwater so long a time?"

"Hull's busted," the Mariner said with a casual gesture. "Hole's so big, there's room to stick your head up and breathe."

"Bad luck," the Asian said, shaking his head. He lowered his hands—cautiously. "But y'know, the Slavers are producin' a good grade of 'poxy these days."

13

The salvage bag of booty was floating past the sloop; did the Asian drifter notice it?

The Mariner said, "But it would cost dearly."

"A handful of dirt—or maybe that wind chime. Or a breeder—if you're the kind of man who deals in flesh."

The Mariner watched his booty bag sail away, caught by the current, that deceptively calm current. "What do you deal in?" he asked the drifter.

"This and that."

"What were you doing waiting alongside my boat?"

The Asian's grin returned. "Just that—waitin'. Waitin' for you."

"For me?"

"For you not to come up." The Asian shrugged. "Then I would have boarded your ship."

The booty bag was still in sight—if his guest would only leave, the Mariner could retrieve it.

But he revealed no anxiety as he said, "Your boat looks familiar. I've seen it before—but not you."

The Asian shrugged again. "Its previous owner didn't need it no more."

"Why is that?"

"He was dead, Anglish. Took it legal—salvage rights." The Asian nodded toward the trimaran. "You had another hour . . ."

"Before you traded up again?"

"That's right." This time he shrugged with only one shoulder. "Just improvin' my means. Can't blame a man."

"At least you waited. I owe you that much."

Raggedy half-gloved hands rubbed the air. "No, no . . . you owe me nothin', Anglish. I got all the supplies I need. See, I just come from an atoll . . . eight days due east, if you're interested."

The Mariner nodded, and looked toward the eastern horizon, watching his salvage bag drift away. Almost absently, he said, "Two of our kind meet, something's got to be exchanged."

"I know the code as well as you, Anglish."

The Mariner's eyes remained on the horizon; but the bag was no longer his main concern. Casually, he said, "You could have taken my boat. I should repay you . . ."

The Asian waved that off, too readily. "Tell ya what—give you this one for free."

Something else out there, on the horizon. "Nothing's free in Waterworld," the Mariner said.

Two puffs of smoke curled from two distant dots on the water. But across that water came a sound that seemed much closer than those dots: engines.

Missing badly, but at full throttle.

The Asian heard it, too, and whipped his head around, toward where the Mariner was watching.

"Smokers," the Asian whispered hollowly, eyes wide with fear. He wet a finger to the air, checking the wind. "Just enough wind to get away clean . . ."

Luck to you," the Mariner said.

"And to you!" the Asian said, swinging the boom

out, adjusting his sail, and immediately the scraggedy sloop was tacking off.

The Mariner was looking at his floating salvage bag, and now the Asian paused in his zigzag course long enough to spot it, as well.

"It's not worth it, Anglish!" he called, shaking his head so violently his body shook, too—and two small, almost round green objects tumbled out of his ragged shirt onto the sloop's deck.

The Mariner flashed a look at his lime tree—and saw it had been stripped of its so-very-valuable fruit.

But the sloop was on its way, now—and its raggedy captain was again shrugging and flashing his colorful, tooth-scarce grin.

"See, you paid me after all, Anglish!" he called.

The Mariner didn't waste a curse on the sea scum—he had other things to do.

Turning to his steering console, he threw levers that converted the ship into something quite unexpected: the eggbeater sail folded into the mast, which extended to twice its height, and a boom appeared from out of the center hull's deck. Sails unfurled—jib, mainsail, mizzen—as the trawler suddenly, almost magically, transformed itself into a sleek racing yacht.

Yanking tiller and lines, the Mariner headed straight for the bobbing booty bag, the trimaran cutting across the glass surface like a speeding arrow.

Others were bearing down on the booty bag, too.

Those dots on the horizon had blossomed into a horrible quartet. The four barely dressed brutes were, as the drifter had rightly called it, Smokers—as fierce as they were stupid, they rode go-juice–burning water sleds (known in ancient times as "jetskis") whose snarling, smoke-pluming engines tore the placid after-noon to shreds as they bore in on the bobbing pouch.

The Mariner knew how savage these dim-witted, muscle-bound marauders were. Being smarter wasn't enough—he'd have to be faster, too. He worked the tiller, trimming the sails, doing the work of an entire crew in fleeting instants. . . .

The trimaran was flying at forty knots when the ship rounded the salvage bag. A long gaff pole in hand, he scrambled out onto an outrigger hull and snagged the bag, even as the ship was coming about hard.

Then the trimaran was going in the opposite direc-tion.

And the four pirates on jetskis almost tumbled off their perches, bringing their little crafts around to take pissed-off pursuit, making foamy wakes, their curses a blur of guttural sound blending with the growl of their air-fouling engines.

Up ahead he could see her: the Asian drifter's sloop. He charted a collision course and was damn near on top of the drifter before the half-dozing man, a half-eaten lime in one lazy hand, realized those crystal-clear engine sounds weren't coming to him across the water, but were perilously close.

The Asian tossed the lime like it had suddenly turned red-hot and tried desperately to trim his sails, yanking sheets to pick up some speed; but the Mariner's trimaran was closing on him.

And the Smokers were ripping across the water, zeroing in on the Mariner's stern.

The Asian let out a pitiful yelp that didn't have time to turn into a scream as the trimaran, on its collision course, suddenly sheeted in on one side, drenching the sloop's deck and its captain, lifting the nearest outrigger hull over the sloop like the wing of a bird.

But that wing snapped the smaller boat's mainmast, cracked it in two.

Looking back at the crestfallen captain of the now-floundering sloop, its mainsail an impotent thing flapping on the deck, the Mariner raised a scolding finger and sent the man a stern look.

You don't break the code.

It was a lesson the drifter was unlikely to live to profit from, considering the whooping war cries of the savages who were now bearing down on him.

The Smokers had, as the Mariner knew they would, abandoned their pursuit of him in favor of swooping in on this easier wounded prey.

"You shouldn't have taken the limes," the Mariner said to the air.

After all, nothing was free in Waterworld.

3

They say that atolls once were islands, rings of land surrounding lagoons; these atolls often consisted of rocklike skeletal marine deposits called "coral." The atolls of Waterworld were skeletal as well, only these atolls were shaped by man, not nature, from the skeletal remains of that earlier industrial time in the Land Days.

A week and a day after his encounter with the drifter and the four Smokers, his trimaran converted to trawler mode, the Mariner—having set an eastern course—approached the sprawling atoll, which emerged jaggedly on the ocean like a mammoth floating trash heap, absurdly golden in the glow of a glorious afternoon sun. The walled circular city—with its occasional jutting guard towers and central lagoon—rose from the hulls of derelict boats. Haphazardly constructed from scraps of metal, wood, plastic, and canvas, settlements like these were cities of odds and ends . . . and that included the population.

As he neared the massive twin gates with their pair of skeletal wood-and-steel, canvas-canopied guard towers, the Mariner could see a desiccated, near-naked man in a one-man bowl of a boat, bobbing in front of the damlike gates of the water city. This pitiful wretch—his excuse for a boat merely one of any number of similar tiny, shabby craft bearing the rabble of Waterworld—was trying desperately to bargain his way inside.

The two gatesmen wore stitched-together-from-this-and-that apparel, typical of atoll dwellers, but matching in a manner that made their rags a "uniform," giving them an official bearing most other Atollers lacked.

The gatesman at left, heavily bearded, scowling, was hollering down at the wretch in the bowl boat. "*Quittez mi camino! La! Departez* my way! *Bizeff!*"

But Polyglot didn't seem to take on the ears of the wretch, who looked up at the gatesman helplessly, shaking his hairy head.

"How many ways can I say it?" the bearded gatesman shouted down nastily. "Go'wan! Beat it! Hit the swell!"

"These hair!" the wretch called back.

An Afrikaner, the Mariner figured.

"These hair," the Afrikaner continued, fluffing that snarled mass like a beautiful woman showing off flowing locks, "to you, I give! Then I take *hydro*—just one small cup!"

The bearded gatesman looked across the way at his

less hirsute comrade in the opposite tower. "Whaddya think?"

The other gatesman nodded, saying, "He does have some bush on 'im."

"You wanna cut a side barter," boomed an imposing voice, "go right ahead. . . ."

The voice belonged to a broad-shouldered, burned-brown muscular figure who walked along a parapet, heading toward the bearded gatesman. On his passage, he nodded to a worker who was hammering lethal looking bone stakes into place along the top of the atoll's protective wall, pointed reminders to keep out. Vested in typical atoll patchwork leather and canvas, this massive figure with the commanding voice needed no uniform for the Mariner to know who he was: every atoll had a guardian at the gate—an Enforcer, they called him.

The man who made sure nobody crashed the party.

". . . 'cause barter makes Waterworld go round," the Enforcer went on. "Just don't open the gates to do it."

There was no menace in his matter-of-fact tone; there didn't have to be. This was a man who could tear your arm off and beat you to death with it.

The bearded gatesman nodded to the Enforcer and began tying a pouch of water on a line. The Afrikaner had himself a deal—but no entry into the atoll.

The trimaran, its eggbeater sail slowly turning, glided into the concave area before the imposing twin gates. The Mariner hoisted the green flag of the trader;

his booty was laid out for inspection on the prow: hubcaps, a "yo-yo," a broken object called a clarinet (apparently a musical instrument), the silver discs labeled CDs, and more of the ancient trash that had become modern treasure.

The Mariner had made himself presentable, as well—in his armless leather-and-canvas jacket, fish-skin pants, and the ski boots he had salvaged last week, he looked a prosperous trader.

Which was, after all, how he saw himself.

Slinging a leather pouch on a strap, he stepped forward on his netting deck and looked up hopefully at the bearded gatesman; the Enforcer stood nearby. Neither of the gazes they sent down to him seemed much impressed.

The Mariner said, *"Quel lang?"*

The Enforcer said, "I'd say yours is Anglish, drifter."

The Mariner nodded respectfully.

"Anglish it is, then," the Enforcer said. All business. "Afraid the flag's down, drifter. We got enough traders in Oasis."

So that was the atoll's name: Oasis.

The Enforcer raised his voice for the farewell: "Move along."

Time to pull out the heavy artillery.

The Mariner lifted the strap, pulling up the leather pouch, and removed the lid from the heavy jar within. He dipped a hand into the jar, scooping up a handful of the priceless substance therein, and allowed it to trickle through his fingers back into its container.

The aroma wafted on the afternoon breeze and tickled the nostrils of the bearded gatesman and the burly Enforcer; they could not repress their smiles. The scent of the stuff within—the real grade-A thing—had an almost aphrodisiac effect on most people.

"Dirt," the gatesman sighed.

The Mariner smiled—just a little.

"Open the gates for him," the Enforcer muttered. He seemed almost woozy from it. Nothing on Waterworld—not the tastiest grilled fish, not the most voluptuous perfumed woman—could compare to the scent of the landed past.

"Hit the water cannons," the Enforcer said casually, and the gatesman followed orders, pelting the Afrikaner and the other rabble in their pitiful boats with wet blasts, keeping them from entering as the tall iron gates swung open for the trimaran.

The four canvas-covered blades of a windmill churned the air lazily, and this looming tower cast its considerable reflection on the lagoon's surface. The windmill was the electricity source of this floating village, and was its highest, most dominant structure.

Even in trawling mode, the Mariner's ship's easy glide and sleek design caught the eyes of the Atollers, solemn, sullen people, their patchwork clothing running consistently to dreary grays and browns, bereft of decoration or jewelry; some wore Asian-style wide-brimmed straw hats, hiding faces as well as eyes.

Moving along walkways from one lashed together boat or barge to another, the Atollers wandered; few seemed to be working at anything much, though a pair of fishermen were stripping the meat off a hanging, gutted shark, the bones of its rib cage poking the air like enormous teeth.

There were no greetings from these water city citizens; no waves, nor hellos. Merely stares—some curious, others openly distrustful. The Mariner offered no greeting, either—just coldly returned their stares.

He gave no sign of noticing, but the Mariner was well aware that the brawny Enforcer had been shadowing along behind him, moving from one walkway to another. That was to be expected. The law always kept an eye on strangers, and the Mariner had spent a lifetime being a stranger. He was used to it.

Before long, the trimaran slipped alongside a sprawling, multitiered, outhouse-dotted organo barge—a pungent fixture in any atoll. Part compost heap, part fruit garden, part cemetery, it was at the moment serving the latter function. Under a tree as mournful as it was massive, a handful of the grieving and a clutch of church Elders—in bizarre seaweed gowns and caps of dried jellyfish—surrounded the corpse of an elderly woman; one of those attending her was in the process of shearing the old girl's hair and depositing it in a pouch.

A somber voice rang across the water as one of the

Elders—a cadaverous individual with an imperious bearing—gave an oratory, as the now-bald corpse was deposited on a mound of organic mush.

"Bones to berries," the Elder bespoke, "veins to vines . . . these tendons to trees, this blood to brine."

The old woman's body began to sink as the mourners revealed garden hoes and began tending rows of fruits and vegetables around her. Then, without so much as a burp from the compost heap, she was gone.

"Too old for life she was, this woman does now leave us. . . ."

The only thing the Mariner hated more than funerals was sermons. He glided on, but the Elder's voice followed him.

"Body recycled and enshrined . . ." The Elder's voice rose grandly. ". . . in the presence of Him Who Leads Us!"

"Right," the Mariner said, and guided his craft toward a grillwork dock. These Atollers were a superstitious lot, the Mariner knew. Living day to day, clinging to survival, they needed something, however silly, to believe in. The Mariner preferred to believe in himself.

He was securing his ship when a menacing shadow fell across him, and the Mariner looked up at a man who seemed taller than that central windmill.

"Remember me?" the Enforcer asked casually.

The Mariner stood, and stood his ground. "I know who you are. What you are."

"Good."

The Enforcer thrust a small iron sundial stake into a hole on the dock.

"You got two hours," the Enforcer said.

"I only need one."

"Less is your choice. More is an infraction. Understood?"

The Mariner nodded.

The Enforcer stood watching as the Mariner, his valuable jar of dirt in the pouch slung over his arm on its strap, yanked from the deck a canvas bag of salvaged treasures; he opened this and plucked out a diagonal rearview mirror from an ancient go-juice land boat.

He started down the dock and stopped one of two tattered kids—boys—who were chasing each other around. The other tumbled into his playmate as the Mariner asked them which way it was to the trading post barge.

"Over there, mister," said the one in front, the one he'd stopped. The boy's eyes got wide at the sight of the diagonal mirror. "What you got there, mister?"

"Something you can see yourself in that isn't water."

"Wow," the boy said. His friend crowded around the shiny object and two dirty faces looked back at their owners.

"Crabs of hell!" the other boy said wonderingly.

The Mariner slapped him on top of the head, not hard. "Don't curse. It's not civilized. . . . This is called a mirror. And it's yours."

"Which one of us?" the first boy asked.

"It's for both of you. You know how to share, don't you?"

"Sure!" the second boy said, liking the sound of getting a piece of the other kid's treasure.

"Well, it's yours," the Mariner said, pointing back at the trimaran, "if everything's here when I get back."

The boys nodded their assurances as he tucked the mirror back in his canvas bag.

The trading barge was nearby, and as he made his way there, a Pied Piper's trail of Atollers followed behind him. Word of his jar of precious dirt had spread across the village like fire chasing oil.

The trading post was part tavern, part store, its high open beams covered with netting that gave the sprawling, expansive room a gauzy openness. There were tables where men traded, and others where they ate and/or drank. One counter served as a bar for the dispensing of various grades of hydro; another, off to one side, served as a sort of bank.

It was at the latter that the Mariner conducted his business.

The dirt from the jar, poured out on a scale, was weighed precisely and handled with the delicacy deserved by so precious a commodity by a portly banker whose eyes were wide with amazement and greed.

"Seven point nine kilos," the banker whispered. "Pure."

A crowd of Atollers had gathered to watch the

transaction, and at this pronouncement, a collective gasp went up. Long ago, gold and silver had been considered precious; those here, on this gently rocking barge where a quantity of dirt was being measured, would have found that notion absurd. Gold and silver had no practical use—and both would sink like the stones they were.

But dirt? Now, there was something wonderful. . . .

"How'd you come by so much of it?" the banker asked.

The Mariner shrugged. "'Nother atoll."

"Which one?"

"Thirty horizons west."

"Hmmm," the banker said. He was mesmerized by the pile of earth on his scale. "Where'd *they* get it?"

"Didn't say."

From the crowd, a scrawny male Atoller called, "I heard about that place! Smokers raided 'em!"

Another atoller called out in agreement: "Yeah! They was all *killed*!"

"That's why they didn't say," the Mariner said.

Worried murmuring passed across the crowd like a wave.

The banker narrowed his eyes, gazed at the Mariner. "*Was* it Smokers, killed them?"

"Don't know," the Mariner said. "Coulda been Slavers. So what's it worth to you?" He pointed at the pile of dirt balancing on the scale. "Are we talking, or trading?"

"How about we tally it like it was pure hydro?" the banker offered, with a smile that tried too hard.

"It's worth more than hydro and you damn well know it."

The banker cocked his head; his smile settled in one chubby corner of his face. "That'd work out to sixty-two chits. That goes a long way, here in Oasis."

"Twice that goes farther," the Mariner said. "And that's what I want."

And that's what he got.

4

At the rear of the trading post, the tavern area was tended by its owner, a strikingly beautiful woman called Helen. Her large, clear eyes were as dark as her lovely hair, which was braided back from a face of carved sensitivity, the gentle sweep of her neck decorated by a beaded necklace, her slender shape housed in clinging net fabric. Many a male tavern-goer sat long after his final cup of hydro was bone-dry, just to continue gazing at her uncommon beauty, those full lips, the swell of her womanly bosom above the leather bodice.

Many in Oasis—as in any atoll in Waterworld you might happen upon—had long since lost all hope, desperately clinging to what Helen well knew was a dying civilization.

What kept her going? What set her apart?

Her belief in the ancient myth of a place called Dryland.

Only to Helen, Dryland was no myth.

That belief—and the very special orphaned child she had been raising—gave her courage to believe in a better tomorrow.

Right now she was serving a pair of scruffy traders who were leaning against the bar, perhaps to get a better peek down that leather bodice. She didn't deny them the view, as long as they kept their distance. Should one risk putting a hand on her, however, she might just have to use the blade beneath the bar, and toss the bloody thing back to him.

"What's so great about dirt?" the younger of the two traders was asking the other.

"You can't eat it," his slightly older companion was saying.

She poured them each a murky tumblerful of grade-three hydro. "You can eat the fruit or vegetables that grow from it," she offered.

"True enough," the younger trader said. "But the amounts you can find won't grow you much of anything." To make his point, he gestured dismissively to a scrawny tomato plant in a pot on one of the nearly bare shelves of the store area, back of the bar, that Helen also owned and tended.

"Can *you* afford that plant?" she asked him with a sly smile.

"That's not the point! The point is, the stuff is highly overvalued, if you ask me!"

"Gullshit," his older companion said. "You'd kill for the stuff, same as me."

"It isn't what you can *do* with the dirt," Helen said.

"It's what it stands for . . . what it reminds us of, in some deep, secret place *born* in us. . . ."

Both traders' eyes had glazed over, hearing these words; she spoke a truth that was basic to Waterworlders.

"Besides," she said, "there's the *promise* it holds."

"Promise?" the younger trader asked.

"Yes," she said, "and the question the dirt asks . . . '*where did I come from?*'"

"Dryland," the older trader said, his voice soft, his tone almost holy.

"That was some dirt that drifter had," the other trader sighed, shaking his head.

"Never seen purer," the older trader admitted.

"A jug," a harsh voice said.

Helen looked up into the hard, cold blue eyes of a muscular, sharkhide-garbed trader with shoulder-length blond hair, and features that would have been handsome had they not been tinged with cruelty. Under the tan, the flesh was fair; he was a Nord.

"Grade two," the Nord said.

She fetched the netted jug, but left her hand on its neck, saying, "Three chits."

He dug out the coins, gave her a lecherous smile, and grabbed the jug from her, going over to a table where a pitiful, balding, tattered wreck of a hydroholic was waiting.

What was a thriving trader doing consorting with a beggar like that? she wondered. Much as she felt sorry for the old man, she'd had him thrown out of the tavern on too many occasions. She had long expected him, like so many hydroholics, to turn up some morning, a floater, after resorting to guzzling salt water.

Now the old boy was sitting at a table with a prosperous looking stranger, apparently about to share a jug of hydro, the Nord buying. Helen didn't like it. She didn't know why, but it made the back of her neck tingle.

As she scrubbed the bar with a rag, the two men began to talk. Helen could not hear this conversation, and that was too bad—because it did, in a not-so-roundabout way, pertain to her.

The Nord, sitting side by side with the raggedy old man, poured a murky tumbler of hydro, while the old man watched with grinning glee.

But when the old hydroholic reached for the glass, the Nord gripped the man's bony wrist—hard.

"That wasn't the deal," the Nord said.

Then the Nord dipped a finger into the jug of water, and licked and sucked the moisture off. The old man watched this with a grotesque combination of pain and delight.

"First," the Nord said, "you tell me."

"It's the child," the old man whispered.

"What child?"

"That woman." The old man pointed.

The Nord looked toward Helen, who was serving another round to the two traders at the bar.

"Are we talking about a woman," the Nord said impatiently, "or a child?"

"Both!"

"Well, then. What *about* them?"

"It's her child, y'see. Well, it's not *her* child. Crabs of hell, I can't think, I can't talk, not without a drink . . ."

The old man reached for the glass again, and the Nord wristlocked him—even harder, this time.

"First info," the Nord said. "Then hydro."

Licking his parched lips, the old hydroholic muttered, "She's raisin' a child. The child ain't hers; she's from somewheres else."

"Another atoll, you mean?"

"No. That's just it . . ." Now the old man's eyes opened, and though they were as murky as the hydro in the glass before him, those eyes glittered. "Dryland."

The Nord snorted. "Dryland's a fairy land."

"Maybe. But this child, she's got marks . . . tattoos, inkings . . . on her back. I've *seen* 'em!"

"Some Slavers mark their women that way," the Nord said with a shrug. He lifted the glass to his own lips and sipped. "That's nothing special. Not worth a glass of hydro, that's for damn sure . . ."

The old man leaned closer; it wasn't just the glass of hydro, close by, that had stirred him up. "But these aren't *Slaver* markings! These markings . . . they say, if you know how to read 'em . . . it's like a *map*. Lead you all the way to Dryland . . ."

35

The Nord let out another derisive snort. "That again. You talk dry rot, old man. . . ."

But the old man was staring at him intensely. "There are some around who still believe. I heard . . . but I ain't gonna tell you what I heard, not if you're gonna be so stingy with that hydro."

"I can be generous. Try me."

The old hydroholic leaned in, even closer, his voice a parched whisper. "Well . . . I heard some traders say that . . . *certain* people got an eye out for the child. They been lookin' for her. See, they heard the stories, too. About the map."

"What 'certain people'?"

"You know. Smokers."

"Smokers, is it?"

The old man nodded gravely.

The Nord smiled at him blandly. "Well . . . we wouldn't want to cross *them*, would we? Best keep all of this to ourselves, old man. What say?"

And he pushed the glass of hydro toward the old man.

"I say you are a generous and kind man, sir!"

The old man began greedily gulping down the fluid, even as another trader was walking up to the bar.

The trader with the shell earring who had caused such a stir with his high-quality pure-grade dirt . . .

As the stranger stepped to the counter, Helen was careful to hide her interest in him. He was a roughly handsome sort, yes, but men didn't interest her. It was the dirt he'd brought with him to Oasis, and its inherent promise of Dryland, that meant so much to her . . . that meant *everything* to her. . . .

But she was all business as she asked him, "Help you?"

He was looking around, as if lost. "Yeah—you run the tavern, right?"

"Right."

"Maybe you could direct me to the store."

She knew how pitifully bare the walls behind her were—wood-and-metal shelving was mostly barren, the netted hanging baskets empty.

"Afraid you're lookin' at it," she said with glum good humor.

"Crabs of hell," he said. "You don't have much to offer."

"Speak for yourself, drifter!" another trader laughed.

Helen didn't offend easily, and normally this wouldn't have embarrassed her. But something about this stranger's demeanor made the moment awkward, and she felt her face redden.

"Can I get you somethin' to drink?" she asked.

"How much hydro you got in storage?"

"Six Gs."

He nodded, the shell earring swinging easily. "I'll take all of it."

"You'll close me down. . . ."

"You'd run out sooner or later, wouldn't you? You're in business to sell it?"

"Yes, but . . ."

"Well, I'll buy it."

37

". . . Okay."

"Got any canvas? Any line?"

"We got line," she said, "but it's hair. No canvas."

"Any bread?"

"No."

"Wood?"

"Just the shelves on the wall, stranger."

His eyes flared. "How 'bout . . . magazines?"

That was rich!

"If I had magazines," she said, "they'd be sold long ago, and I'd be retired."

Magazines were the one thing more valuable than dirt, in Waterworld. Actual pictures of the Land Days . . . what could be more precious?

The stranger slumped, disappointed that his chits could buy so little here in Oasis.

Helen felt a wave of sympathy for him. "How about that drink? I still got a few bottles you didn't buy. . . ."

He nodded, leaning against the counter. "Make it a tall one."

She poured from a jug into a glass, filling it with murky swill.

"What's that, grade two?" he asked.

"Yes . . ."

"The good stuff." He threw a chit on the counter. "Pure."

She reached for another jug and was pouring him a tumbler of clear water when that Nord trader suddenly sidled up to the bar. Next to the stranger . . .

38

"*Skol*," the Nord said to the Mariner. "*Quanto tiempo vous parti?*"

The Mariner ignored this intrusion. He raised the tall glass of hydro to his nose, savored its bouquet. Then he took a small, slow sip.

"*No habla vous Polyglot*, huh?" the Nord was saying.

The Mariner downed the glass in a succession of gulps, like a man who hadn't had a drink in a week.

"How about Anglish, then?" the Nord asked.

The Mariner lifted the empty glass and said to Helen, "One more."

The Nord touched her wrist. "Make it two, sweet one. A man this rich'll buy a glass outa courtesy for a fellow outwater, I'm sure."

She pulled her wrist away and frowned at the Nord.

The Mariner said, quietly, "Just one."

The Nord stared at the Mariner with blank menace that slowly blossomed into a smile. But Helen didn't believe the smile: she had a feeling the stranger's slight would not go soon forgotten by the Nord.

She refilled the glass and went back to cleaning up the bar.

The Nord said to the Mariner, "Some boots you got there."

"They're not for trade."

"Shame. You don't mind my admiring them, surely?"

The Mariner said nothing.

"So, Dirt Man," the Nord said, "how long you been out?"

39

The Mariner looked coldly at the Nord, still said nothing.

"Talk is free," the Nord said.

"Nothing's free in Waterworld," the Mariner said.

"How long you been out? I'm just asking. Making friendly conversation."

The Mariner turned his eyes away from the Nord and sipped the second tumbler of hydro. "What lunar is it?"

The Nord frowned in thought. "Well, let's see . . . Farch, Mapril, June . . . Saugust, isn't it?"

The pair of traders down the bar, half listening to this, nodded agreement.

"That's right," the Nord said, nodding. "Saugust. So. How long you been out, 'tween atolls?"

"Fifteen lunars."

This rocked the Nord. "Fifteen lunars? Holy Provider! Are you kidding?"

The Mariner turned to look at him, slowly. "Does it look like I 'kid'?"

"You're serious. Fifteen lunars . . . don't you like people?" The Nord laughed incredulously, shaking his head; then something caught his attention. His eyes narrowed to cutlike slits. His expression froze.

The Mariner looked to see just what it was that had gotten such a reaction from the man.

It was just a child.

A child coming from behind the tarp doorway of the storeroom behind the counter . . .

She couldn't have been older than seven. Her skin

was darker than that of the lady bartender—the woman was not likely the child's mother, though both were handsome enough. Her netting apparel was similar to the woman's, but the child's midriff was bare; this, and the dreadlocked hair, gave her a look apart from the other Atollers of Oasis. The Mariner thought perhaps the child was Nepali.

The girl moved to a stove—in this weather, it was of course not lighted—and swung it open and dug inside, fishing out bits of charcoal.

As the girl bent over the stove, the back of her netting tunic slipped down, revealing something, what? A birthmark?

No, the Mariner thought, *those are tattoos* . . . a dark circle, a jagged peak, an arrow, and lettering within and around the circle that looked oriental . . .

The Mariner was not the only one who noted this. The Nord's eyes were wide and frozen, and he had moved so close to the counter, he was damn near climbing over it.

Helen saw this.

"Enola!" she called to the girl.

"I want to draw some more," the child said.

Helen knelt and guided the girl to her feet, pulling the tunic up, covering the markings. "C'mon, baby . . ."

"But I need more!" Enola said.

"I'll bring it to you," Helen said, steering her to the rear. "You just stay in back, now . . . only grown-ups out here, you know the rules . . ."

With a loving pat, Helen guided her to the back room and lowered the tarp behind the girl. When she returned, Helen caught the Nord nodding over at the table to the old hydroholic, who was nodding back. *What did that mean? Had they seen the markings? Could they know their significance?*

There was nothing to worry about, she told herself. But the back of her neck was tingling again. . . .

"So," the Nord said to the Mariner, conversationally, "as I was saying, if you don't like people, why would you think these Atollers would give a shit about—"

The Mariner stopped him with a look—a cold, deadly look.

"Why are you talking to me?"

The Nord's grin had nothing to do with smiling. "Just being friendly."

"I don't have friends," the Mariner said.

The Nord thought about that, then seemed to come to a conclusion about his course of action. He shrugged, threw a "what's-wrong-with-*this*-character" look to the pair of traders at the bar, and wandered away from the counter, and out of the trading post.

"You ready for another?" Helen asked the Mariner, nodding toward his near-empty glass.

"This'll hold me." He looked past her, toward the mostly barren shelves. "That plant . . . it's a tomato plant, isn't it?"

She smiled, impressed. "You have a keen eye."

"Saw a picture of one, once. How much?"

"The dirt it's in goes with it, you know."

"I know. And the pot. Otherwise it wouldn't be a plant, would it?"

She thought for a moment, then said, "Half your chits."

He nodded without hesitation. What the hell else was there to buy in this bleak little Oasis?

She was plucking the plant off the shelf when he added, "I'll take them, too."

"Take what? You bought everything but the shelves!"

"That's what I mean," he said. "I'll take them, too."

5

The shelving in a netting bag over his one shoulder, the meager potted tomato plant under his other arm, the Mariner stepped from the trading post into the afternoon sunshine. Gold was dappling the lagoon's surface, turning the reflection of the lazily churning windmill tower into something pretty—pretty as a picture in the ancient magazines. Around him was the milling life, the people of the community that was Oasis—fisherwomen repairing their nets, some men patching a hole in the wharf, kids running and playing, their voices echoing off the water.

But this wasn't for him. He was an outsider here, as in any atoll; he headed for home—his trimaran.

Rapid footsteps clomping on the wharf behind him made him twirl—was it that Nord, looking for trouble?

No. Just the woman. The tavern keeper with the big dark eyes and nice shape. What had he heard her called?

Helen was startled by how quickly he turned to her, but she masked her fear. A woman alone in Waterworld either learned to conceal emotions or wound up taken advantage of. Or dead.

"Something wrong?" he asked her. "I paid you in full, didn't I?"

"Yes . . . of course. I just . . . wanted to talk to you, away from the others."

"Why?"

"You said you were out there . . ." She pointed across the golden lagoon, toward the gates to the outwater. ". . . fifteen lunars."

"Yes. So?"

"That's a long time between atolls."

He looked her over. She was pretty enough, and he hadn't been this close to a woman in a long time. But he could tell this one was more trouble than she was worth. The smart ones always were.

She flushed at his looking her over, and said crisply, "That *wasn't* an offer . . ."

"What was it, then?"

"A question. Or really, a question I was leading up to . . ."

"Ask it, then."

Her eyes were alive and her smile was wonderful. She hadn't let herself be beaten down, like so many Atollers. Like most Atollers. The Mariner found himself liking her, despite his better judgment. . . .

Breathlessly, she asked, "What have you seen out there, in your fifteen lunars?"

"And what might I have seen, besides fish and ocean and an occasional boat?"

"An end," she said, her voice a hopeful whisper. "An end to all this damn water . . ."

"You're asking the wrong person."

"What do you mean?"

Now he pointed across the lagoon, at the side where the organo barge floated. The funeral was breaking up, the gardeners spreading precious dirt over the grave. He wondered if it was the dirt he'd sold the atoll, earlier.

"Ask the old woman they buried," he said. "She found the only true end."

Her face fell. "I don't believe that."

"Good for you."

Her eyes flared. "You don't have to be nasty about it."

"I meant the words," he said. He nodded to her and moved on. He listened for her footsteps, but she wasn't following him. He wasn't sure how he felt about that.

One of the two tattered boys he'd left to watch the trimaran rushed up to him.

"Can I have the reflector now, mister?"

"It's called a mirror. Not till I check my boat."

"You got people waitin' to see you. Give it to me, here, now, would ya, please?"

"Why?"

"In case you're in trouble."

The Mariner stopped. "Who is it that's waiting for me?"

"Committee of Elders. The big shot's there, the really old one—Priam, they call him."

"Okay," he said, and handed over the mirror. "But remember to share it with your pal."

"Yes, mister!"

The boy scurried off, and the Mariner wondered if he'd been scammed; but then, as he rounded the dock and his trimaran was in clear sight, he saw them: a reception committee of half a dozen Elders in their seaweed gowns and dried-jellyfish caps. Silly asses.

As he approached, the cadaverous one who had officiated at the funeral—and who the Mariner correctly assumed to be the "big shot," Priam—stepped forward with folded hands and a somber smile.

"A proposition for you, sir," Priam said.

"I've finished my trading here."

He tried to move past Priam, but the group of Elders shifted so as to block the walkway.

"Look," the Mariner said to them, coldly exasperated. "I was given strict orders by your Enforcer to be out of here in two hours."

Priam said, "I'm in a position to overrule that order."

"I'm leaving," the Mariner said.

"But you haven't even heard our proposition yet . . . or, rather, *seen* it."

The group of Elders parted, like curtains opening, to reveal a woman. Or, really, a girl—she couldn't have

48

been far out of her teens, if at all. She wore filmy netting apparel that didn't conceal her well-rounded attributes, and her face was pleasant, if frightened.

"What do you think, hmmm?" the cadaverous Elder asked.

"I think you boys run an interesting religion around here. Excuse me . . ."

"But she's agreeable enough, isn't she?" Priam pressed. "And they say you've been out fifteen lunars . . ."

"Just out of curiosity . . . what do I have to do, to earn this fee?"

Priam frowned—and on that face, a frown was a symphony of wrinkles. "You don't understand. She *is* what we're asking you to . . . do."

"What?"

Another Elder stepped forward. "You may have noticed us burying a citizen today. You understand, we maintain strict population control here."

"Yes? So?"

"So," Priam said, "one citizen's death makes room for one more."

"Well, *I'm* not staying."

"We're not asking you to. All we want is your seed."

He sighed. "My lime plant is not for sale. And I just spent half my chits on this tomato plant, so . . ."

"No, no, no," Priam said, quietly amused. "*Your* seed."

The Mariner glanced at the girl, who smiled timidly

49

at him. Now he understood. And he'd had worse offers. . . .

"We could look to our own for impregnation," another Elder said, gesturing with open palms, "but too much of that gets . . . undesirable. That's why we've outlawed it."

The Mariner was confused again. "Outlawed what?"

" 'It,' " Priam said. "How *else* do you think we can control our population?"

"Once she's with child," another Elder said, "you can go on about your way, with all the supplies you need."

"You don't have anything I need," the Mariner. "I already cleaned out your only store. This place is dying. I want no part of it. . . ."

The Mariner pushed past them. As he approached the ship, he could hear the Elders muttering behind him: *no man stays out fifteen lunars and turns down a woman; maybe he's a Smoker spy; is he hiding something?*

Not good.

He glanced behind him. The Elders were staring after him with expressions that ranged from fear to suspicion, and his confrontation with them had attracted other attention, too—a crowd of Atollers was gathering on the wharf nearby.

Crabs of hell.

The trimaran was just up ahead as a hard hand grabbed his shoulder from behind. He flicked the hand off, turning to face whoever it was, hoping it wasn't their brawny Enforcer.

It wasn't; but who it was was bad enough.

The bearded gatesman, his breath a foul mixture of low-grade hydro and smoked fish, said, "When the Elders give the word, you can leave. Not before."

The Mariner swung the netted bag of shelving into the gatesman, knocking him on his ass, and moved quickly on; then the other gatesman was suddenly there, one hand on a stubby speargun holstered on his hip, the other grabbing the Mariner's arm.

The Mariner reached out his free arm and squeezed the trigger of the holstered speargun and sent an arrow streaking down, skewering the guy's foot, pinning him to the dock. His yowl of pain was accompanied by a reflexive release of the Mariner's arm, but the Mariner's freedom was short-lived. Powerful arms locked him from behind—the first gatesman had gotten up off his ass—pinning the Mariner's arms back, causing the net bag of shelving to clatter to the dock. His precious scrawny tomato plant tumbled there as well, without much dirt spillage or the pot breaking, he noted thankfully.

The Mariner sent a sharp backward head butt into the gatesman's face, shattering the man's nose, unleashing a torrent of blood and another howl of pain, and another reflexive release of the Mariner.

Again, freedom was fleeting. A trio of male Atollers, doing the Elders' bidding, group-tackled him, dragging him to the dock, wood scraping his flesh, fists flying into him randomly, fingers clutching his neck in a choke hold that threatened death.

The Mariner twisted his neck, fighting the grip, working his mouth around to where he could get at one of those hands choking him.

And took a big, deep bite. . . .

The guy screamed shrilly and released the choke hold, but grabbed with both hands at the Mariner's long hair, and yanked up, as if trying to rip the Mariner's head off his body. Instead, the seashell-shaped earring got torn from the Mariner's lobe, and the hair fell away from his neck, revealing to one of the men wrestling him the secret there.

The gill behind the Mariner's ear.

"Shades below!" the Atoller said. "He's a *mute-o*!"

And he was looking up into three horrified faces.

And he could hear an alarm being raised as the voice of Priam shouted, "*Mutation!*"

The cry echoed across the water, rang through the atoll. He didn't have to be able to see it to know the crowd of Atollers would be swarming—curiosity inbred with fear. . . .

If he didn't get away, *right now*, he was dead.

He lashed out with a hard fist at the nearest face, and began throwing kicks and punches with savage speed, and then he was on his feet, hands, arms clinging to him, but he hammered blows and kicked and squirmed and thrashed his way free.

He'd have to forget the trimaran, for now at least—he needed to get under that water, where he could breathe and they could not. He paused and grabbed deep breaths as he chose a path to that gold-dappled water.

"Don't let him get to the water!" Priam cried.

Blocking his way was a clutch of Atollers ready to bring him down in another gang tackle. They outnumbered him, yes, but they were hunkered down, getting ready to spring.

So he sprang first.

He leaped right over the imbeciles, clearing them only by inches, but inches were enough, as he splashed into the deep, clear, cold, wonderful freedom of the lagoon. He could swim under that gate and survive out there, until some trader gave him a lift. . . .

But echoing above the water was a voice, a voice he couldn't make out, though he knew it was Priam's, and could guess what was being said: *"The nets! Cast out the nets!"*

He was a fish for them to catch, now. Well, let them try. . . .

Underwater, the sound of the splash of the first one who came after him was muted, but no less ominous. If he'd been up to speed, the Mariner could have outdistanced any of them, easily. But he was still getting his underwater bearings when the hand clutched his ankle, and an Atoller, his clothes streaming in the water, was clawing at him.

The Mariner glanced back and saw the flash of a blade in the Atoller's hand, and spun, and dove deeper, as the knife narrowly missed him.

Altering his spin, curling sideways, he grabbed the wrist of the oncoming Atoller, using the man's own momentum to drive the blade back, and down, into his belly. Red gushed and immediately thinned into crimson trails.

Then, above him, all around, were splashes and spurts of foam as more Atollers, so many, dove in, surrounding him. And a net large enough to snag the trimaran itself came cascading down. He whirled, hoping to dive deeper than the net or the Atollers could follow, but it was too late.

The net was around him, and they were yanking it tight.

Like a fly in a spider's web, he was caught, squirming, using his own knife to try to cut at the netting, getting nowhere.

Soon, men on the dock above were hooking the net—and him—with their gaffs, pulling him in, tugging him up on the dock, just another flopping fish. Their big catch. . . .

Through the grid of the netting he could see them—not just a crowd, but a mob now. Angry faces, frightened faces . . . only one face, one sympathetic face, could he find: the woman. Helen. She was upset for him. . . .

But that wasn't worth much when the rest of the mob was screaming: "*Kill him! Kill him! Kill him now!*"

The net came off as a rope looped him around the

neck, around the gills, and yanked tight. The bearded gatesman was his keeper.

Priam, his seaweed skirt blowing in a gentle breeze, strode solemnly up. He looked at the Mariner, but his words were for the mob, squeezing in behind.

In a voice deep and funereal, the High Elder said, "He almost poisoned our strain."

The Mariner knew a death sentence when he heard one. So did the Atollers, who screamed their assent.

The rope around his neck began to tighten; he struggled, but was weak and battered from the fight, and—whether man or fish—having his oxygen cut off was turning the world red, and then the red began to darken to black. . . .

The *swish* that saved him was that of a machete slicing through the rope.

The Mariner fell to his knees, gasping for air.

Above him, glaring at the gatesman, was the Enforcer, huge blade in a sledgehammer fist. The brute was the last person the Mariner had expected to save his life. . . .

"By what right—" Priam began, stepping up to the Enforcer. The Elder's frown was as regal as it was disapproving.

The Enforcer wasn't impressed by Priam or his frown. He said, matter-of-factly, "You pay me to keep the peace. This ain't it."

Another Elder spoke, indignantly: "He's killed one of ours!"

"Defending himself," the Enforcer said.

"It's not your place to judge that," Priam said.

"Is it this mob's?" the Enforcer asked.

The Elder did his best to look down his nose at the bigger man. "He needs to be destroyed."

"That may be," the Enforcer said. "But not here—and not like this."

The Mariner watched as Priam thought that over.

"If you're not going to follow your own damn laws," the Enforcer said, "I'll seek out another atoll. I'm sure my services will—"

"That won't be necessary," Priam said quickly.

Good Enforcers were hard to find.

"Cage him," the High Elder said.

Then they hauled him away, with the ugly, muttering mob following along. The Enforcer took charge of the Mariner's property—the netting bag of shelves and the potted tomato plant.

The Mariner did not see the one person in the crowd who stayed behind—Helen. Nor did he see her as she noticed something on the dock, and bent to scoop it up, and concealed it in her tunic.

The Mariner's shell earring.

6

The sprawl of the organo barge was nearby, its pungent waste odors a constant reminder of where the Elders of Oasis intended to dispose of him. In the moonlight, the barge had a silvery beauty, the gnarled mournful tree there extending its many arms over the paltry gardens like a ghost unsure whether to haunt or protect.

Battered, bleeding, the Mariner was suspended over the pier in an iron cage, large enough for him to stand in—just barely—and small enough that he could not lie down without curling into himself. He had tested the bars and the padlock and saw no means of escape. Swaying in a cool evening breeze, he hung helpless in the cage like that gutted shark he'd seen, just another beast pulled from the sea.

The post that suspended him extended up through a latticework platform; an open stairway gave the townspeople access to a half-circle metal walkway that was uncomfortably near the cage, should they be of a mind to gawk at their prisoner, or curse at him or pelt him with things.

Three scroungy boys—one of them the lad he'd given the rearview mirror to—had been goading him for quite a while. The sun had still been up when they began, and they persisted through dusk, and now the moon was on the rise. He ignored them. He didn't blame them: the right parents would have seen to it these boys were home by now. He knew all about having the wrong kind of parent.

Two of them—not the one he'd given the mirror to—had bamboo fishing poles they were poking at his cage with. One of the poles had on the end of it a fish on a hook—bait. The other boy was simply jamming his pole at the cage itself, and occasionally landing a blow.

There wasn't much power in it, but the Mariner's patience was wearing thin.

"You'd like this, wouldn't you?" the boy with the baited pole was saying, waving the fish in front of the cage, just out of the Mariner's reach. "Take a nibble . . ."

The Mariner ignored him.

"Poke him again," the boy told his friend with the unbaited pole.

The second boy poked at the cage, and the pole nudged into the Mariner's side. He gave no reaction.

"He sure is quiet," the second boy said, giving up. "Not the shark he was this afternoon . . ."

The third boy—the rearview mirror boy—stood

shuffling his feet on the platform, not looking the Mariner's way. He seemed uneasy. Not having as much fun as his pals . . .

"Why don't you let up on him?" the third boy said. "You might hurt him."

"So what?" the first boy said. "He's just a big fish."

"Aw, come on—let's just *go*. . . ."

"No!" The boy leaned over the rail of the parapet and poked his baited pole closer to the cage, and grinned tauntingly at the Mariner. "I *know* you're hungry . . . I *know* you want it . . . or maybe you don't eat your own kind?"

The boy laughed at his own joke, and so did his pal with the other pole, but the laughter soon caught in the kid's throat.

The Mariner reached an arm through the cage and caught a handful of the boy's long scruffy hair and yanked him over the side of the platform. The pole clattered to the wharf below and the startled boy's arms and legs pumped as he swam in the air, and began howling in pain. His two pals reached across the railing, eyes wide with fear; they flailed at him, grabbing at him, finally catching him and pulling him away from the Mariner's grasp and over the rail and back onto the platform, like fishermen struggling with a floundering catch till they'd pulled it up into a boat.

The footsteps of the boys were a mad clatter as they ran away, down the platform, the lad who'd been dangling weeping and clutching his head where a fistful of hair was now missing.

As the footsteps and crying died out, the Mariner could make out a gentler, more musical sound: laughter, lilting laughter, echoing melodically across the moon-reflecting water.

He looked toward the laughter and saw the face it belonged to.

In the window of the windmill tower was the child—that dark, pretty, mysterious child from the tavern, her delicate face and dark eyes caught by the moonlight, her teeth flashing white as her childish laughter fell trippingly on his ears like the wind chimes on his boat.

His eyes met the child's, across the distance. Her laughter settled into a tiny smile; then her face returned to its perfect, enigmatic state and she slipped away from the window.

What had that tavern wench, Helen, called the girl? Enola.

The name was as lovely as her laughter.

A loud groanlike creaking startled him, and then he realized it was only gears within the windmill as it picked up speed, its canvas-bound blades cutting the air as if the atoll were a single large boat struggling to leave port. Soon he knew the why of this power surge: coils within jars atop poles along the wharf walkway came gradually alive, until brightening pools of yellow light glowed here and there, giving the floating city an after sundown lease on life, and an otherworldly beauty as the harsh angles of its patched

60

together wood-and-steel structures were softened in a luminous electrical blush.

Not every atoll had street lamps. He might have been impressed, had he not been suspended in a cage near a barge of shit.

With this added light, he could make out his trimaran much better from here. His ship. His home. In sight, but so out of reach, it might as well have been fifteen lunars west.

Crabs of hell!

There were people on his deck! They'd boarded under the cover of night, and were now exposed by the street lamps.

He stood, clutching the bars of his claustrophobic prison, and it swayed, almost swung, and his mouth opened to yell an objection . . . only what good would it have done?

Helpless, he watched as Atollers hopped off the trimaran with armloads of his possessions—his lime tree, tools, bags of booty—scurrying away like rats into the night.

"Hard luck, Dirt Man," someone said.

The Mariner's eyes traveled to the lagoon nearby, where a little dinghy was being rowed past him by the grinning Nord. The blond trader waved, but the Mariner didn't return the gesture, and watched impassively as the dinghy eased its way to the main gates, which groaned open just wide enough to give the Nord passage, then rumbled shut.

The muffled echoing of voices traveled to him from

61

a converted Chinese junk off to his left. Earlier, he had seen Atollers and the Elders themselves gradually entering the structure; that tavern keeper, Helen, had been among them. Perhaps it was a kind of meeting hall.

Perhaps his fate was being decided within, even now.

He grinned, shook his head. That said it all, about Oasis, didn't it?

You didn't even get invited to your own trial in this damn atoll. . . .

Within the meeting hall, the High Elder—Priam—sat with his brethren at a main table as Atollers, some seated on benches, others standing, crowded around, milling with the excitement, the afterglow, of catching and trapping a mutation.

"The evidence speaks for itself," Priam said. "We must dispense with the mute-o as soon as possible."

There were nods and murmurs of agreement, but one voice rang out above them: *"Why?"*

Helen stepped from among the crowd and onto the platform, facing the seaweed-gowned tribunal.

"Helen," Priam said gently, "he killed one of our own. You know the law. He has to die."

She stepped forward, urgency and passion a vibrato in her voice. "But he brought *dirt!*"

More murmuring crossed the crowd. She turned to them, playing to them.

"Dirt the likes of which," she said, "we haven't seen in years. . . ."

"We have seen dirt before," said the Elder at Priam's right hand, "from other traders. . . ."

"Not like *this*," Helen said. "Not since Enola came. . . ."

"So it's pure dirt," the Elder said dismissively. "So what?"

"So . . . it had to come from somewhere," Helen said. "What if it came from Dryland?"

The crowd's murmurings rose to a roar. To some, the word stirred dying hope; others considered it blasphemy, and there were shouts, and boos.

"Please don't start with your—" Priam began.

"He came from the west," a voice interrupted boldly.

Eyes turned. It was the bearded gatesman who had brought the Mariner down. But the word Dryland had roused something in him.

"The west!" a male Atoller shouted, standing, raising a fist. "That's where the Smokers come from!"

"From the west," a woman agreed. "I heard that, too!"

"Smokers come from Dryland?" a confused old Atoller asked the air.

"Please, please!" Priam boomed, patting the air. "Calm yourselves."

"Perhaps the ichthy man *is* a Smoker spy," the right-hand Elder said.

All eyes turned to him.

"If so," he continued, "he could give away our position . . . our weaknesses."

"You have no evidence of that," Helen said, her head high. "This is all supposition."

"Perhaps," another Elder said, the man on Priam's left. "But even so, he's still a mute-o apt to contaminate our community."

"Then why not just let him go?" Helen asked. "The life he took was, as your own Enforcer said, in an act of self-defense."

"He might contaminate other communities in Waterworld," the Elder intoned pompously.

"*What* other communities?" Helen's laugh was harsh. "We haven't seen or heard from another atoll in over a year!"

Priam was patting the air again. "Let us please keep to the issue at hand."

Helen shook her head, disgusted with this self-important tribunal. She turned to the crowd and spread her arms and addressed them.

"Every year, every month," she said, "it gets worse. Fewer atolls . . . fewer traders . . . our gardens are dying, our trees bear less fruit . . . machines breaking down. . . . This place, this whole way of living—it's coming to an end. Doesn't anyone else *see* that?"

The crowd's murmur was insistent this time. The voice of an old man rose above it: "When I was young, there were lots of atolls! In one day, you could visit two, three of 'em."

Now Helen turned back to the council of Elders.

"What have you been doing about these problems? Praying! Praying for help! Well, don't you know an answered prayer when it stares you in the face?"

Priam frowned. "What is your meaning?"

"We have someone in our midst," she said, "who might actually be able to show us the way to a new place, a new *land*, a man who—"

"He is *not* a *man*," the right-hand Elder said.

She sighed in exasperation, shook her head, raised her palms. "It doesn't *matter* who or what he is. I say, if he knows the way to Dryland, don't *kill* him—make him *show* us where it is!"

"People have searched for centuries for Dryland," Priam said, not unkindly. "You know what they found, Helen. Death is what they found. It's all they found."

Her chin trembled; tears welled in her eyes as she shook a defiant fist at the council. "Well, at least they died trying."

Priam's kind demeanor vanished and he lashed out at her: "Dryland is a hoax! A myth, a children's fairy tale! This has been discussed and discussed, again and again, and decided, for once and for all, long, long ago . . ."

And now the High Elder thrust a pointing finger at her, as if it were a spear.

"And it is long since past time, Helen," he said, "that you accept that fact. The sooner you do, the better off we'll *all* be!"

The bearded gatesman stepped forward but Priam had doused the kindling hope the man had evidenced earlier. "We'd be better off if we got rid of that *child* of hers, too!"

The murmuring was back again—uglier now. The same human sharks that had gone after the stranger were circling *her*, now.

"Those marks on her back," the gatesman said, "they attract talk—they attract trouble! It's said the Smokers are *looking* for her . . . I heard it from a trader!"

Priam patted the air. "Please! One matter at a time . . ."

From the crowd came an angry male voice: "I say we get rid of *both* of them—the mute-o *and* the girl!"

The murmuring was rising into something loud, something fevered. If this crowd didn't start killing each other, they'd soon find somebody else to kill.

The stranger.

Enola.

Fear clutched Helen's chest. She gave up all hope of reasoning with this rabble, and rushed from the meeting hall.

Perhaps Old Gregor would know what to do. . . .

7

In a loft workshop within the tower of the windmill, a white-bearded, slightly stooped old man gazed through one of his own inventions: a good-size makeshift telescope aimed, as any good telescope should be, into the heavens.

Around him in the workshop were wheezing bellows, the skeletons of fish, various fruit-grafting experiments, bottles and tubes and flasks on tables (and similar tables were scattered below, along the rustic walls of the windmill tower).

Gregor was his name, and despite his eccentricities—and a constantly distracted state that made him seem almost addled—he was granted by the Elders this generous space, and had been able to collect these incongruous remnants of what the ancients called "technology," because he was, after all, the designer of the windmill whose gears powered the atoll's electricity.

The Elders, all the Atollers in fact, considered him

brilliant—a "genius"—but Gregor viewed himself as anything but. He felt himself a stupid man, though he was not: he was a brilliant scientist in a time when science was a distant memory. That was his problem: even the most gifted carpenter needs tools.

And Gregor's tools were odd gathered bits of this and that left over from a vanished age.

Yet to Gregor, gazing through the glass, searching the sky (". . . Polaris to Orion . . . then perpendicular from . . ."), the answer to the most crucial question in Waterworld lay just out of reach, just sitting there. . . .

Or, to be more precise, it rested on the back of a child.

She was forty feet below him, in the living area (which was littered with experiments and inventions in progress), sitting at a table, by a window, hunkered over there, at her favorite pastime—drawing.

Using a piece of charcoal—a "drawstick," as the child put it—she drew directly on the table, conjuring up fabulous visions of things no one in Waterworld had ever seen, outside of the few who had seen those precious manuscripts called magazines—and the only magazines this child had laid her eyes upon were the handful in Gregor's own meager library.

But Gregor recognized a good number of the images—he'd seen them in the magazines of others, and knew that these fabulous images, no matter how childlike the girl's scribbles might seem to the uninformed, were glimpses of life on land. . . .

Plants and waterfalls and birds and beasts . . .

Could these all flow from the child's imagination?

As he moved down to her, along the winding wooden walkway—did the creaking emanate from the wood slats, or his old bones, or a mingling thereof?—he wondered if the things she saw were visions, and if so, were they visions of the past, of the future . . . or some tangible present, just beyond the horizon?

As he approached the doodling child, Gregor knew the answer: this was not a child recording her dreams. The charcoal sketches reported things this girl *had seen* . . . just as right now she was putting the finishing touches on a crude drawing of a man in a hanging cage.

The stranger, the "mute-o" whose case Helen had gone to plead at the Atoll Council Meeting, was unwittingly posing for the young artist through the window by her table.

Gregor stroked the child's hair and she looked back up at him with wide eyes, a deep, dark blue that only the ocean at its most dangerous depths could rival.

The old man, patting her shoulder, said, "Lovely, child, lovely . . . you've drawn our fish-man, and so very well!"

"Thank you."

She returned to her drawing.

"I don't mean to bother you, child," he said, lifting her long hair and tugging down her tunic ever so slightly from her shoulder to have another look at the markings, just below the nape of her neck.

The path he had just traced in the sky—three stars that when connected created a straight line on a dawn horizon to . . . dare he even think it? . . . *Dryland*—he now traced over points of the tattoo.

But what had matched up in his mind fell short in practice.

He sighed, shook his head, stared at the tattoo. Was it a map? A calendar? Or something his insufficient intellect hadn't even yet thought of!

Tugging her tunic back in place, smoothing her hair back, he said softly, "You'd tell me, child, if you knew its meaning? Wouldn't you, Enola?"

She looked back at him again, her expression at once impassive and sad and wise. . . .

"Of course," she said.

Now she was drawing an ancient beast, which Gregor recognized from his readings of magazines in the collections of others; such beasts ran on four legs and had manes that flowed in the wind. These beasts had been called "horses."

"Do you know what that is, child?"

She shrugged. "No."

"Do you remember it? Or did someone show you a . . ."

"I don't know."

A side door opened, and without looking, he knew it was Helen.

"Back from the meeting so soon?" Gregor asked. "I presume you talked sense, and they didn't listen. Come see the prodigal child's latest visions!"

Helen crossed the room, skirting the central metal throne that was actually part of Gregor's latest—and most vital—project, as the smokestack tucked behind the chair hinted.

The slender woman was minus her usual bounce, and her brow was troubled. When she reached the child, Helen stroked Enola's long hair and returned the smile Enola flashed at her; but when the girl turned away, Helen's smile turned grim, her face frightened, bloodless pale.

She whispered to Gregor: "We've got to get out of here."

He took her gently by the arm and walked her away from the doodling child. "I take it the meeting did not go well."

"To say the least," she sighed. "They're putting us adrift, Gregor."

"They wouldn't dare cast me out," Gregor said indignantly. "I'd shut down their power so fast . . ."

"Not you." She whispered again. "Enola and me."

"They won't hurt you," he assured her. "They know I'd turn their lights off if they did!"

She cast her eyes toward the odd metal throne and its incongruous smokestack. "How long till we leave?"

He looked upward, thought about it, calculated.

"Another week," he said. "Ideally."

"We don't have a week," she said. "We'll be lucky to have tonight! You know better than I that we could take off *any* time. . . ."

His shrug was elaborate. "But, Helen—I don't know where to *go* yet!"

They looked toward Enola, as the child sat drawing with her piece of charcoal. The riddle needled onto her back remained unsolved, for all Gregor's elaborate celestial calculations.

Helen gestured to his tabletop library—the only one in Oasis: a coverless *People* magazine, a *Chilton's Manual* for 1964–68 Ford Mustangs, and the Tacoma, Washington, yellow pages. He had pored through these treasures time and again, using the reading skills his grandmother had taught him.

Helen asked, "What do your books tell you?"

"There's nothing there," he said. "I know the child bears the answer we seek—if we could just solve the puzzle on her back." He shook his head. "I just don't know *how*. . . ."

"Maybe," the child said, "*he* does."

The girl had stood at the table and was leaning forward, looking out the window. Gregor hadn't realized she was even listening to their sotto voce conversation! But there she stood, pointing.

To the man . . . that is, the mutated man . . . hanging in the iron cage, washed in moonlight.

In the shadow of its towering twin, a much smaller windmill's four blades churned the cool night air; this windmill was atop Gregor's cap, and—via a cable that looped around his sleeve—it powered the glow-coil in the lantern he carried, in one hand, before him.

He went up the stairs of the platform to the metal half-circle walkway and paused at the railing, at the closest possible point to the dangling cage—and its silent seated occupant. He raised the lantern to get a better look. The stranger stared in the opposite direction, not deigning to even acknowledge Gregor's presence.

The old man fished a magnifying glass from his loose, patchy clothing, leaned against the rail, and used the lamp to help get a closer look at the mutated man . . . specifically, at his feet.

"Ah, yes," Gregor said, not to the stranger, but to himself. "Oh, my, yes! They *are* webbed, aren't they? Seven, eight, nine, ten . . . all ten digits. Isn't that *wonderful. . . .*"

The stranger now turned a sullen gaze on the old inventor, who shifted the lamp, now, and the magnifying glass, to get a look at the creature's neck.

"Let's see . . . isotropic gills. But are they vestigial? No . . . no . . . they're *functional!*" He beamed at the impassive mutation. "You're the genuine article, all right! Ichthyus Sapien! *You* can breathe in *water*."

But the Ichthyus Sapien did not reply; he might as well have been carved from stone. Perhaps Gregor's third-person manner had been too distancing, too cold, too impersonal. . . .

"I know you can speak," Gregor said, not at all unkindly. "Helen told me. Please try to understand. I'm only here to *help* you."

The Ichthyus Sapien suddenly seemed about to say something!

And then spat in Gregor's face.

With a sigh, the old man wiped the spittle away with a sleeve. "Don't like humans much, do you? Can't say as I much blame you. But are *all* your kind so foul tempered?"

"I have no kind," the Ichthyus Sapien said flatly.

"Oh, fishrot," Gregor said, as casually as if this conversation had been two-sided all along. "I'd be shocked if there weren't others."

That perked the mutation up. Had he never found others of his kind? Had he been looking for them, even as Gregor and Helen dreamed of finding Dryland?

"If there *aren't* any of your kind right now, my boy," Gregor said, "there will be, there will be . . . eventually. Give nature a little time to catch up with you."

The Ichthyus Sapien turned away.

"Don't pout, now. It's not your fault—just bad timing on your part, showing up so early. Rotten luck, really." Gregor could hardly keep from staring at those fabulous isotropic gills. "Anyway, I've come to ask . . . that dirt of yours, where'd it come from? Not Dryland, by any chance?"

And the Ichthyus Sapien's gaze returned to the old man; was the creature smiling, however faintly?

"*Is* there such a place as Dryland?" the old inventor said, unable to conceal the desperation in his voice.

But the creature only turned away again.

Gregor tucked the magnifying glass back in a pocket and found something else, a folded piece of paper—rare stuff, paper—and this drawing, though in charcoal, wasn't the work of the child, not exactly: Gregor had drawn this himself, moments before he set out with his windmill cap and his lantern.

It was a rough replica of the tattoo on Enola's back.

Never before had he and Helen dared to put this on paper, but here it was . . . so that it could be conveyed to this fish-man.

"Do you know what it means?" Gregor asked, tremulously. "Can you read it?"

The Ichthyus Sapien cast his eyes indifferently toward the paper.

"The ancients did something terrible, didn't they?" Gregor asked. "Something terrible that caused all this water . . . hundreds and hundreds of years ago?"

After a pause that seemed an eternity, the Ichthyus Sapien said, "If I tell you, will you open this padlock?"

Gregor frowned. "But I haven't a key."

The fish-man's eyes traveled to the windmill cap. "You look pretty resourceful to me. There's a mooring cleat down there . . . see it?"

75

Gregor leaned over the railing; he could see the metal scrap down there, a broken mooring cleat on the wharf walkway.

"That should be as good as any key."

"If I do let you out," Gregor whispered, "can I trust you?"

"I won't hurt anyone," he said. "I'll just answer your questions . . . and leave."

Soon Gregor was heading down the stairs to the walkway, where he snatched up the cleat. He reached a hand up to the stranger, who was reaching down from his cage, when a voice boomed out: *"Gregor!"*

He dropped the cleat as if it were red-hot, whirled toward the sound, and was immediately caught in a lance of light. Shouting from a watchtower, shining a spotlight of Gregor's own creation on the old man, was the atoll Enforcer.

"What's your business there?"

"Nothing! Just having a look at your captive!"

"Well, get inside! It'll soon be curfew."

Gregor looked beseechingly up at the Ichthyus Sapien.

"I'm sorry," the old man whispered. "I'm not a brave man. . . . If you know anything about Dryland, I beg of you, tell me now. Don't let it die with you!"

The Ichthyus Sapien turned his back on the inventor, settled himself in his cage, and closed his eyes.

Gregor stood there for several long moments, searching for the words that might stir this creature, swinging in his lonely cage.

Then the watch bell clanged across the water, echoing through the atoll, announcing curfew.

And, defeated, the old man dragged himself home, following the path his windmill cap made for him.

8

The golden glare of the sunrise had a tinge of blood red in it, as the atoll's sharp angles and harsh surfaces, aglow here, in shadow there, achieved an unusual beauty. The individual studying this magnificent jagged landscape did so from a considerable distance, through the twin telescopes of an ancient device called binoculars.

He was a striking looking man, his head the shape of a hard-boiled egg, with exactly the same amount of hair, his skin burned reddish brown, like an apple starting to go bad. Though he wasn't tall, his bearing made him appear enormous, and he had brawn enough, though many of his men were brawnier—just not, thankfully, brainier.

His apparel, tattered as it was, seemed vaguely official, even military. The shoulders of the antique garment he wore—a "sport coat" with lapels—were wide with remainders of epaulets long since shredded in battle. In fact, his camouflage-colored attire was loosely entwined with bits of chain, loose thread, and dangling rope, giving an impression of a warrior draped in seaweed.

Or, perhaps, of a man coming undone. Unraveled.

His smile was white and dazzling, his eyes bright and crazed. He stood on the deck of his fleet's refueler barge and gazed at the craggy way the Oasis cut the horizon.

"Time for breakfast, boys," he said to the barbarianlike Smokers around him, who hung on his every demented word.

His name was the Deacon.

He thought of himself as a warrior prince, which was only fitting, because if Waterworld had such a thing, the Deacon was it. Around his neck, on a thong, was a cross. Its precise significance was lost in the mist of time. But he knew it was a religious artifact of the Land Days, and that was enough for him.

For the Deacon preached of a day when men would walk on the land again, as they were meant to. Dryland was no myth: it was out there. He would find it.

Even if it took killing every living soul in Waterworld.

Footsteps, falling like little pebbles, nudged her awake. Helen's eyes opened slowly. She patted the bedside beside her.

The girl was gone.

Fear immediately clutched her chest and she sprang

from the bed, the threatening words of the Elders and Atollers echoing in her brain.

"Enola!" she called. "Eno—"

But there the child was, at a window. The walls around her—all of the walls in their living quarters behind the tavern area of the trading barge—were littered with charcoal images that had leaped from the child's imagination . . . or memory.

Gregor had identified them for her, and Helen— who could read, and had seen her share of books and magazines—recognized some of the images herself: *trees, huts, mountains, flowers*. . . .

Helen went to the window and touched the girl lightly on the shoulder. Normally, the child would have bestowed a smile on Helen; today her lovely little face was a mask of sorrow.

"What will they do to him?" she asked.

Out the window, they both could see the procession of Elders, in slow marchstep, Priam at the lead, of course, with Atollers falling in behind them. They were approaching the stockade platform, where the stranger stood clutching the bars of his dangling cage, staring down at them defiantly.

"You shouldn't watch this," Helen said, tugging the girl's arm, pulling her gently away.

But the child would not budge. "They're going to bury him, aren't they?"

"Don't watch." She slipped her hand gently across the girl's eyes.

With surprisingly strong fingers, the girl gripped Helen's wrist and removed the woman's hand.

"Not watching won't make it not happen," Enola said. Then she slowly turned her dark blue eyes and fastened them on Helen's face.

"We should help him," the child said.

The Mariner stood facing the tribunal, who stood along the half-circle walkway of the platform. There was an easy breeze that riffled their seaweed gowns. The one called Priam raised both hands in a sort of benediction.

Only it was something else.

"After considerable deliberation of the evidence," Priam said, "we have come to our decision. . . ."

"Nice of you to let me know how my trial came out," the Mariner said. "Sorry I couldn't be there."

Priam raised his head, ignoring the prisoner. "This . . . 'mute-o' . . . does indeed constitute a threat to Oasis and to Waterworld itself. Therefore, in the best interest of public safety, and the greater good, he is hereby sentenced to be recycled. . . ."

There were murmurs of assent from the crowd.

"Proceed," Priam said, "in the customary fashion."

An Atoller in uniformlike garments resembling those of the gatesmen began working a pulley. The Mariner heard the grinding of gears and felt his one-cell prison shifting, swaying. Above him, a boom was swinging him out, carrying him toward the organo barge.

And *over* the organo barge.

"Bones to berries, veins to vines," Priam intoned, "these tendons to trees, this blood to brine. . . ."

Lowering him, now.

Dropping him, cage and all, into that foul compost stew of theirs; right into the damn goo. . . .

"Too strange for life, he was," Priam said, "this mute-o does now leave us. . . ."

The ooze was coming up through the iron bars of the cage's floor; he began climbing the sides of the cage, but there just wasn't room to go anywhere.

"Recycled and entombed . . ." Priam went on.

The only glimmer of hope was the snail's pace of the process . . . at least he was sinking *slowly*. The stuff was as thick as it was foul, and this would take a while.

Though suffocating shouldn't take long at all. . . .

"In the presence," the High Elder solemnly intoned, "of Him Who Leads Us . . ."

If there was such a person or entity, the Mariner thought, as the cold brown muck filled the bottom of the cage, now would be a good time to show himself.

In a watchtower, through a viewing scope, a watchman did what watchmen do: kept watch. In Oasis, there could be no more boring job, no task more dull than studying that endless, unchanging sea. For days on end, your eyes could search the water and see only . . . sea. So rarely did anything turn up on the horizon, that—

But right now something had turned up, not visible

at first because it was dead in line with the sun: tendrils of smoke curled skyward, seeming to rise from the water.

Smoke.

"Smokers!" the watchman screamed.

The slime was up to his ankles now, and the Mariner— his mind on other things—didn't make out the word the watchman screamed.

Everyone else in Oasis did.

The Atoller working the pulley lever stopped in midcrank, and everyone—including the normally dignified Elders—scattered in every direction, like pieces of a shattered glass.

The Mariner was a problem instantly forgotten.

Forgotten by all but the organo heap itself, which was sucking the cage and its occupant slowly, inexorably down, deep down into its graveyard of sludge.

Out on the ocean, closing in on the floating city, was the Deacon's armada of Smokers, flying across the surface of the sea, skimming over it as if the water were a mere inconvenience to determined men with motors.

A beat-up seaplane, the armada's scout plane, led the way for hovercraft, swamp skiffs, speedboats, and jetskis, some of the latter bearing one Smoker, other bigger jetskis carrying a pair of the brutes, some with prow-mounted machine guns or chainsaws. Of the speedboats, the larger crafts contained four to six

Smokers, with a gunner sometimes perched riding an angled scaling ladder, others hanging off the sides as if eager to dive into battle, clutching their clumsy looking but deadly firearms, fused and/or taped together pieces of this ancient weapon and that, making each gun different, though their goals were common.

As the vehicles of various size bore down on the atoll, belching diesel smoke, the engines ripping the world apart with a collective senses-destroyingly loud rumbling roar, they cut across a deep blue ocean that seemed almost white. Having the sun behind them did that. It made them seem an awful vision, a nightmarish hallucination.

But, like Oasis itself, they were all too real.

Within the floating city, the denizens were taking battle stations; the embattlements with water cannons were manned almost instantly. Elsewhere, storm shutters were dropped, fire buckets doled out, and nets of living weapons were reeled in: jellyfish for catapulting.

Down in the armory, a process repeated in many a practice drill was now a grim reality as men, women, and children plucked and pulled weapons from shelves and racks—bows and arrows in quivers, blades, spearguns, mallets, lances . . . no guns, no firearms, though all knew they'd be facing the firesticks of these fiercest of foes.

A frantic boy, face smudged with soot, bumped into

Helen as she and Enola quickly exited the armory, carrying bow and arrows and crossbow, respectively.

"I . . . I can't find my Dad!" the boy blurted.

"He's probably at his station." Helen thrust the crossbow in the lad's arms; no better time to become a man. "Now get on a wall and *fight*!"

A horrified cry from a watchtower cut above the din of the encroaching diesel-burners and the burps of gunfire. *"Berserkers!"*

A chill coursed through Helen as she returned to the armory for a weapon. She found a speargun and a quiver of ammo for it and followed after Enola, who was scurrying up a walkway with her bow and arrows to a wall to defend.

Berserkers, Helen thought, scurrying into position. The horrible stories about these brain-damaged semi-human Smokers had seemed so unlikely. Legends. Tall tales . . .

Yet there they were, out on the sun-whitened water, huge, mostly bare brutes on water skis who shot off moving ramps in order to catapult themselves into the air, hurtling themselves into flight, simpletons soaring blindly over the walls of the atoll, where they would land inside—*anywhere* inside.

It seemed unreal, as she ducked down, a human rocketing over her head to go splattering against the armory roof. She turned and saw the Berserker sprawled there in a reddish smear, dead on impact. Other Berserkers hit walkways and walls, and—when they survived—instantly infiltrated the fortress Oasis had become. Those Berserkers that did not overshoot landed safely, more or less, splashing into the lagoon itself.

If they did not catch an arrow or a lance first, these Berserkers divested themselves of their skis and swam to the shore that was the wharf, and became part of the hand-to-hand combat breaking out all around the atoll, as Atollers battled Berserkers who had survived their suicide mission landings.

Helen fired her speargun with deadly accuracy at other Berserkers, turning their soaring entrances into exits. . . .

The cage had stopped sinking. That was the good news. When the sludge barely got to his ankles, it had stopped sinking. The bad news was, all around him carnage and battle reigned, and the Mariner could neither protect himself nor anyone else; though the ideal solution here would be for both sides to wipe each other out, superstitious Atollers and barbaric Smokers alike.

But even that wouldn't get him out of this damn *cage* . . .

He was a stationary target here, and it would only be a matter of time before—

A Smoker stood before him, his grin as yellow as it was idiotic, pointing a handgun at him, a grotesque looking weapon inbred from who knew how many pistol parents. Dripping wet, the bastard was probably a Berserker.

Well, the Mariner thought, *I don't have far to go to get to the graveyard. . . .*

But he would have preferred to die out there, on his trimaran, or better still, in the water, where he really belonged.

The Berserker shuddered, a shudder that shook his whole body, his eyes widening till they popped.

Then he flopped on his face on the walkway, a spear sticking out of his back. The Mariner hadn't heard the spear thunk home over the tumult of battle.

When he fell, the Berserker revealed—standing a few yards behind him—another brutish figure, but not another Smoker: the atoll Enforcer, speargun in hand.

The man looked at the Mariner, who nodded a barely perceptible thanks, then yelled, "Let me out of here! I can fight!"

But the Enforcer moved on.

"Crabs of hell!" the Mariner screamed. "Let me—"

His words were cut off as a screaming Berserker on skis, flying over the wall, came crash-landing onto the Mariner's cage. The impact killed the Berserker at once, but it did something else, as well. . . .

It knocked the cage, at an angle, deeper into the organo pit . . . *and now the cage was sinking again. . . .*

The muck climbed to his waist so fast he could barely fathom it. The Mariner reached a hand out through the bars, up and around, and tugged a knife off the belt of the dead Berserker.

He began working on the padlock, attacking it, before it, too, got enveloped by this organic slime. . . .

Helen and the child remained at the battle station, the two females killing without hesitation the savages on skis streaking over the atoll walls. The Atollers were fighting back effectively: water cannons knocked jetskiers off their mounts, live jellyfish were dropped onto Smokers scaling the walls, and down below, bucket brigades were putting out spot fires, and when it took two or more Atollers to kill one Berserker, that's what they did. This was war.

A barrage from behind chewed up the wall next to her and shredded the Atollers fighting there, tossing them to the walkway like blood-spattered rag dolls. Helen wheeled around, stood with her back to Enola, blocking the child, and faced a dripping wet Berserker, standing there on the walkway with a taped-up firearm that took two hands to use.

But after that impressive burst, a burst that had turned half a dozen Atollers into so much organo, the ugly weapon was silent in the Berserker's hands; he looked down at it, stupidly, then grabbed a ramrod from somewhere and tried to clean the jammed weapon.

Helen was out of spears, but the dead Atoller next to her wouldn't be needing that lance. She grabbed it and raced toward the Berserker at a dead run.

Just before she reached him, the Berserker gave up on making his weapon functional and tried to club her with it; but soon his heart was no longer in it—not with Helen's spear in his heart.

"Helen!" Gregor's voice called across the engine noise, the gunfire, the shouts, the screams. *"Helen!"*

The old man was waving to her from the window of the workshop.

"It's time!" he called. "It's time!"

"You old fool," she muttered. "If you leave without us . . ."

She yanked Enola by the hand, but the stubborn child took a moment to pick up a "drawstick" she'd dropped, and then they ran, dodging bodies, skirting skirmishes, heading for the windmills, mere steps— and a lifetime—away. . . .

The Mariner was up to his neck in shit and ooze, but he had the knife's blade in that lock; it was under the surface of the slime, but he was working it in there, if he could only . . .

And then the blade snapped.

9

On the outskirts of the battle, on the deck of the oil-drum-strewn refueler barge, leaning on his mace of office—a Spaulding five iron—the Deacon inhaled his unfiltered smokestick. Back on the *'Deez,* the mother ship, he had in his storehouse of spoils many cartons of the prehistoric sticks—Camels, Marlboros, Chesterfields, all fresh enough to smoke after hundreds of years, thanks to their crisp, crackly plastic wrappers. The ancients had been very wise.

When he wasn't inhaling the smokestick, he was breathing in the fragrant fumes of destruction, as his Smokers—and those lovely, dedicated boys, the Berserkers—did his bidding.

Jetskis and small attack boats were scurrying back to the refueling barge's go-juice berth at the bow. Some of his Smokers did not have jetskis and had been rigged to be self-propelled, with go-juice pumped into rubber bladders they wore on their backs. The naive lads were unaware they were human bombs.

But what Smoker didn't enjoy going out in a blaze of glory?

Still, despite a lovely, smoke-streaked sky, the Deacon grew weary of the way this game was going. He was, frankly, irritated that his casualty rate was so high, going up against primitive Atollers who apparently had no firepower whatsoever. Bows and arrows, spears and lances.

How embarrassing for what should have been a savage raid to turn into a pitched battle.

He took a practice swing with the Spaulding, aiming his imaginary golf ball at the Oasis, then motioned a flag boy over.

"Key to the city," he said.

The boy nodded and went to the edge of the deck and began working the signal flags, flapping the word to the Deacon's favorite toy.

The Hellfire Gunboat was a barge onto which the Deacon had bolted the remains of an ancient vehicle called a "truck"—the word "Mack" was on its prow—and on the truck's flatbed, manned by the Deacon's best gunner, was a wonderful weapon. This death-spitting mechanical demon gave the Hellfire Gunboat its name: the elephantine machine gun had a cluster of rotating barrels that discharged .20mm rounds successively as they rotated around an axis.

The result was, simply, hellfire.

At the flag boy's signal, the gunboat's driver—sitting in the cab of the truck—hot-wired the vehicle's transmission, pumping pistons to life, in turn feeding shells into the massive weapon.

From the refueler barge, the Deacon's ears rang gloriously as the gunboat unleashed its hellfire on the atoll. His smile curled in a perfect half circle around his erect smokestick as he watched tracer rounds chop off the top of the atoll's precious central windmill.

"Yes!" the Deacon shouted. "A hole in one! And on a water hazard, yet . . ."

Scruffy Smoker soldiers around him nodded as if they understood; they had learned long ago the wisdom of going along with the Deacon's every word, every whim.

The Deacon cackled with glee as the rounds ripped through walls, turning embattlements to flying fragments, the Atollers defending those shattered embattlements dropping into the sea like target-practice birds shot from the sky.

The growl of the truck engine being floored by the gunboat driver roared across the water to the Deacon's delighted ears as the ammo loaded faster and faster and the hellfire weapon wailed at full crank, spewing, strewing devastation.

A section of atoll wall vanished—turned to powder—before the Deacon's rapturous gaze.

Well, now, that was better. He was enjoying himself again, the weary feeling replaced by exhilaration. He took another practice swing with the Spaulding, and as if he had caused it, another section of atoll wall powdered under hellfire.

Now if only the prize he was seeking turned out to be within those crumbling atoll walls, he would be back on his game. . . .

Was Gregor even still *alive*?

Helen and Enola had watched with horror, and dived for cover, as the top of the windmill exploded under a hailstorm of gunfire, raining down fiery fragments, the roof gone, as if it had never been. Could Gregor have survived this disaster?

Hope and fear fought for control as Helen, her heart pounding, trying to beat its way out of her chest, clutched Enola's hand and wove along the wharf walkway through the hand-to-hand combat and the scattering of Atoller and Smoker corpses, until they reached the windmill. At least the structure had not caught fire, though question marks of smoke curled from the irregular opening where the rooftop had been.

Had they been mere moments earlier, they would have found him in the workshop, sun streaming down on him as he frantically piled his precious books, magazines, and charts into the stowing area underneath the thronelike chair with its two side seats for Helen and Enola. He had already attached the steering mechanism and affixed the propeller onto the crude engine with its smokestack on the back of the strapped together chairs.

But when they entered the windmill workshop, the

putt-putting sound of the engine told Helen a terrible truth: they were too late.

Gregor was leaving without them.

She looked up and saw him, rising like an apparition, the quiltwork bag filled with hot air, the contraption—according to Gregor, it was a small "dirigible," a steerable balloon—already six feet off the ground.

"Gregor—wait!"

"I waited as long as I could!" the old man cried, his voice anguished. He had a hand on the steering device, but reached the other down to them. "A blast unmoored me!"

"Gregor!" Helen screamed. "No!"

"You can still make it!" the old man called.

But he was already too far above them—seven feet, easily.

"Please don't go away!" Enola called.

Helen jumped, tried to reach his hand. So did Enola. Helen's hand scraped Gregor's clutching fingers. But just for a moment. . . .

They ran up the circling walkway, trying to catch him.

No use. No use.

"Forgive me!" he cried. "Forgive me. . . ."

Then they were looking up, and the despondent Gregor was looking down, as the dirigible floated away, through the smashed roof and into the sky.

Taking hope with him.

Leaving fear behind.

• • •

The Deacon was the first to spot the cigar-shaped flying balloon.

"What *is* that thing? Blast it out of the sky!" He slapped the flag boy on the head. "Alert them! *Today*, you moron!"

The flag boy flapped his flags, signaling the gunboat driver, and soon the gunner had wheeled his immense weapon around, powerful arms swinging it up to take aim, squeezing the trigger on a perfect line of fire . . .

. . . that was entered by a leaping Smoker on skis with a bladder backpack of go-juice, which detonated in a fireball that was like a sun exploding, leaving a smoke cloud so large it obscured the path of the escaping dirigible, which emitted its own stream of smoke from an engine that was powering the gizmo.

By the time the cloud cleared, the balloon contraption was well out of range, on its way to being a dot in the distant sky.

"I don't suppose there's any chance that Smoker survived," the Deacon said.

"No, sir," the flag boy said. "Did you want to reward his bravery with a medal?"

"No," the Deacon said, lighting up another smokestick. "There was something I wanted to do down his neck, after I ripped his head off."

The Smoker who'd been hit by the hellfire barrage intended for the dirigible did not survive. His fiery black corpse hit the organo barge like a meteor, setting its central tree on fire.

Helen, from a window in the windmill tower, witnessed the late Smoker's fiery landing, but her mind was awhirl, and it took Enola pointing out the window at the stranger in his cage, all but sunk down under the ooze, to jog her back to life. . . .

Gregor was gone, and with him, hope of finding, of reaching, Dryland.

But someone else knew of Dryland, and that same someone else just might be capable of getting her and the child out of here, away from this burning devastation and an Oasis whose inevitable death was only being hastened by the Smoker attack.

Helen grabbed Enola's hand. "We're not through yet," the woman said defiantly. It was something she needed to say to herself as well as the girl.

And they ran from the windmill.

Death, foul-smelling, sticky death, was oozing in all around him. He had always known his death might be violent; that was Waterworld. But a man—or whatever it was he was—with webbed toes and gills does not expect to die a drowning death. And drowning in shit, at that. . . .

So he didn't give up. He would die trying, at least. Struggle was his way. He kept his face pushed up to the top of the cage, where there was still air, where . . .

. . . he saw a lovely face.

The tavern keeper!

She had laid a hunk of plastic board across the organo pit and was crouched there, her eyebrows arched, something like a smile tickling her full lips.

"If I get you out of here," she said, "will you take us with you?"

He could make out the child, standing at the edge of the ooze.

"Take your time thinking it over," she said.

"If I get the boat," he said, "can you get the gate open?"

She nodded.

Then she took something from alongside her: a crowbar.

It was in his hands just as the muck swallowed him, and his cage, entirely.

10

A blurp of sludge signaled the disappearance of the cage and the stranger within, as the pool of muck swallowed them both. Helen, perched on the plastic plank, gasped; but then Enola said, "Look!"

And a gooey brown arm emerged, along one solid edge of the organo pit, a slimy hand gripping hold. The stranger, covered in brown-gray gunk, looking more monster than man, pulled himself up, onto his feet. His eyes took in the raging battle, the atoll gates shrouded in water cannon mist, several Smokers scurrying about the deck of his trimaran, scouring it for plunder, not knowing the Atollers had earlier beaten them to it.

He looked toward Helen, who was already moving away from the organo pit, Enola in tow.

"The gates," he reminded her. "They'll have to both be open, or my ship won't make it through. Understand?"

"I understand," Helen said.

"Good," he said.

Then he dove off the barge, into the lagoon.

The water turned muddy, where he went in, and then he was gone, swimming deep. Helen held Enola's hand as they traversed the walkways toward the gate. Smokers were storming through a breach in one atoll wall, and hand-to-hand fighting was breaking out everywhere, the Atollers grossly, tragically outnumbered.

From the walkway over the armory, Helen could see children being shackled, for Slaver barter; a Smoker chainsawing down the tree on the organo barge; hydro being pumped out of desalination tanks into Smoker containers.

She saw something else from her high vantage point: an all too familiar face.

A cruelly handsome figure in sharkhide, blond hair so long it brushed his shoulders, strode down a walkway, leading a swarm of Smokers toward the trading post barge.

The Nord.

So *he* had been the Smoker spy.

The Elders had consigned the wrong stranger to the organo cemetery. But they had had little time to regret it. Even now, on the far ramparts, Smokers were slaying them, the Elders not even fighting, just looking to the sky for an answer that was not forthcoming.

She paused for a moment as she saw Priam standing among his fallen brethren, even as Smokers clambered over the walls behind him. The High Elder—wounded, dazed—looked down upon his floating city with dismay.

His anguished cry rang across the water: "All is lost!"

Helen shuddered, turning away as a Smoker's weapon turned its firepower upon the old man, validating his final prophecy.

The Nord strode into the trading post as, around him, Smokers trashed and pillaged the place. From his previous visit here, he knew there was little worth taking.

"Is this her?" a voice called.

He turned to see one of his Smoker lieutenants dragging in a fair-haired little girl with traumatized eyes.

"No, you idiot," he said. "You heard the Deacon's briefing. The one we're looking for is dark. With markings on her back!"

"Yes, sir," the Smoker said, hanging his head.

"She's here somewhere," he said. "Keep looking."

"Yes, sir."

The Mariner, cleansed by his plunge, swam deep, cutting a sleek path toward the trimaran. Above him, bullets pinged the water, Smokers on jetskis streaked; but underwater, these sounds—like those of the battle raging up there—seemed distant and unreal.

Soon, bursting from the water like a leaping dolphin, the Mariner landed on the stern of his ship, almost at the feet of a looting Smoker, who swung a speargun up to shoot.

Quicker than an eye blink, the Mariner knocked him cold with a hard fist to the jaw, plucking the speargun from now-limp hands. He snatched a blade from the Smoker's belt and, with casual power, nudged the bastard overboard, in a dead-weight splash.

He attached the dragline at the stern to the speargun and shot a spear across the lagoon, thunking into the walkway near the smoking windmill ruins. Then, at his steering console, he threw levers, starting the eggbeater sail turning. The dragline pulled taut, and soon the trimaran was pulling itself into the lagoon, allowing him to line up the ship on a course with those massive gates, which were as yet still shut.

With Smokers streaming in through breaches in atoll walls on almost every perimeter, there was nothing left for the gates to guard. Atollers were desperately attempting to shore up a wall weakened by the thunderous barrage of gunboat gunfire when a Berserker cannonballed through, collapsing the wall, crushing the defenders there under the wreckage.

He had the trimaran on course now. *Where was that woman?* Then he saw her, climbing a walkway, nearing one of the twin gatesman towers, the child trailing along.

He hit levers and gears, then rushed to the stern with the Smoker's blade in hand, severing the towline, even as the trimaran began its transformation.

∙   ∙   ∙

From the walkway high above, Helen felt a small hand grip her arm.

"Look!" Enola said.

Below, in the lagoon, on course for the closed gates, was the stranger's trawler—only it was suddenly something more than just a trawler.

The mast was telescoping upward, the windmill blades snugging themselves flush with the mast, sail rigging beginning to unspool, a mainsail unfurling from within the mast. . . .

The stranger's trawler had turned itself into a sleek sailboat!

"Wow," Enola said.

Looking past the transforming trimaran, Helen could see a far less inspiring sight: through a breached wall near the stranger's boat, Smokers were swarming in, casually slaying, along their path, various Atollers who had fallen to their knees, praying to the smoke-streaked sky. More practical Atollers were diving into the lagoon's waters, some in canoes, others in barrels, some swimming along in life buoys.

They needed the gates opened, too.

It was up to her, if any of them were to survive.

But at the entry of the gate tower, the bearded gatesman—damp with blood, drunk from blood loss—staggeringly guarded his post. Weak as he was, he seemed to have little trouble training his speargun on her.

"Zed," she said softly, kindly, approaching as if her

footsteps might set off a deadly explosion, "the enemy's already inside. . . . See for yourself. . . ."

Weaving, he said, "If you . . . you or anybody tries to open these gates . . . so help me, Helen . . . I'll drop you where you—"

And a burst of stray gunfire caught him, tossed him aside, his eyes blank with death as he toppled from the gate-tower bridge.

She bent to Enola, looked at the little girl, hard. "When I throw that lever, and the gate begins to open, we have to run . . ."

She pointed to the narrow catwalk attached to the back of the gates; right now, the walkway was one continuous bridge. But when one gate parted, the walkway would split in two, as well.

". . . and we'll have to jump. Understand?"

The child nodded.

"Can you do it?"

The child nodded again.

"Try not to be afraid," Helen said, and squeezed the child's shoulder.

Another nod, and the child said, "You, too."

Helen took a deep breath, then went inside the gate tower and shoved the lever, and gears ground their teeth as the first gate began to rumble its way open.

"Let's go!" she yelled, grabbing the girl's hand, and—against a backdrop of screams, smoke, and gunfire—began leading her down the narrow, moving catwalk.

The gate slowly began to open, but the Mariner knew he could not find passage until the other side swung open as well. Watching the woman and child scurry across the moving walkway, he guided his ship, keeping down, bullets pinging the water and clanging off metal on the trimaran. It would be a miracle if he didn't catch one.

He heard a thump behind him and whirled to see a Smoker, having leapt from a jetski onto one of the pontoon hulls of the ship, climbing to his feet, gun in hand. The Mariner bolted toward him and kicked the Smoker in the face, knocking him back into the lagoon.

But the Smoker's riderless jetski was still moving— flying, in fact—and it crashed right into the unopened section of gate.

"Hurry!" he called up to the woman and child.

They had paused at the edge of the catwalk—where it ended, and where it was moving away from its continuance on the other gate.

"Jump!" he yelled.

They jumped, but as they did, random gunfire stitched its way across the wreckage of the crashed jetski, hitting the go-juice tank, which exploded in a minifireball that rocked the gate, knocking Helen and Enola off balance, sending them toppling off the walkway.

The child screamed.

Then Helen was hanging by both hands from the

105

edge of the walkway, with the child clinging to her; they swayed there, dangling precariously as smoke rose from the explosion below.

As the smoke cleared, the Mariner could see that the bottom half of the gate had been blasted apart. Not big enough a hole to sail through, but he cruised toward it anyway, and into it, letting his mast bump jarringly up to a halt against the upper remaining portion.

Then he clambered up the mast and leapt onto the catwalk.

"Thank heaven!" Helen gasped, the child dangling around her neck like a human necklace.

But he jumped over where Helen's fingertips clung to the edge of the catwalk and ran along the walkway to the open gate tower. He found the lever that sent the counterweight falling, and the gate—or what was left of it—began to swing slowly, rumblingly open.

As it did, he ran down the moving rampway toward the woman, her expression one of relief . . . until he leapt over her and threw himself at the trimaran mast, sliding down the pole onto the ship.

"You bastard!" the woman screamed.

He was already at the helm, guiding his ship into the rain of water cannon mist. The nearest breach in the atoll wall made a doorway Smokers on jetskis were racing through, with the Mariner their clear objective.

The sail whumped as the woman, child clinging to

her, dropped herself from the catwalk onto the full, passing sail of the trimaran, and she and Enola came sliding down, landing on the netting deck, in a graceless pile, though neither looked any the worse for wear.

She glared at him and he just looked at her. He left the helm momentarily to hike out to her. She seemed about to say something, till he brushed past her to get at what he'd seen: that potted tomato plant he'd bought from her, bobbling in the water amidst various floating rubble.

He fished it from the water and returned to his helm, steering the boat out into the open sea. As he got his bearings, the Mariner was pleased to see that the Smoker's gunboat—with its massive machine gun that had wrought so much of the devastation here this morning—was behind them, the weapon aimed at another section of atoll wall.

But he was not pleased to see another craft before them: a sprawling Smoker-populated barge where jetskis and small boats were refueling.

On the deck of the refueler, the Deacon—in a benevolent frame of mind—was handing out smokesticks to the Smoker soldiers. Lighting up amidst all that flammable fuel, the Smokers gleefully sucked on these tobacco medals of honor, even as the Deacon's charitable expression melted into something foul.

"What craft is *that*?" he growled.

A three-hulled sailboat was crossing his view, sailing away from the atoll as if on a pleasure cruise.

"Did one of our men commandeer that boat?" He slammed his Spaulding into the deck, and his men jumped. "I don't remember saying anyone could leave in the middle of the battle! Did I say that?"

None of his men had answers to any of these questions, and their gleeful expressions turned sheepish.

The Deacon slapped the cigarette out of his flag boy's mouth. "Signal the Hellfire Gunboat, you moron! Tell them to blow that sailboat to shit and gone!"

But the flag boy couldn't catch the gunboat's eye. The Deacon began yelling and whistling to get the gunboat driver's attention, or the gunner's. . . .

"I hate sailboats," the Deacon said, shaking his head in disgust. "A man without a motor isn't a man!"

And now the gunboat was starting to turn, not that its gunner even noticed. Face and goggles black with diesel soot, the gunner was in a blind-killing mode, the huge weapon jumping with flame, spitting death and spent cartridges, and whether man was controlling machine or vice versa was anybody's guess. The gunboat crew cringed on deck, hands plastered to their ears, as the massive weapon roared on.

The Deacon smiled and lighted up a cigarette, savoring the thought of what that big mother gun would do to that candy-ass sailboat, once the gunboat got itself swung all the way round. . . .

· · ·

The situation was not lost on the Mariner, glancing back at the gunboat. He turned to Helen, who continued to glare at him.

"Steer for me," he told her.

"Why should I trust you?" she asked him.

He just looked at her, then she grimaced and dove for the helm as he grabbed a line and swung out to the bow harpoon station. Drawing a careful bead on the Hellfire Gunboat, he fired.

The harpoon caught the gunboat in the bow, and the harpoon line drew taut.

The trimaran had a catch.

Soon the Mariner's boat was towing the gunboat, pulling it and its careening crew around, the bullet-and-fire-belching machine gun still carelessly shooting up the ocean, to where the refueler would be its next, if unintended, target.

The Deacon saw bullets tracing paths in the surface of the sea, and said, "Could someone tell me why that boat is still firing? Signal him, you moron, flag him!"

And the flag boy frantically issued a cease-and-desist order, but the Hellfire Gunboat's gunner gunned on. Right now he was cutting down an emerging pack of Smokers on jetskis, turning them into bloody mist and fish chum.

The hurricane of gunfire was swinging closer and closer to the refueler, shredding the water ahead of it.

The geometry of it was inevitable.

While his Smokers stood there stupidly, the Deacon had the foresight to jump off deck, though his jump was accelerated somewhat when, as the Hellfire Gunboat's hellfire tore into the refueler's bow, the barge detonated like the floating bomb it was, disappearing in a startling fireball that scorched the Deacon's departing ass.

On the trimaran, the Mariner used a Smoker knife to cut the harpoon line, then returned to the helm and sailed through the rain of fiery debris and a fog of smoke that soon began to thin, and clear.

11

The endless empty stretch of lazily rolling ocean made an eloquent argument for a world without people.

Unintentionally presenting corroborative evidence, a lonely battered tugboat carved a disruptive path through the gently white-capped blue, dragging the remnants of a once-proud Smoker armada—riderless jetskis, smaller boats, even barges. These were damaged craft in some cases, go-juiceless in others (the refueler barge having exploded). Clinging to these craft, aboard, alongside, some even hanging onto towropes and struggling to stay afloat, were Smokers as battered as the tug, many of them wounded, clutching makeshift bloody bandages to injuries inflicted by the inferior force at Oasis. Some of these men would not make it home to the *'Deez*.

The Oasis atoll carved a different pattern against the horizon in the aftermath of the attack: whole sections of it were gone, and tendrils of smoke slithered into the sky like crawling charcoal snakes. As a Smoker patrol boat grumbled its way into the lagoon, its prow bumped into floating debris, some of it human, nudging it out of the way.

Soon the Deacon stepped off the patrol boat onto a stable section of dock that elsewhere had gaping holes like missing teeth in an awful smile. The Warrior Priest of the Smokers looked as battered as his men: his head was wrapped in a blood-soaked bandage that rode his bald skull like an off-kilter bandanna, covering his left eye (or what had been his left eye, before the refueler explosion). His uniform, which had before an unraveled, seaweed aspect, had been reduced to charred ribbons.

A Smoker everyone referred to as "the Ledger," carrying the big black balance book he'd been named for, rushed up to the Deacon.

"I heard you were wounded, sir. Terribly sorry."

The Ledger was small for a Smoker, and smart for a Smoker, too—that was why the Deacon had given him the responsibility of keeping the books.

"Make me feel better," the Deacon said.

Adjusting his wire-frame eyeglasses, the Ledger filled his hands with the big book and held it open and began to read as if the words were holy.

"Six hundred sixty Gs of hydro salvaged, three-quarter grade or better . . . one hundred twenty keys of assorted edibles—jerked fish, plankton cakes . . . sixty keys of lamp oil . . . forty-four old-growth grapevines . . . ten assorted fruit trees."

"Reloads?"

The Ledger looked up from the book and winced. "Sorry, sir. Zero reloads. No ammo storage at all on this atoll, just spears and bows and arrows. . . ."

"Primitive little shits."

"Zero go-juice, too. No refining capability."

"Barbarians." The Deacon shook his head, then regretted the gesture, touching his face below the bloody bandage. His voice was more melancholy than pained, however, as he said, "These little excursions used to be *fun*. How long's it been since we had a really good crusade, Ledger? Tell me—how long?"

The Ledger frowned and began flipping through the pages, apparently not wanting to express an opinion without documentation.

"Don't look it up," the Deacon sighed. "It was a rhetorical question."

"A what, sir?"

The Deacon sighed again. His human ledger book was smart for a Smoker, yes; but that was faint praise.

"Used to be a new atoll on every horizon," the Deacon said wistfully. He extended an arm and his fingers stretched toward the sky. "Where the hell are they all going?"

The Ledger glanced around the smoking scorched ruins of the atoll, and seemed about to answer him, then thought better of it.

In the remains of what seemed to be a factory of some kind, the Nord improved the Deacon's mood with a discovery.

"Found this." The Nord sneered a smile as he held out a jar with netting. "It was among the effects of the atoll Elders. . . ."

The Deacon eagerly opened the lid, dug his hand down in the earth. How rich it felt! About a third of the dirt was gone, probably wasted in ceremonial use by these primitives. He withdrew his hand and held it to his face, and got almost giddy from the aroma.

"We're getting warmer," the Deacon said. "And the girl?"

The Nord shook his head. "Not here. She may have gotten away."

The Deacon swung a fist at the air. The Nord and the other Smokers began to back away—they knew about the Deacon's temper.

"She's what we *came* for!" He began to pace, his boots clomping on the slat floor. "We didn't do this for practice. We didn't lose machines and go-juice and men so we could sack a poverty-stricken floating garbage heap for a few Gs of hydro and a handful of damn fruit trees!"

"Couple heartbeats inside," the Nord offered, tentatively. "Not saying much."

"Take me to them. *I'll* question them personally . . . show you candy-asses how a real man conducts an interrogation. . . ."

Their wrists lashed to a large gearbox, two Atollers— one of them an Elder in the characteristic seaweed gown, the other a gatesman—were slumped, barely conscious, heads hanging; both were smudged and mussed and bleeding, their apparel in shreds. A pair of Smokers were guarding them, but the prisoners weren't going anywhere.

The Deacon held out an open palm to either Smoker guard and they knew at once to fill those palms with a handgun off their belts.

The Nord just behind him, the Deacon stood in front of the two prisoners, between them, and raised a handgun to the nearest temple of either man. Their eyes widened and both men began to beg for mercy, their words a frantic jumble.

"If you both talk at the same time," the Deacon said, like a scolding teacher, "I'll *shoot* one of you!"

They fell silent.

"Good," the Deacon said. "Now . . . if you'll notice the arterial nature of the blood coming from the hole in my head, you can fairly assume that I'm having a bad day. And you can ask my men, if you doubt me . . . but when the Deacon has a bad day, *everybody* has a *really* bad day."

The Smoker guards were smiling a little, nodding at each other. The Nord and Ledger were exchanging nods, too.

"So," the Deacon said, "here it is: I need to know about the tattooed girl."

The two men began talking again, blabbering all at once, each trying to talk louder than the other, their words piling on top of each other, making an awful blur in the Deacon's pounding skull.

He flipped a metal coin, then blew the gatesman's

brains out in a shower of gore, the echo of the gunshot thundering through the factory.

The Smokers around him didn't flinch. They knew the Deacon's ways.

"All right," the Deacon said quietly. He addressed the Elder. "You won. Now, start over."

The Elder, shocked into silence, splashed with blood, looked beseechingly at the Deacon, whose gun barrel was still pressed into his temple.

The Deacon took the gun away. "Yes, you can talk. I want you to talk. If you don't talk, you're gonna get blown away, too. Got it?"

"I saw the girl," the Elder said, his voice a raspy whisper.

"Where?"

"I'm not sure . . . the smoke was so thick . . . but she was with Helen, the one who raised her. . . ."

The Deacon frowned. "What are you talking about?"

"The tattooed girl! She got on a boat. With Helen."

"*What* boat?"

"The three-hulled one."

Rage turned the Deacon's face crimson. That was the boat that blew up his refueler! The boat that cost him a thousand Gs of go-juice. . . .

"*Whose* boat?"

"The mute-o's," the Elder said.

The Deacon's frown turned puzzled. "'Mute-o'? What the hell sort of word is that?"

The Elder was working hard to earn his life. "He's

116

got slits behind his ears . . . like fish gills. He wasn't really a man. 'A fluke of evolution,' Old Gregor called him."

"I'm sorry," said the Deacon, the soul of patience and goodwill. "A fluke of what, did you say?"

"'Evolution,'" the Ledger said.

The Deacon turned to smile at his human balance book; the Ledger looked away. It was the sort of smile that was frequently followed by a blow.

"I heard the man," the Deacon said.

"Sorry, sir," the Ledger said.

"Tell you what. Let's have an intelligent conversation—I'll talk, all of you listen. . . ."

The Smoker guards, the Ledger, the Nord, all gave the Deacon their rapt attention, while the Elder just dangled from the gearbox, trembling.

"In the beginning," the Deacon intoned grandly, "the Provider said, 'Let there be water,' and the seas came forth. He created everything we know—the sun, the air we breathe. He made man, he made fish. But no combination thereof. The Provider does *not* abide the notion of 'evolution.'"

The Smoker guards, the Nord, and the Ledger joined in to say, "Amen."

The Deacon said, "Bless you, my children," and put the gun back against the Elder's head, cocking the hammer back.

The Elder's eyes were huge and terror-stricken. "But . . . you said you wouldn't kill me!"

"Did I?" He looked back at his men. "Witnesses—anybody? Speak the truth, now. Did I?"

Shrugs all around.

"You *did*!" the Elder said. "I *heard* you—you said it!"

The Deacon backed away, uncocked the gun. "You know . . . I may have. And a man is only as good as his word, after all."

The Elder gasped in relief. "Provider be praised. . . ."

"Provider be praised," the Warrior Priest said, and handed the gun to the Nord with a nod, and walked away as a second gunshot thundered through the ramshackle factory.

When the Nord caught up with him, gun smoking, the Deacon said, "When we get to the '*Deez,* tank up the sky boat. Get it out on patrol. . . ."

The blood was running from under the soaked bandage; he yanked it off and exposed the ghastly gaping scarlet cavity where his left eye used to be.

"I want that Ichthy freak! Find him, and we'll find the girl."

The Nord nodded.

"And damn it," the Deacon said, "somebody get me a fresh bandage! Do I have to do *everything* myself?"

12

The swell of the sea was increasing, but the trimaran—
its deck littered with debris, including charred pieces
of the Smoker refueler that had exploded—was sailing smoothly, especially considering its battered condition. With a spare sail in hand, the Mariner dove
from the ship into the icy waters and swam under the
main hull to plug up a hole blown there in the battle.

That should hold her—for now.

Soon he was flopping back onto the trimaran deck,
dripping wet; he reached for his plastic bottle of
murky three-quarter-grade water and swigged, once.

He turned his gaze on the woman, Helen, who sat
nervously beside the mast, its broken lines and tattered
sail swinging just above her.

She'd had the opportunity to pilfer a drink from the
plastic water bottle, while he was down plugging that
hole. But she hadn't taken that opportunity—either
out of fear, or trying to show him she could be trusted.

Not that he gave a damn, either way.

"I know what you're thinking," she said, glumly.

He said nothing. Instead, he glanced at the child, who sat silently on the stern, staring across the sea back in the direction they'd come from, her perfect little face blank with shock and horror. Without even looking at what she was doing, the girl was scribbling drawings on the hull with a piece of charcoal— explosions, hand-to-hand combat, violent images no child should ever have been subjected to. He felt bad for her.

But it didn't change the reality they would soon be facing.

"You're thinking," she said, "how much longer that hydro of yours would last if there wasn't three of us on this boat."

Actually, it had been much earlier that he thought of that.

"Well," she said, in a reasoning, reasonable tone, "Enola won't drink much, and I won't . . ."

He screwed the cap back on the water bottle. Maybe she thought he'd reward her honesty with a sip. If so, she was wrong.

". . . I won't drink at all," she said. "Not till we get there."

He frowned. "Get where?"

"Wherever you're going."

"And where would that be?"

"Wherever you got your dirt."

So that was it.

He said, "I salvaged it off an atoll the Smokers hit. The dead Atollers didn't say where they got it."

"Nice try," she said, with a nasty little smile, shaking her head. "Smokers don't leave *anything* behind after a raid—*especially* dirt."

He said nothing.

"And I never saw dirt like *that*," she said.

Her eyes searched his.

"You've been there, haven't you?" she said. Her voice was hushed, barely audible over the lap of waves against the ship. Hushed, and almost wistful.

"Where?"

Now urgency throbbed in her voice. "*Dryland . . .* you *know* where it is."

Almost amused, he moved over, next to her. "Yeah. Sure. I know where it is."

Her eyes exploded with surprise. It was as if she'd been struck in the head by a swinging boom.

"I *knew* it," she said. "And we . . . we're *going* there?"

"You and I are," the Mariner said. Very softly, he said, "The kid we gotta heave over the side."

Now her expression fell; she seemed confused, then horrified. "What?"

He nodded toward the main hull. "We're taking on water. My boat got tore up in that fracas. My desalinator got bunged up. . . ." Now he nodded to the contraption of hoses and globes and filters and valves that recycled his urine. "We'll be lucky to get half a hydro ration out of that."

Her eyes were tight. "I said I wouldn't drink. . . ."

"For twelve days? I don't think so."

She moved away from him with a shudder. "Maybe the Atollers were right. Maybe you are a monster. . . ."

He whispered: "Better one of you dies now than you both die slow. You're strong. You have a chance. That kid is doomed. Face it. Live with it."

He got to his feet and she reached out and grabbed his ankle. "Wait!"

He looked coldly down at her. "There's nothing more to talk about."

"We saved your life! Without us, you wouldn't've got out of there. . . ."

"You got me out," he said, "so you could get out. That makes us even."

She scrambled to her feet. "Look, I can fish . . . I can cook. . . ."

"So can I."

Her eyes were flashing with desperate thought. Then her fingers flew to her neck, removing her necklace. She held it out to him.

"Take this, then," she said. "It's worth . . ."

"I got better ones below deck." He grinned for half a second. "The looters didn't find everything."

She sighed, shook her head. "Listen . . . I can understand after what happened to you back on Oasis, why you'd be bitter . . ."

"I'm not bitter."

"Well, angry, then . . ."

"Do I look angry?"

"But she's just a *child*. . . ."

He said nothing.

Her face lost all expression; her eyes turned hard and clear.

"Is there . . . something else I can barter, then?"

"Like what?"

She wet those lips. Parched or not, they were full and lovely. "You said yourself . . . you've been out a long time. . . ."

She was a vision, haloed in the afternoon sun . . . her mouth so full . . . her shape so womanly and yet girlish. . . .

The thoughts must have shown in his face, because she smiled a little—to use her word, it was a bitter little smile—and she called out to the girl: "Enola!"

"Yes?"

"Enola, go below deck. I need to . . . speak to our host, privately."

"Yes, Helen."

And then the woman was standing before him, tugging the tunic off a round, tanned shoulder.

Enola jumped down inside the cramped cabin. Like any kid, she couldn't resist exploring, snooping, and almost immediately she touched a latch that sent a board slamming open.

Jumping back, cringing, she cocked an ear, expecting the sound to attract the grown-ups' attention, and get her a scolding. . . .

But they must have been busy up there, because no scolding came.

The piece of wood that fell from the wall made a sort of desk, and on it was pinned a homemade chart—a map, though that was not a word Enola knew. There were shelves and square cubbyholes in the space the board had been hiding. And more charts were rolled up there—paper! Precious paper!

Even Old Gregor hadn't had such a wealth of paper.

And in one of the cubbyholes, she found a box. She could not read the words on it—CRAYOLA CRAYONS—64 COLORS—but she knew at once, as any child would, what the objects within were made for.

They were of various sizes—some used more than others, some broken in half—but Enola knew treasure when she saw it. She snatched a crayon—labeled "Cyan"—and made a test line on one of the water-stained, ancient pieces of paper—turning it over to the blank side, first. She didn't want to spoil the drawing someone else had made.

She was not a bad child, Enola.

But she was a child, and a child with a box of crayons, at that.

The test line turned out beautiful, and she hunkered over the paper, images spilling out of her mind; she would use first one crayon, than another. She'd never had *color* drawsticks before, and now she could make color pictures!

And they were wonderful images—birds, horses, people in their huts, mountains—with shadings of this hue and that one. The stark charcoal images of battle had been left out on the hull.

She stepped out of the tunic.

Her flesh was lovely, perfect, not a blemish, hardly any scars, even—unusual for anyone in Waterworld. Her breasts were full, held proudly high, her rib cage prominent (good for childbearing), her stomach hard and flat and muscular, her legs muscular, too, but their shape pleasing, as she boldly, unashamedly stood with her feet planted firmly, legs apart.

She obviously didn't like having to offer herself like this, but once that decision had been made, she went with it. He had to admire that.

And he certainly admired the looks of the woman.

Without him consciously willing it, his hand reached out and touched one lovely, round breast; barely touching the supple skin, he felt himself stirring . . .

. . . and withdrew his hand.

"No," he said.

She was astounded. "No?"

"It wouldn't be right," he said acidly. "I'm not your kind."

She clutched his arm, saying, "I'm not like the others . . . I never . . ."

"You air breathers are all alike." He removed her hand. "You know what I was *really* thinking? Why shouldn't I drop you both in my wake, right now! You got nothin' I need."

She covered her breasts with her arm—as if suddenly realizing she was standing there naked—and he brushed by her, as if she were just another flapping sail, and headed for the stern. He heard her gathering up her clothing behind him, even as he bent to clear off some of the rubble littering the deck. Then he began working the sails.

Her voice came from behind him, and there was a new edge in it; a harsh edge.

"You're taking us to Dryland. *Both* of us. . . ."

He turned slowly and looked up at her. She was back in her tunic again, but in one hand was something new: a weapon. Where she'd got it from, he had no idea; she'd sneaked it aboard, somehow.

Small, one shot only, the wrist speargun was aimed directly for his heart.

"Killing's a hard thing to do well," he told her, still working with the sails. "And, believe me, I'm not the one to start on."

But her expression was steely and determined, and the tiny speargun in her hand could not have been more level. If she was nervous, it was well hidden.

"Maybe you wouldn't be the first man I killed," she said.

"Maybe. But just how long do you plan to hold that thing on me?"

"As long as it takes," she said, unflinchingly. "From here to Dryland, if—"

He shoved the tiller hard over, making the boat point sharply up, the jib crackling; then he flicked a pawl holding the jib halyard, and—suddenly loose—

the sail billowed aft, smothering the woman within its canvas blanket.

He grabbed a boat oar and thumped the lump in the sail's middle—her head—one good hard whack.

The lump slumped.

Then, in one easy motion, he reached under the canvas, fished out her lifeless arm, and yanked the wrist speargun from her hand.

Now maybe he could concentrate on sailing, and make a little time, before those Smokers came looking for them.

13

The Deacon's castle—the *'Deez*—was a sprawling cargo ship that in ancient times had been called a "supertanker"—three hundred tons of rust-pitted, barnacle-encrusted steel. A towering smokestack at the stern billowed black fumes, but the ship seemed almost stationary. It had been adrift for centuries, and at this stage of its existence was more atoll than vehicle.

Deep in the bowels of the *'Deez,* in the ship's infirmary, Doc—the Deacon's personal physician—was tending his patient. The small, emaciated Doc did not look well, his sickly appearance accentuated by the tubes permanently installed up his nostrils. The tubes extended to gas tanks on a wheeled cart, which provided the addicted Doc not with oxygen but with a recreational mix of various gases, a nasal cocktail that he adjusted via handles on the tanks, according to his mood.

In the small, filthy cabin, where the Deacon sat in a

leaned-back chair (whose metal plate included the following markings: "Dental Implements, Inc., Philadelphia"), several spectators gathered around to view the procedure. Among the onlookers was the Deacon's second-in-command—the Nord—as well as a handful of filthy feral children.

The Doc complained of these human baby rats intruding on his sanctuary ("Unsanitary!" he would say); but to the Deacon, children were tomorrow—they were the future! So he gave the little vermin the run of his ship.

Into a metal tray next to the lean-back chair, containing various antiquated medical instruments as well as a number of ball bearings of varied size, the Doc deposited the final tool of the operation: a fine-tipped paintbrush.

"There!" the Doc said, pleased with his handiwork, sucking in gas. "All done! Good as new—*better*!"

The Deacon pulled down the device above him that included a mirror and had a look at his new eye. The ball bearing that rode his left socket had a pupil and iris painted on; the Doc's artwork gleamed wetly.

But the Deacon was afraid the Doc was an even lesser artist than he was a physician.

The Deacon climbed out of the lean-back chair, picked up the putter that had become his new mace of office (the five iron, tragically, was missing in action), and struggled to get his balance.

The Doc steadied him. "There may be some small problem in depth perception. . . ."

"This better not screw up my short game," the Deacon said ominously.

"You'll soon adjust!" the Doc said. He laughed nervously. "A man of your intellect, your natural artistic skills, why in no time——"

"Well?" the Deacon said, turning to the Nord, gesturing to the ball bearing eye. "What do you think? Be brutal."

"Uh . . . not bad," the Nord said. "Yeah. Not bad at all."

"I don't mean to boast," the Doc said, touching his chest, "but I do believe I prefer it to your *real* eye."

The Deacon turned to one of the feral kids. "What do *you* say?"

"Looks like shit," the little punk said.

The Deacon beamed at the lad. "See? That's what I love about kids. No guile. No gullshit. Just the plain, utter truth."

He thrust the putting end of the putter into Doc's chest and the little man blanched.

"It *does* look like shit," the Deacon said accusingly. "And it feels like *cold* shit. . . ."

Just as the Deacon was weighing whether or not to turn up those valves and overdose the Doc in payment for his services, a voice from behind him caught his attention.

"'Scuze me, Deacon!"

The Ledger stood framed within an ungainly doorway cut out of the bulkhead.

"What is it?"

"There's a problem in the pit. Maybe you should come."

The Deacon fished out a pair of swimmer goggles from a pocket. He had blacked out the left lens, making a temporary eye patch of it. But now that the Doc had failed so miserably in coming up with a suitable prosthesis, the damn goggles would have to do. He tugged the goggles on, black lens covering his bad eye, the other lens riding his forehead.

He caught his reflection in the chair's mirror and, modern pirate that he was, thought himself rather dashing.

"Let's drive," the Deacon told the Ledger.

The Deaconmobile—as its master liked to refer to it—was cobbled together from six different land yachts of those glorious ancient days; rusted out, rolling on the now misshapen rims of its tireless wheels, multiple air horns riding the hood, an obstruction clearing prow attached to its nose, the Deaconmobile was a chariot fit for a god.

He climbed into the right front seat.

"The pit," the Deacon said to his Smoker chauffeur.

Smokers appeared from somewhere to line up behind the Deaconmobile and push. The chauffeur popped the clutch, the vehicle lurched to life, spewing exhaust, sending the Smokers pushing it into coughing spasms.

"And don't bother with the scenic route," the Deacon told the chauffeur, as the Deaconmobile rumbled down a corridor.

But every route within the labyrinthian recesses of the *'Deez* was scenic. Over there, huddled over an oil drum fire, a Smoker finished a rusty can of Spam and threw it onto a trash heap, only to have a handful of dirty feral kids leap for the can and fight over it, like the animals they were.

Kids, the Deacon smiled to himself. *So natural. So pure. . . .*

Soon they passed through an area of the dark ship where, looking down, the Deacon could see a crew of Smokers cutting plates out of an iron wall with grinding, sparking tools. Now and then a plate would slip through a hole in the floor, and a clang would be followed by a howl of echoed protests from workers on the floor below—these protests, of course, were ignored. Here and in the distance, flickering welding irons and the glow of white-hot iron being poured from portable forges into bullet molds were bursts of light in the vast, shadowy near-darkness, a mystically moody sight for the Deacon's proud eyes . . . or eye.

To a less biased eye, this area of the interior of the *'Deez* might seem ravaged, as if metal-eating germs were destroying the inner stomach linings of the decaying beast. But even in his foulest (or most pragmatic) frame of mind, the Deacon considered this work a necessary evil: the Smokers needed ammo, and if melting down their own walls was what it took, so be it, and Provider protect us.

The Deaconmobile pulled up by the door to the storeroom. The Deacon waited while the Ledger (one of the handful of others with access to the vast chamber of goods) unlocked the heavy steel door; then he, the Ledger, and the Nord went in, leaving the chauffeur behind.

Stacked against the walls and on shelves were the spoils of countless Smoker raids: diminishing cases of prehistoric canned meat, smokesticks, and beer (canned and bottled). The Deacon knew that, with the atolls disappearing, opportunities to replenish this thinning repository were getting fewer and farther between.

Their footsteps must have indicated their presence to the tenant below, because suddenly a desperate voice came echoing up through the floor: *"Somebody! Anybody! Take it off! Hey, up there!"*

With a tickled little smile, the Deacon knelt over the steel cover plate in the middle of the floor and screwed the spigotlike valve, swinging the plate up so he could look down into the blackness of the "home" of the Smoker with, hands down, the worst job on the *'Deez*.

"Yes?" the Deacon said.

And though he spoke softly, his voice reverberated off the steel walls of the cavernous chamber below.

"Your Deaconship! Hello!" the lonely Smoker called.

Twenty feet down, floating on a dingy dinghy in a pool of black sludge, his body slickly, wetly black from the rib cage down, the Deacon's human depth gauge was waving his hands, like a shipwreck survivor on a raft trying to flag down a plane.

"What is it?"

"Good morning! Or is it night? Whatever the case may be, greetings to you, sir!"

The Deacon was bored already. "Get on with it. I'm a busy man."

"I thought you should know," the depth gauge hollered up, his voice bouncing off the steel walls, "we're down to exactly four feet, nine inches of black stuff!"

The Deacon moved away from the opening, nodding to the Nord to screw the cover back in place.

"Your Deaconship!" the human depth gauge was calling. "Is there a possibility for relief—"

But his words were cut off by the scraping of the cover being wound back in place.

The Deacon stood and gave the Ledger an openly troubled look. "How many Gs is that? After refining?"

The Ledger's eyes rolled upward as he did some quick calculating. Then he looked warily at the Deacon and said, "Maybe three refueler loads."

"If we *had* a refueler," the Deacon said disgustedly.

"Sweet Joe," the Nord said. "Is that all? We'll burn through that in two lunars. . . ."

"It doesn't matter," the Deacon said.

"Doesn't matter . . ." the Nord began.

The Deacon raised a silencing hand. "The only thing that matters is the tattooed girl. Don't spare any go-juice finding her. I don't care if we run through every drop of the stuff . . . just don't waste it on *anything* else."

The Nord nodded.

The Deacon placed his left hand on the shoulder of his right-hand man. "My friend, Dryland is the mother lode. The first person who gets there is king. Got it? Not captain of some dying ship. *King*."

Next stop for the Deaconmobile was the theater, where he rewarded his loyal Smokers with screenings of a half-dozen films, Land Days artifacts even more precious than magazines, culled from countless raids. He stood on his speechifying balcony, overlooking hundreds of his men as they sat in the darkness watching the scratchy images of a war film starring the legendary Land Days leader, John Wayne.

Fighter planes battled the skies, with John Wayne and his Smokers riddling the planes of their Asian opponents, sending them flaming from the sky. The Deacon's Smokers cheered wildly and were a mad chorus shouting every long-since familiar line of dialogue in tandem with the screen.

The Nord had sent for the Deacon's staff, twenty Smokers who constituted the best and brightest of his army, but this was of course not saying much. An ancient Land Days proverb popped into the Deacon's mind: "In the land of the blind, the one-eyed man is king."

"If it wasn't for me," he whispered to the Nord, "this place would be absolute chaos. Anything from our scout planes?"

The chief Smoker pilot, wearing a dilapidated, moth-eaten pilot's cap, stepped forward and said, "Nothing yet."

"Tracker sharks deployed?"

The Nord nodded.

"Good," the Deacon said. "All right. Shut 'er down."

Soon the projector bulb below dimmed, then died, the sound slowing and droning to a halt. The Smoker crowd erupted in protest.

The angry shouts, however, died upon the clicking on of two great klieg lights that bathed the Deacon in white.

The Smoker army, hushed now, turned en masse to their leader, eyes on the balcony from which he had dispensed so much wisdom in the past.

"Let me hear a witness!" the Deacon's voice boomed. "Are we going to Dryland or not?"

The crowd erupted again, but this time in approval, hooting and hollering its support.

"Let me hear it!" the Deacon cried, his voice echoing across the hall. "What will we do when we get there?"

And the voices, in almost perfect unison, began the litany: "*Plow it and paint it . . . Pile it and pave it. . . .*"

"Mine it and depine it!" the Deacon added, his fist threatening the air. "And don't forget the height of our ambition, that ancient symbol of Earthly power! What puts the shine in our shinola? The Dryland Experience!"

He yanked a cord and his Smoker staff stood to one side as curtains parted to reveal a huge chart (labeled

"Architect's Rendering") of an eighteen-hole "golf course" spreading over rolling green hills.

The Smokers went wild, their cries almost orgiastic, resonating in the metal chamber.

"Eighteen holes," the Deacon said, reminding them (for he had given this speech many times before), using his putter as a pointer, "world class . . . fifth hole a par five, six hundred and thirty yards with two doglegs."

Cheers rose from the Smokers below.

Now the Deacon returned to the railing of the balcony and leaned over and stared down at his men with one wide, wild eye.

"But none of that happens until we find the fishman that has the little girl . . . right?"

The word "right" returned to him in overlapping unison.

"She's the deed to the property," he shouted. "Finding her is Job Number One. And the first guy that spots 'em gets *this*. . . ."

And from a pocket he withdrew—and held high—an object as rare as a magazine or film: a videotape.

"Operation Desert Storm," the Deacon said seductively. Then his voice rose to booming heights again: "The Air War!"

The crowd roared and stampeded out of the theater to seek out their under leaders to volunteer for scouting duty. Even the eyes of the Deacon's staff had lighted up at the thought of this precious prize, his chief pilot scurrying off to climb aboard his plane.

138

It had occurred to none of them, the Deacon noted to himself with wry amusement, that the only VCR on the ship was communal . . . and that whoever got the tape would end up sharing it with the rest of the men, anyway.

But he had learned to accept that his men were morons, and that wasn't all bad.

Would men with brains be this loyal?

14

The trimaran was shipshape now, or as close to it as could be expected, spliced lines speeding through pulleys, frazzled sails snapping shut.

The Mariner shifted his attention to repairing his hydro recycler; he was patching some of the tubing as the woman came across the netting deck, her face a mask of quiet disgust as she bore two jars of yellowish fluid. Even with a welt on her head (from where he'd oar-whacked her), and a couple of jars of piss in her hands, she was a handsome woman.

He took the jars of urine from her, poured first one, then the other, into the funnel; then he poured a jar of his own in and cranked the pump. The machine was still leaking, but not as badly, and in a few moments, a trickle of nearly clear water flowed from the spigot and spattered into the glass beaker.

"Why don't you just use sea hydro?" she asked. There was a tiny sneer of distaste on the full lips.

"Salt's too hard on the filters," he said.

When the last recycled drop fell, he held the beaker up to the sunlight—its color was right, or right enough. He took a drink.

Not bad.

He drank some more, till the beaker was half-empty.

"Can I have some?" she asked.

"I thought the idea of drinking recycled urine made you sick."

"It's not for me. It's for the girl."

He took another swig, swirled it around in his mouth, then spit it out on the soil of the tomato plant.

"Part of that came out of me, you know," she said indignantly.

He handed her the beaker with the remainder of the hydro and watched her cross the netting to where Enola sat near the mast. The woman knelt by the child, smiled, and made her drink all of the water.

At least she kept her word, the Mariner noted. *Didn't take any for herself. . . .*

The girl's voice was soft, and intended for Helen only, but he could hear the child say: "Is he taking us to Dryland?"

And he heard the woman, not so softly, say, "Yeah. He is."

He spliced the torn dragline on the stern, biting the rope to test its strength. It would hold. Then he sat coiling the rope, and sensed someone approaching.

The child came slowly across the springy netting deck, her face solemn, her dreadlock braids swinging in the breeze, the cloth of her tunic doing likewise.

142

Then she stood before him, staring at him.

He stared right back at her, continuing with his coiling.

Finally the girl spoke; it was a whisper, barely audible above the wind. "Thank you for not killing us."

She bent forward and kissed him on the cheek.

He couldn't have been more surprised—or unnerved—if she had struck him a blow. He got to his feet, brushing her aside, and she fell on the netting, on her behind, not hard, bouncing. He really hadn't meant to knock her down, and even though it hadn't hurt the child, chagrin spread across him like a rash.

He moved quickly away from the child, from both of them, finding the farthest corner of his boat—to be as far away from them as possible.

"Just stay away from him," he heard the woman advise the girl.

Despite an undercurrent of hostility, the woman was doing her best not to cross him; she'd lend a hand, whenever she could, working hard, obviously trying to earn her keep, and the child's. Once, coming down from a point high up the mast where he'd been making a repair, he had stopped to watch her as she sat sewing a patch onto a spare sail. She had grace, and a supple, womanly way about her that made him ache, somewhere deep inside him—and not just his loins.

Then she caught him looking at her, and again embarrassment spread across him, and he turned quickly away and went to his steering console, to check the boat's course.

The child, bent down doing something, was sitting there, in his path.

"Move," he said.

"Enola!" the woman called.

Helen was gesturing for the child to get out of his way, and she did, bounding off a few steps on the springy net deck. As she went, he caught a glimpse of the strange markings on her back. He'd noticed them before.

And he did wonder what they were.

But asking about them would bring him closer to these two, and he did not really care to be any closer to them than he already was. He'd never had to share his ship with anyone before, and this clutter of humanity was driving him crazy.

He took his seat at the console, plucked his telescope from its scabbard, and began slowly scanning the horizon. Then something was blocking his sights, and he lowered the device, and realized Enola had wandered into his line of vision.

"For the love of Poseidon!" he swore. "You're in my view!"

"Enola!" the woman called. "Get *over* here!"

At least the child was quick to obey.

But as she scurried away, he noticed something clutched in her hand: one of his crayons. Had she been in his things? Grimacing with irritation, he turned to complain to the woman, but before the words came out, he noticed something else.

Drawings—right on the hull! Violent images

sketched not in easily removed charcoal, but with crayon . . . Smokers pierced by arrows, Atollers wounded in battle. . . .

"Hey," he yelled.

The child was sitting, now, using the Crayola to scribble more images right onto the central hull of the boat. Dozens of drawings! Damn. . . .

He stalked over to her. "What the hell are you doing?".

She didn't look up at him, shrugging a little. "Decorating your boat. It's ugly."

He picked her up—she almost flew out of his hands, she was so light; she weighed almost nothing—and set her aside roughly, snatching the Crayola from her hand. He found a cloth and knelt and rubbed at the drawings. And rubbed.

They didn't come off.

He stood, wadding and tossing the cloth to his feet. He shook a scolding finger at the child. "You don't touch *anything* of mine."

She looked up at him placidly; her eyes were wide and deep blue. "I drew it for you."

He bent over and shook a fist at her. "You don't draw on *anything* of mine. Understand?"

She was expressionless, and not at all frightened.

Exasperated, he shook his head—and his line of sight caught something else: the nearby sail, covered with Crayola drawings. Covered as far as the child's reach, that is.

He grabbed her by the arm. Not hard—just to get her attention.

And then, trying to crack the child's placid countenance, he said harshly, "This is my boat. I keep it the way I like it. If I wanted pictures drawn on my things, I'd draw them myself."

"Maybe you don't draw as good as me."

"You take up space," he snarled at the child, "and you slow me down!"

"She's just a little girl," the woman said.

He hadn't seen her approach; it was as if she had materialized, a guardian angel suddenly hovering over the child.

"This is my boat," he said.

"She doesn't know the rules," Helen said.

"You want to stay?"

The woman, a hand on the girl's shoulder, swallowed hard, and nodded.

"Then teach her," he said, and he went to the tiller.

Again, he heard the woman's warning to the child: "Stay away from him."

But not five minutes later, there the child was, standing looking at him, bluer-than-blue eyes staring unblinkingly at him from that carved-mask face of hers.

"You know what?" the child asked.

He didn't answer.

"You're not so tough," she said.

He didn't look at her.

"How many men have you killed?" she asked.

He didn't answer.

"Ten?"

He didn't answer.

"Twenty?"

"You know what?" he asked.

She didn't answer.

"You talk too much," he said.

"I talk too much," she said, "'cause you don't talk enough. . . . How many?"

"How many what?"

"Have you killed?"

"You mean, including children?"

She studied him, trying to figure out if he was kidding her, or if it was a threat.

Then she said, "I'm not afraid of you. . . . I told Helen you wouldn't be so ugly if you cut off some of that hair."

That did it.

He scooped her up like a sack of booty and said, "You talk all the time; it's like a storm when you're around," and he heaved the wide-eyed child over the side.

The splash summoned the woman, who looked over the side at the girl, thrashing in the sea, and yelled, "You bastard! She can't *swim*!"

And then the woman dove in after the child.

Crabs of hell, he thought. *Two of them in the drink, now!* Of course, leaving them there would solve a lot of problems. . . .

But instead, he headed aft, kicked the mainsail winch, collapsing the mainsail, gibbing around to pick them up. The woman swam well enough—she had the child in tow—and he had to admire her spirit, jumping in like that, without a thought for her own safety.

A pop caught his attention. He swung his face above the swimming woman, looking to the horizon, and heard another backfiringlike pop. He had meant to help the woman back up into the boat, but then she was boosting Enola up on the pontoon and swinging herself up there, wringing wet and hopping mad.

"You son of a bitch!"

He wasn't looking at her; he was looking at the horizon.

"I swear," she was saying, "if you ever touch that child again, ever lay a hand on her, you'll go to sleep that night and never wake up. . . ."

As she trailed off, she clearly sensed that he was on alert. He ducked under the boom, and his eyes searched the opposite horizon. Not a boat in sight . . .

But there was a droning sound, not unlike the mechanical drone that announced the speedboats and jetskis of . . .

"Smokers?" Helen asked.

He turned his attention to the sky.

Engine missing, buzz-sawing over the water, spewing smoke so badly it might have been crashing rather than cruising, the battered seaplane loped into view, then looped in and began circling the trimaran.

"Can we outrun him?" Helen asked.

"Not with my sails down," the Mariner said. "They may not open fire. They're just scouting us . . ."

"Are they Smokers?"

The plane circled them, then swooped down toward the bow, and as it came around, they could see him: the goggled tail gunner, aiming a grotesque looking machine gun their way, and then it barked at them, bullets stitching their way across the water and nibbling at the outboard pontoon.

The three of them ran for the main hull, heading for the recess of the main cabin, and the roar of the seaplane engine told them the plane was coming around for another try at them. The child ducked behind the mast, taking cover, and the woman was right behind her, but the Mariner stopped in his tracks, looked back, and turned and quickly ran toward the rear of the ship, diving down the stern hatch.

He could hear the woman's voice shout over the seaplane's rumble: "Hey!"

It was an accusation of cowardice, not that he gave a damn; he was down snatching a double-barrel speargun off the bulkhead. He whipped out his knife, sliced the line connecting spears and gun, and leapt back up onto the hull.

The machine gun was silent, though the plane was swooping in for the kill. The Mariner caught the frantic face of the gunner, ramroding the clogged barrel of the jammed weapon. This might buy them a little time. . . .

But just as he was thinking of how to best use it, he saw her: the woman, Helen, hunched over the harpoon gun mounted on the bow. She had the thing cocked, and was swinging it around, taking aim on the circling plane.

Her face was tight with determination and he admired her courage, even as he knew the disaster she was sowing, and he screamed, "*Nooooooo* . . . !"

She either didn't hear him, or didn't care about his opinion, because she fired the gun, and its big harpoon streaked into the sky, trailing its line, and just as the gunner was swinging his fierce, and now unjammed, weapon around, bringing it back to bear on the trimaran, the harpoon stabbed through the plane's fuselage.

The Mariner almost had to admire her aim—or her luck—as he saw the form of the gunner slumped bloodily over the now useless gun; she hadn't just got the plane, with her shot, she'd skewered the gunner, as well. The pilot was looking back frantically at his dead gunner . . . and at his wounded plane.

Only the plane wasn't just wounded: it was harpooned like an airborne whale.

Attached to the trimaran by an uncompromising umbilical cord.

And as the plane flew, the line connecting it to the harpoon gun began to tighten, until finally the line was taut, and the expression on the woman's face was one of dawning horror as she realized what she'd done.

Knife in hand, the Mariner ran toward the bow, even as the ship lurched with the plane fighting the restraining line, and the deck around the harpoon gun began to whine and groan like an injured beast. Helen had backed off and now stood shielding Enola, and he flew past them, his blade just touching the line . . .

. . . when the entire harpoon gun and its stand ripped free of the deck and went flying over his head, as he landed bruisingly hard.

Like a fish that had taken bait from the sky, the harpoon gun and stand rode its line upward, shredding and tearing sails and lines as it went, only to lodge in the spreaders.

Caught there.

The line was wrapped around the mast, the Mariner noted bleakly as he got to his feet, and now that plane up there was circling . . . and the line was *winding* around the mast!

He gave the woman a sneering, murderous look and ran to the base of the mast, stabbing his free hand through a wrist lanyard, pulling on a counterweight; but it was tangled in the harpoon line circling the mast.

"Crabs of hell," he muttered.

The double-barrel speargun was on a strap, so he tossed it around his shoulder, stuck his knife in his teeth, and began climbing the teetering pole.

The higher up he got, the more nauseating the sway of the mast was, as the plane yanked the boat from side to side. The winding line was making a mess of the mainsail, but he was nearing the spreaders, where he could get at that vibrating harpoon line and cut the trimaran free. . . .

A bullet tore through the sail next to him. Not from

the machine gun, but something smaller caliber . . .
a pistol! Was that damn pilot taking potshots at him?
He grabbed a line, swung out from the mast, and
yanked his speargun off his shoulder. Drawing a bead
on the plane, he sent a spear winging toward the son
of a bitch. . . .

He could hear its thunk, which meant he'd probably
hit the plane, not the pilot, but maybe the guy would
be distracted long enough for the Mariner to swing out
and cut the shuddering harpoon line, setting them both
free. Four pistol shots stitched across the sail next to
him, and as he ducked the bullets, the knife slipped
from his hand and went tumbling, then clattering, to
the deck.

Shit!

He still had one spear in the speargun. He leaned
out, took careful aim as the plane closed in on him.

He could see him, see the pilot leaning out, pistol in
hand. The Mariner took aim. . . .

The pilot shot first. Only the shot wasn't aimed at
the Mariner, but rather the harpoon rope that bound
plane to boat, or which *had* bound plane to boat,
because the Smoker plane now lurched free, and the
remains of the rope fluttered after it.

The recoiling mast tossed the Mariner, backward,
through the tattered trimaran sails, and into midair,
and finally dropped him in the water as if he were an
engine that had fallen off the retreating plane.

He was underwater when the harpoon gun and stand
fell to the deck and crashed through it; he heard the

sound, both amplified and muffled, but didn't realize what it was till later. When he bobbed to the surface, he was so hot with anger, it was a wonder the water around him didn't boil.

He swam quickly to the boat and hauled himself aboard.

He glanced around his ship. It looked like hell.

He glared at the woman; she stood sheepishly, the child cowering behind her.

"I'm sorry," she said. "I was just trying to . . ."

His look silenced her.

He picked up his knife from the deck and moved toward her. The woman gasped as he reached out and stretched the long mane of hair tied behind her; as he brought the blade down, the child screamed. . . .

And the Mariner tossed the braid of hair onto the deck.

"The next time you touch anything on my boat," he said, "I'll choose something else to cut off."

The woman dropped to the deck in an exhausted pile, body heaving; but she wasn't crying.

Lower lip trembling, the child stepped forward and blocked his path.

"She said she was sorry," the girl said.

He stepped around her and tried to find some corner of the boat where he could be alone for a while, before he once again began repairing his home.

15

The Deacon's spacious quarters on the *'Deez* had once been a conference room; the captain's quarters had not been spacious enough for a man of the Deacon's magnitude. Not that the Deacon was physically imposing, but his personality, and his appetites, were huge.

He had decorated the suite himself, with trophies from this conquest and that one. The grand crystal chandelier had once upon a time lighted an opulent hotel ballroom, in Land Days—or so said the Elder who presented it to him, as a sort of duty offering if only the Smokers would spare the Elder's atoll (which was called, if memory served, Pardise).

The Deacon—who had been offended by the very idea of one man of religion attempting to bribe another—had, of course, directed the Nord to slowly torture the Elder, in order to pry loose the locations of any other of the atoll's hidden treasures. Nothing else of much value turned up, however, and before long the

Elder—and the rest of the atoll and its inhabitants—were sent off in search of another Paradise, courtesy of Smoker guns, blades, and fire.

Other treasures, gathered from this plundered atoll and that one, made the Deacon's quarters a veritable palace: the orange shag rug, its vivid color spreading like a glowing memory of days when the world wasn't shades of blue and gray; the purple, plastic-cocooned couches another colorful reminder of a superior time and culture; and artworks, including his vivid painting on velvet of the Land Days religious icon, Elvis, and a more prosaic if peaceful portrait of some unidentified Land Days personage, said to be the work of an ancient artist named Rembrandt.

But he would gladly trade it for a John Wayne on black velvet.

The size of the room lent itself to his putting range—too bad, in a way, his orange shag was not green—and, wearing sunglasses, he bent over his putter, lining up a shot. The damn ball bearing eyeball fell out and clicked against the sunglass lens.

"Damn it," he muttered, sliding a hand under the sunglasses to push the prosthesis back in place, and then he gently, expertly putted the ball into the cup.

"Nicely done," the Nord said.

The Deacon, chuckling with delight, sheathed his putter in his golf bag, and said, "And I wasn't even using my good eye."

The Nord had been patiently waiting. Now he risked interrupting the Deacon's game.

"You said to bring the pilot," he said, "when he returned."

"He's back? Good."

Urgency in his face, the Nord stepped forward. "He spotted them. There was a skirmish . . ."

"Bring him in!" The Deacon snapped off his sunglasses. "Let him tell me himself."

And soon the pilot, holding his battered cap in both hands, looking exhausted and emotionally wrung out, slumped before his master.

The Deacon placed a paternal hand on the pilot's shoulder. "Tell me what happened."

"They . . . they killed Ed. . . ." The pilot choked back tears.

"Tragic. So very tragic. The child? Did the fish-man have the tattooed girl?"

The pilot nodded. "Yeah, and some atoll bitch. She's the one that shot Ed. Harpooned him!"

"There are many bad people in Waterworld," the Deacon allowed, with a somber shake of the head. Then he slipped a supportive arm around his chief pilot, and gave him a manly hug. "But we both know there's plenty more where Ed came from. Now . . . which way were they heading?"

The Nord answered the question: "West-southwest."

The Deacon, pulling the shuffling pilot along with him, joined his second-in-command at a conference table, where antique charts were spread out. The Nord was working out speed-distance computations on one of them.

"Show me," the Deacon said.

The pilot nodded morosely, and pointed to a spot on the chart. "From here."

"Good. Now, get some rest."

And he shoved the pilot away, nodding to a Smoker guard to haul the pitiful creature out of his sight.

"Now, it seems to me," the Nord said, "if we launch *now*, we can run him down about . . ." He pointed to the chart, thumped a spot with a finger. ". . . *here*. Unless he changes course. . . ."

"Not likely," the Deacon said.

"He's a tricky one."

The Deacon nodded sagely. "Oh, yes, a wily one, our Ichthy demon. If he knows he's been spotted, he'll expect us to expect *him* to change course."

A smile slowly blossomed on the Nord's cruel, handsome face. "Which is why he'll keep on his heading."

"Exactly," the Deacon said. "So the real question is—*where* is he headed?"

The Nord's eyes narrowed.

"And does he know," the Deacon further offered, "just how precious his cargo is?"

Smoker guards on the periphery were not able to wrap their tiny minds around the Deacon's thoughtful analysis. But the Nord was keeping up.

"Dryland?" the Nord whispered.

"Dryland," the Deacon said. "Salvation. Room to grow!"

The Deacon hunkered over the chart, his eyes

burning. He stabbed a finger at the chart. "I say he's headed *here*. . . ."

And the Deacon stabbed the chart again, at another point.

"Which means," the Deacon said, "we'll take him here. . . ."

And the two men exchanged satisfied smiles.

Just over the Nord's shoulder, Elvis was smiling, too.

16

Its sails in tatters, the trimaran limped along courtesy of a breeze from the west-southwest. The Mariner, who had made all the repairs he could with what little he had to do them with, plucked a tomato from the scrawny but ripening potted plant.

He walked past the woman and child, sitting on the deck, and they recoiled in fear as he walked by. Women! What had he done to *them*?

On a small, square wooden block that he often ate his meals from, he used his knife to cut the tomato into four segments; the blade was razor-sharp and made clean cuts, but a little juice still squirted out onto the wooden board.

He ate the segments slowly, savoring them, then he licked the juice from the wooden block. He was wiping the excess juice from his face, about to lick his hand, when he noticed the dot on the horizon.

At his steering console, he unsheathed the telescope and had a look: a trawler, smaller than his, weathered but seashape, was piloted by a scruffy bearded drifter, who was waving at him, smiling, pointing upward . . .

. . . to the green flag atop his mast, flapping in the breeze.

"Who is it?"

The woman was suddenly beside him.

"Just some drifter," he said.

"Doesn't that flag mean he wants to trade?"

"Yes."

"Aren't we stopping?"

"No." He put the telescope back in its scabbard.

She smirked at him. "I thought you drifters all had to stop for each other. Isn't that your 'code'?"

He brushed past her.

"Maybe he has food," she said behind him. "You know, the child isn't like you—she needs to eat *every* day. . . ."

He looked at his sorry ship and wondered if stopping to trade with the scruffy drifter wasn't worth the risk. But after all he and his poor pummeled trimaran had been through, what did he have to trade?

Behind him, she was saying, "We may not see another boat for days. . . ."

He turned, glared, and said, "Sit down and shut up."

She did.

Before long, the Mariner was yanking a rope tight into a knot, securing it to the rail of the trimaran, where the drifter's boat was pulled up alongside.

The drifter boarded the Mariner's ship, but stayed close to his own vessel, as the trade got under way.

First, some socializing, as the drifter said, "Nice to run into somebody who still follows the rules." A grin flashed in the furry face. "You don't find many who honor the code, these days."

"Make it quick," the Mariner said. "What business do you have in mind?"

"What else?" The drifter shrugged. "Barter."

"Got any sail?"

The drifter eyed the trimaran and snorted derisively, shaking his head at the notion. "You ain't got enough to tempt me."

"I had enough for you to raise a flag."

"Just followin' the code . . . courtesy of the seas. . . ."

"This was your idea," the Mariner said coldly. "Get on with it."

From behind the Mariner came that nagging voice again: "How 'bout food?"

He glared at the woman. Didn't she know it wasn't her place to speak up in a barter? But she wasn't looking at him, she was smiling, cordially, at the drifter.

"Food?" the drifter said. "Great idea! I haven't eaten in two days. What've you got?"

Her smile fell; apparently that wasn't the answer she was looking for.

But the drifter's smile—and eyes—only got bigger, as he took in her womanly shape. "You the cook? Or maybe the waitress? 'Waitress' was always my favorite food. . . ."

She shivered as the drifter roared at his own lame joke. Her expression turning contemptuous, Helen slipped a protective arm around Enola, who huddled to the woman, confused about just exactly what was going on here.

The drifter was shopping—casting his gaze around the deck of the trimaran.

"Like you said," the Mariner conceded, "I don't have much."

But the drifter's eyes again landed on the woman; he looked her up and down, greedily. "On second thought, I don't know if I'd agree with you."

The woman moved back several steps, taking the child with her.

The drifter nodded toward the tomato plant. "How 'bout we start with that orchard you got over there?"

Pretty soon, a trade had been made. First, there was the ceremony of the Mariner offering the drifter a glass of his hydro, and the drifter doing the same from his own hydro storehouse. After dickering, the tomato plant and two rearview mirrors were at the drifter's feet, and the Mariner had, at his feet, a coil of rope.

Finally the drifter got around to it. "Got yourself quite a little harem going," he said.

The Mariner said nothing.

"What do you want for the females?" the drifter asked.

"We're not for sale," the woman almost shouted, hugging the child to her, her chin high but trembling a little.

164

"I'm not buyin', darlin'," the drifter said, "I'm tradin' . . . and everything's up for barter in Waterworld."

"Our business is done here," the Mariner said.

"They a pair?" the drifter asked, ignoring this statement, "or would ya consider sellin' 'em separate?"

"We need to move on," the Mariner said. "Thanks for the trade. . . ."

"How 'bout jus' rental?"

The Mariner thought about that. "You got sail, or resin, you can part with?"

The woman, child clutching her, stepped back another pace, taking the girl along.

"I told you already," the drifter said, "don't have any to spare. Haven't seen neither for trade in lunars."

"We're finished, then."

The drifter's eyes glinted. "I've got somethin' *else* that'll change your mind, though—somethin' you *can't* pass on. . . ."

Reaching inside his tattered shirt, the drifter withdrew a small, sealed bottle; within were a few pages from an ancient magazine—writing and pictures, both. "Picks and Pans" were the words at the top.

The Mariner's scalp began to tingle.

"Took it off some Atoller refugees," the drifter said. "Life savings of the whole clan. Been savin' it . . . for a *special* trade. . . ."

"Don't do it," the woman said. It wasn't a demand, but a plea.

The drifter sneered toward the woman. "Maybe I'm talkin' to the wrong person, here. Maybe this is *her* boat. . . ."

The Mariner extended his hand, and the drifter, eyes gleaming, mouth damp from spittle, filled that hand with the bottle, the pages within beckoning.

"Half an hour," the Mariner said.

"No," Helen gasped.

"Half an hour?" the drifter said, frowning, and he snatched the bottle back. "There's two pages in here! You could buy half a dozen girls with this!"

"Then go where you can do that. On this ship, you get half an hour. You trading or not?"

"Don't do this," the woman said softly.

"Shut up," he told her.

"I'd just as soon take the little one," the drifter said. "The other one talks too much. . . ."

The Mariner shook his head. "You can't afford the child. Half an hour with the woman."

"Please . . ." Helen said.

But he silenced her with a look. And he told her with that look that this was the price for her fare, and the child's; the price for what she had put him through.

And something passed across her eyes—almost as if something flickered and died—and she dropped her chin, dropped her gaze, too.

She knew she had no choice.

The Mariner held out his hand and the drifter tossed him the bottle.

"Come on," the drifter called to Helen, gesturing to his boat; dutifully, she began to move forward.

But the Mariner blocked her with an arm.

"My boat," the Mariner said.

The drifter shrugged. They both knew the protocol of barter. "Fair enough," he said.

The woman headed toward the hatchway door of the recessed cabin in the main hull, and the drifter, licking his lips greedily, followed after her. Enola began to follow as well, her face tight with confusion and concern.

"Helen!" the child called.

The Mariner reached out for her arm and gripped it.

"Sit down," he told the girl.

Without looking back, just before she disappeared down the hold, the woman said, "Enola—do like he says."

Then the drifter slammed the cabin door and the sound of it shot through the Mariner's head like a spear. He stood on deck, putting his head in his hands, as the child's confused expression turned itself on him.

Helen faced the drifter in the cramped cabin.

"Don't take 'em off," he said, nodding to her tunic, approaching her. "For what I paid, I'm gonna rip 'em. . . ."

She backed up. "No need to get rough. I'm not going to fight, as long as you—"

"Shut up." His grin was yellow and green, like

some awful strain of seaweed. "You might as well know, I plan on taking the little one, too. . . ."

She grabbed a breath that might have turned into a scream, but the hatchway door yanked open and the trimaran's captain dropped into the cabin in a shaft of sunlight. His face was expressionless, but his eyes were wild.

"Trade's off," he said.

The drifter turned and almost snarled his response: "What? *Why?*"

"I changed my mind."

She moved quickly around the brute, getting behind her unlikely savior.

"Do I hear you right?" the drifter said, his eyes narrow and hard, his face clenched like a fist.

"Do you? Trade's off."

"You can't *do* that. . . ."

Her champion tossed the bottle, with its precious pages, to the drifter, and bit off the words: "I just did."

The drifter tossed the bottle aside, and filled his hand with a gleaming knife.

"Well, I'm sorry," the drifter said, "but I got my needs and I won't take no for an answer."

"Get out," her savior told Helen.

"Yeah," the drifter said. "Go on, move! Just don't go far. This won't take long. . . ."

And she scurried out of there, just as the drifter was saying, "Pretty stingy, aren't ya, for a man who's got everything. . . ."

Then the cabin door slammed shut, and Helen ran to

Enola, clutching the trembling child to her as the sounds of a terrible battle below deck shook the trimaran like a gale—screams, and the sounds of objects and men smashing and crashing. . . .

She searched around deck until she found the double-barrel speargun; it was loaded. Good. Then she turned toward the hatch, as it opened . . .

. . . and the drifter crawled out.

If he was the victor, it had been a losing battle, for the drifter was bloody, carved up by his own knife, and whatever humanity he had left in him was pooling up in his eyes as he looked beseechingly toward the woman he had intended to rape.

"Take me . . . take me . . . back to my . . . boat. . . ."

He lurched toward her, and she backed up to the mast, aiming the speargun.

"Take me . . ."

He lurched closer, but she was no longer afraid, lowering the speargun.

"Please. . . ."

And the drifter's eyes rolled back, and he flopped to the deck, very dead.

Then his body seemed to lurch once more, but it was only her host, shoving the heavy body up out of the way, clearing the hatch.

She couldn't believe the surge of joy she felt, seeing him. Enola's face was bursting with a smile, as well.

They watched him admiringly as he kicked the

corpse of the drifter viciously over the side. Then he turned to them with a scowl.

"Come on," he said. "Help me."

"Help you?" Helen asked.

"With the three of us pitching in," he said, "we can strip that sorry bastard's boat clean in no time."

17

Plundering the drifter's boat gave the captain of the trimaran what he needed to make minimal repairs, at least; but the drifter hadn't been lying when he said there was no food aboard.

As the boat sailed easily in the whisper of west-southeast wind, Helen sat next to a cross-legged, daydreaming Enola on the main hull. Helen was trying to fix a broken fishing reel she'd salvaged from the drifter's ship. She looked up at her host as he rigged his newly patched sails, not wanting to show weakness by asking him for help, but at the same time wishing she had it.

Suddenly he reached down, plucked the broken reel from her hand, took a quick look at the busted mechanics, and tossed it overboard in a plink of a splash.

Enola blinked out of her reverie and frowned. "Why did you do that?"

Helen touched the child's arm. "Enola . . . please leave him alone."

Back to tending the sails, he glanced down at his two passengers with blank indifference.

"Please," Helen said. "We appreciate what you've done for us. . . ."

Without responding, he turned his back to them, heading to the steering console.

"Why does he act that way?" Enola asked. "I know he likes us."

"He spared us," Helen said. "That doesn't mean he likes us."

"He likes us," the child insisted. "I wish I knew his name."

"I don't think he has one."

The breeze lifted the child's dreadlocks gently. "I have one for him."

"What?"

"Mariner."

Helen frowned. "I've heard that word . . . it was in a poem Old Gregor used to recite. . . ."

Helen remembered the old man reciting the poem, or rather a fragment of it. The words were very old, from early Land Days. How did it go?

"It means 'sailor,' " the child said.

"Actually," Helen said, "I think it means more than that. A sailor comes home to port. But a mariner . . . he *lives* out on the sea. It's his home."

The child was nodding. "It's a good name for him. You can use it, too."

And from then on, that was how Helen thought of him.

A growling emerged from the child's stomach, and Helen stroked her cheek. "You're awful hungry, aren't you?"

Enola shrugged. She was not a complainer.

Helen looked toward the Mariner, at the steering console; he stood so still, he might have been carved there.

"I hope you're right," Helen said to the girl.

"About what?"

"About him liking us."

And she got up and moved gingerly over to him, pausing beside him at the console. "Please . . ."

He didn't look at her.

". . . we don't want to make you angry. But if you'd just give me something to fish with, I'll catch them myself."

"Not in these waters," he said.

"What?"

He looked away from her.

"We don't disappear," Helen said, "just because you turn your back on us."

He swung around and faced her. He didn't look angry. He didn't look *any* way. . . .

"We're hungry," she said. "The *child* is hungry. . . ."

"You don't understand."

"What don't I understand?"

"What fishing is like, around here."

From behind them, Enola's voice chimed: "Maybe he doesn't know *how* to fish."

He shook his head in disgust and stormed away from her, leaping into the recess of the cabin in the main hull.

For a few moments, she thought he was just trying to get away from them, avoiding the problem he considered them to be; but then clattering sounds below deck indicated he was up to something. . . .

He emerged with a strange looking two-headed harpoon gun, larger than the speargun she'd seen before. How many weapons and hidden treasures did he have stowed down there? For a ship that had been looted by both Atollers and Smokers, the trimaran had a wealth of equipment stashed in secret holds by its cunning captain.

What was he up to?

Eyes burning, face flushed with anger, he was fastening a long coil of rusty wire to his trawling mechanism at the stern.

Enola was at her side. "What's he doing, Helen?"

"I'm not sure. . . ."

Now he was securing the other end of the wire around the middle of the harpoon gun.

"Should I ask him?" Enola wondered.

"No!" Helen said.

Then—as if it were the most natural thing in the world—the Mariner, harpoon gun clutched in both hands, threw himself, backward, off the stern of the slowly moving boat, making a modest splash.

Holding, and hanging onto, the harpoon gun as if it were a handle tied to the ski rope of the trawling wire, he lay facedown on the surface of the foaming water, allowing himself to be dragged along behind the boat. His head would bob up from the water now and then, but mostly he stayed facedown in it.

Helen and Enola could hear the sounds only when his head was above water, but the Mariner was emitting strange, dolphinlike squeaks as he skimmed along, pulled behind the boat. Kicking expertly, he swung back and forth across the trimaran's wake, then suddenly began spinning on the end of the wire!

Helen frowned. Like . . . like . . . a *lure*?

Rupturing the surface of the sea, making the ship's wake seem a meaningless trickle by comparison, a huge blue creature burst into view. Thirty feet long, easily, with the body of a whale and seemingly countless rudderlike fins, it leapt with the grace of a dolphin; but dolphins didn't have impossibly huge jaws ringed with pointy, razor-sharp teeth that opened in a yawning oblong entry to hell.

Enola clutched Helen around the waist, and both she and the child gasped, their wide eyes frozen at the sight of the beast swallowing the Mariner in one gulp, snapping the trawling wire. . . .

"No!" the child screamed.

Helen, as confused as she was frightened, soothed the girl, stroking her hair.

The beast had not submerged, rather was languishing on the surface, perhaps savoring its meal for a moment, or digesting it. . . .

Then a tearing, thunking sound emerged from within the beast, and so did a harpoon, right out the side of its grotesque head; then a second ripping thunk announced the other harpoon's exit from the other side of the now-dying beast's ugly skull. Soon a knife blade was emerging from the fleshy area by the jaws, as the Mariner began cutting himself an exit from his catch of the day.

"Oh, my," Helen said.

She really *hadn't* understood about fishing in these waters. . . .

By late afternoon, Helen was keeping her promise and doing the cooking, as enormous whalephin steaks sizzled on a small grill they'd salvaged from the late drifter's boat. She turned the meat with her bare hands, seasoning the steaks with salt and herbs her host provided. The Mariner, returning from cutting from the huge carcass of the whalephin (as he had identified the sea beast) as many steaks as they figured would keep for a few days, sat and waited patiently as the fresh, smoky fragrance wafted enticingly up.

Gentle singing—the child's—floated on the breeze. "There is a girl that lives in the wind," she sang, hanging onto the mast with one arm, "in the wind, in the wind. There is . . ."

The Mariner looked up sharply at the girl.

She stopped. "Don't you like my singing?"

He didn't say anything.

"Helen says you don't like my singing," the child said, "because you can't sing yourself."

"Enola!" Helen said.

The Mariner said to the girl, "You ever stop and just listen?"

Enola seemed puzzled. "To what?"

"To the music of Waterworld."

The child cocked her head, trying to hear something, then shook her head. "I don't hear anything. . . ."

"That's because you're too loud," he said, "and you're either fidgeting around or talking all the time. Try sitting still, for a change."

She frowned; it was as close to a pout as Helen had ever seen Enola come.

The Mariner must have noticed it, too, because he made a peace offering. He went over to the pile of steaks he'd cut, then returned, holding out his palm. "You can have one. . . ."

In his hand were two large eyeballs, formerly the property of the whalephin.

The child recoiled, her face distorted with horror, as he shrugged, took one of the eyeballs and squeezed its juice out into his mouth.

"Don't know what you're missing," he said.

Helen couldn't bring herself to take one, either, and he shrugged and repeated the juice-squeezing process, tossing the slimy residue over the side.

Then he shocked them both even more by pushing his water jug toward them with his foot.

Helen extended her hand, tentatively. "It's all right . . . we can . . . ?"

"Drink all you want," he said. "It's going to rain tonight."

Enola was staring at the foot that had pushed the jug toward them. Helen was slightly repulsed by the webbed toes; her host—like the whalephin he'd slain—was, after all, a mutation.

The child, however, was not repulsed, merely interested. Fascinated, even.

"I wish I had feet like yours," she said.

"Enola!" Helen said.

The Mariner just looked at the child.

"Then maybe *I* could swim," Enola said.

After supper, a contented Helen curled up for a nap; soon she was sleeping soundly, on the first full stomach she'd had since this ordeal had begun—and even before that, as food supplies at the atoll had not exactly been flush.

A nonspecific sound stirred her half-awake. She pushed up on an elbow. A blood-red sun was setting, turning the sea shades of glimmering crimson and gold. She settled back onto the deck and was just drifting off again when the sound repeated, and this time she recognized it.

A scream!

She sat up, flashing looks around the deck—no

sign of Enola, or the Mariner, for that matter. Another scream—a child's scream, *Enola's* scream—sent Helen to her feet.

Out on the crimson-gold water, the Mariner was swimming easily on his back, and Enola was gleefully sitting on his chest, riding along. The screams had been squeals—squeals of pleasure.

The child was having fun, having a wonderful time, but that wasn't the point. . . .

"Enola!" Helen yelled frantically. "What are you doing?! Those monsters will kill you!"

"They're asleep now," the Mariner said, his voice barely audible above the gentle splash of his swimming.

He was taking her by the hand and easing her off of him, as he turned over and swung the child onto his back; she hung on, around his neck.

"No need to be frightened," he was telling her. "I won't let anything harm you. . . . Let the water guide you, listen to it, and it will tell you how to move your arms and legs. . . ."

And for the next hour, she watched as their gruff captain gave the child a swimming lesson. From time to time, Enola would look up for Helen's approval, and Helen would bestow her with smiles and nods.

"Look!" Enola said. "Look, Helen!"

It was a rudimentary dog paddle, but it was a start.

Later, on deck, the sun gone, the sea a deep blue under a dark, cloudy sky, she asked him why he'd done that.

Sitting at the tiller, he shrugged. "I just never met anybody who couldn't swim before."

She didn't know what to say to that, and the silence was getting uncomfortable when she remembered the scrap of cloth in her hand, and said, "We . . . we wanted to thank you . . ."

He just looked at her.

". . . for . . . everything. But we don't even know your name."

"I don't have one."

It was matter-of-factly stated, but to Helen, it was the saddest thing she'd ever heard. He must have sensed her sympathy.

"I never needed one," he added.

She brought the scrap of cloth from around her back.

"I . . . I have something for you," she said.

"What?"

"It's just a scrap of cloth I found on the drifter's ship. Just a rag."

"Rags are useful."

"Well, I hope you won't use this one." She held it up, showing the crudely charming sketch Enola had done of the three of them, on the deck of the trimaran, together. "Enola wanted to give you this, but she was afraid to."

He didn't say anything. But then he reached out and took the rag from her.

"Oh, and here," she said, and handed him the

180

crayon the girl had used to make the drawing. "I took it away from her. She won't do it again."

Now he was looking at her. It made her uncomfortable—it was as if his eyes were boring into her. . . .

Finally he said, "The marks on her back—what are they?"

She had wondered when they'd get around to this; a chill ran through her.

"Nothing," she said.

"They must mean something," the Mariner said. "They're not a birthmark. Somebody put them there."

She lowered her eyes, then brought them up, to find he was still staring at her. "You . . . you wonder about us, don't you?"

"Well . . . you don't look much like her. Unless she takes after the father."

"I'm not her mother."

"You act like it."

The endless sea was black and charcoal and gray and blue and the wind whispered across its surface: *Trust him . . . you can trust him. . . .*

"About six years ago," she said quietly, "a basket floated into Oasis with a child in it . . . a baby . . . a little girl."

"Enola," he said.

She nodded. "Everyone wanted to push her back out to sea—that was the law of the Elders. But I said I'd take her . . . she was so precious, and I had some position, in the atoll, with my store, so they listened to me. But they said if I wanted her so badly, I could never bear a child myself. *She* would have to be my child, my one and only child."

"You agreed to this."

"There was no choice. And I had no man in my life . . . frankly, I never thought I wanted anyone in my life, not anyone in the atoll, anyway."

"But the child wasn't *of* the atoll."

"No. No, she wasn't, and there was no one else who wanted her, who would take her—she would have died otherwise."

He shrugged. "So what?"

She frowned at him. "Have you ever heard the word 'compassion'?"

"No. What does it mean?"

She sighed, shook her head. "Never mind. It'd be hard to explain to somebody who's lived alone as much as you. . . ."

He said nothing.

Not unkindly, she said, more to herself than him, "You know, I pity you, really."

"What's 'pity'?"

"You really *don't* know, do you?"

"If I knew, why would I ask?"

"If you don't know," she said softly, "I'm afraid . . . afraid I could never make you understand. . . ."

He just shrugged and tended the tiller.

And she decided not to tell him any more about Enola, not now, anyway. . . .

She gazed out at the water again. "When will we get to Dryland?"

"Tomorrow, maybe," he said. "Day after, at most. Here."

He handed the crayon back to her.

"What's this?" she said, with a surprised little smile.

"I'm not giving it to the child, understand. It's just . . ."

"A loan?"

He nodded. "A loan. I'm *not* giving it to her."

Maybe he wasn't so hopeless. She hugged her arms to her chest and drank in the clear night air, let the breeze take the tendrils of her hair.

"Is Dryland beautiful?" she asked. "Tell me the truth."

"You'll see, soon enough."

"To me," she said dreamily, "it's like going to heaven."

Then she left the Mariner at his post, and went to Enola to tell her it was time for bed.

The Mariner made sure the woman was asleep—he let her have the cockpit, for night quarters—and ducked down into the recessed cabin of the main hull. He allowed the child to sleep in there, and she was curled up, soundly slumbering.

Secure of his privacy, he opened a secret compartment along the wall and took out his most prized possessions—three dog-eared copies of a magazine called *National Geographic*.

He knew how to read. His mother had taught him—the kindest human he'd ever known. So he pored over the sacred pages, not always understanding but fascinated nonetheless by the articles—"Global Warming A Reality," "Death of the Rain Forests," "Pollution Spiral" (those in a magazine from 1999); "Our Friend the Atom," "Our Marvelous Freeways," "Exploring the Reaches of Space" (from 1953); and, best of all, the most ancient—from 1932!—with his favorite article, his favorite pictures, "Up the Congo with Gun and Camera."

One picture, however, haunted him; it clutched something in his chest, and threatened the bittersweet joy he felt from the other photos.

In a black-and-white photograph, a black native stood in pouring rain just outside a tent. In the tent, a white man in an upside-down bowl of a helmet and short, childish pants cooked a meal on a little stove.

The caption read: "Pity the poor native guide, who must stand in the rain while Professor Matthews enjoys all the benefits of a modern, gas-burning aluminum camp stove."

Outside, the sky rumbled. The rain was coming. He needed to put his precious magazines away and gather containers to catch the hydro.

"Pity the poor native," he said softly to himself, and got on with it.

18

The spire-shaped tower jutted from the horizon like a massive deformed tree, as if metal and wood fragments had grown together somehow. A chimney spiraled black smoke into the clear sky, while much smaller, boxlike structures—attached by lines—bobbed around the much larger one like buoys.

Viewing this through binoculars, Helen frowned. Too small for an atoll. What *was* this place? What was this nightmarish tower?

Out on the prow, the child was squinting at the spire, looming two kilometers ahead. Then her question echoed Helen's thoughts: "What *is* it?"

Helen, standing near the Mariner in the cockpit, looked at the trimaran's captain, even as a cold suspicion began crawling up her spine.

"Barter outpost," he said casually. Not looking at her.

"You said we'd get to Dryland today." She tried not to put too much accusation in the words.

"Today, tomorrow. What's it matter?"

She winced. "What's it *matter* . . . ?"

"I need canvas."

"We *have* canvas," Helen said. "We got canvas off that drifter's boat. . . ."

But he didn't reply.

Something wasn't right. She was about to question him more pointedly when she noticed that *his* expression seemed troubled, as well. Shedding its jib, the trimaran began bearing in on the tower, but one hundred meters out, the Mariner suddenly changed his mind.

She studied him as he veered off, apparently buying a little more time before docking.

He held out his hand and she knew to fill it with the binoculars.

"What do you see?" she asked.

"The traders in the tower are waving," he said. Then he lowered the binoculars and shouted a greeting. It carried right across the water, hailing them in a language Helen had never heard before.

No words came back.

"What language did you use?" she asked.

"Portugreek," he said. "That's what they talk in these waters. . . . Or so I thought."

She plucked the binoculars from his hand and had another look. She could see the traders waving, yes, but there was something odd about it, something . . . wrong.

186

Then she swung her view down to the bobbing boxlike structures, and saw that they were cages.

And in those cages, clutching the bars much as the Mariner had when he was dangling over the organo barge, were pitiful, shabby examples of humanity at its saddest.

Slaves.

Fear clutched her chest.

Lowering the binoculars, she said, "Those are . . . It's a *slave* colony!"

He didn't reply. Was this a surprise to him, too? He certainly seemed to be studying the tower and its inhabitants carefully . . . suspiciously. . . .

Or (and the thought chilled her thoroughly) had he brought Helen and Enola here . . . to *sell* them?

The slave traders in the spiral tower were waving at the Mariner and his trimaran, all right. But they had help.

They needed it—they were dead.

Some had had their throats cut, others had been shot, stabbed, skewered, what-have-you. Still, what they all had in common, to a man, was that they were dead, slain by the puppet masters behind them, working them like corpse marionettes.

While his Smokers waved the dead men's arms, the Deacon stood on a pile of dead Slaver bodies, giving him access to a spy hole in the tower wall, which he poked his telescope through like a snout.

It gave him a lovely view of the three-hulled ship,

a hundred meters out. On its prow, like an exquisite, perfectly carved masthead, was the dark little child.

"Ah," the Deacon said. "*There's* my girl. . . ."

The Mariner moved to the edge of his ship. The woman trailed after him, saying, "Why did you bring us here?"

"Quiet," he said, and leaned out to have a look overboard.

The water gleamed with the faint but telltale iridescence of oil—a sure sign of a go-juice boat, and a strong indication of Waterworld's prime proponents of such vehicles—Smokers.

But there was no sign of any boat, let alone a go-juice boat, let alone a Smoker. . . .

Still, the Mariner had to follow his instincts. Out here, it was the only thing that kept you alive. So he left the woman behind to babble her questions to the wind and moved to the starboard hull, where he ducked below deck, into the crawl space.

Within the womb of the ship, he removed a floorboard and exposed a wet well, open to the water below. Nearby was his portable periscope, which he thrust into the wet well.

At first, all he saw was water. What had he expected? He guided the periscope to give him a full view of the main hull and then—jarringly close— he peered into the hideous face of a begoggled, breathing-tubes-up-the-nose Smoker.

As the startled Smoker paddled away, an expansive

view filled the eye of the periscope with dozens of the bobbling bastards, hiding underwater, straddling jetskis, in goggles and breathing tubes, wearing weighted belts . . . *everywhere*.

Bursting topside, the Mariner ran to the cockpit and leapt into place, blowing out the jib, bringing the mainsail around, the swinging boom damn near decapitating the woman.

"Hey!" Helen screamed, terrified, furious. "What the hell is . . ."

"Smokers!" he yelled.

From the Slaver tower a commanding voice rippled across the water: "Sound it, sound it, *sound it*!"

And, even though set off underwater, the blare of the air horn could be heard on the trimaran deck, as jetskis came alive underwater, the submerged Smokers cranking their engines, then to come roaring, leaping out the water.

The Smokers on jetskis were water-ballet coordinated as they dragged with them a huge gill net, a webbing noose in which they clearly intended to snare the trimaran.

On the prow of the ship, the child was trying to make her way back, but she lost her footing. The Mariner had no time to save her, but the woman shouted out commonsense advice: "Hold on! Get down, and hold onto something!"

And the girl hunkered down, gripping the prow with tight, tiny fingers; her look of determination said she was ready to ride out the battle. He had to admire her tenacity.

Meantime, he had found his wind and was making a run, but with Smokers popping up on both his flanks—and starting to nose ahead—he knew the noose would soon tighten into a death grip. He tacked hard, veering away.

He knew what to do.

"Port side!" he shouted to the woman, as he loped to the port-side bow. *"Now!"*

He untied the hinged ladder and heaved it out, onto the surface of the water, as if the sea were a wall he intended to climb.

"What are you . . . ?" she cried, as she reached the port-side hull.

His answer was to grab her by the wrist and haul her with him out onto the ladder, where they hiked out, doing a dangerous balancing act, adding weight to the ship. He extended the ladder another six inches . . .

. . . and the starboard hull began rearing out of the water, clearing the tightening net noose!

He guided her back, and they centered their weight, the trimaran slamming back down on the water, level again.

The Mariner said, "Centerboard—pull it!"

She nodded and streaked to the main hull, shooting below deck.

Grabbing a line, the Mariner swung around the stern, landing on the starboard hull. He could hear her working the speed crank in the forward cabin below, which would bring the centerboard—the ship's keel—up inside the boat, bringing some stability.

He called to the woman, still below deck, "Starboard, now!"

As he did, he caught sight of a Berserker on a jetski—*not* part of the dragnet team—bearing in on the prow; he was reaching for the girl, who was goggle-eyed with fright.

"Duck!" the Mariner yelled.

She did, and—still leaning out to snatch her—the Berserker slammed into the trimaran's prow, at full speed, shattering a forward crossarm and vanishing beneath the boat and the water without so much as a whimper.

The woman emerged topside and, following the Mariner and his instructions, climbed the starboard hike-out ladder, adding her weight, and the port hull began rising off the water.

When they shifted their weight back again, the boat slammed down on the water—*outside the tightening noose*.

Then, both of them breathing hard, they made their way back to the starboard hull, and he pulled in the ladder.

"You walked us out of that trap!" she said, amazed.

That same commanding voice traveled across the water: *"Cut loose! Cut loose!"*

The Smokers on their jetskis were using machetes to hack away at the net they were dragging—apparently the thing was attached either to them or their vehicles. Either way, he noted with a grim smile, they were slowed by the weight of it.

Jumping back into his cockpit, he kicked open a hatch that would give him the raw speed he needed now. A pedal was revealed, and he slammed his foot on it, firing the foredeck air mortar. His emergency ace in the hole went rocketing over the head of the startled child on the hull.

"What . . . ?" the woman said, looking up after the comet he'd fired. She was beside him again, he noted.

"Spinnaker," he said.

The triangular box kite headsail, like a star in the daytime sky, gave them just the burst they needed. The Smokers were suddenly far behind them. The battle was over.

Then a spear burst through the Mariner's shoulder in a bloody blast of immediate agony.

He whipped his head toward the source of the pain and saw him—the Berserker who had rammed into the prow! The bastard was under the ship, clinging to the deck netting as if it were a wire-mesh cage, half in the water, half out. And on his ugly head, he wore a two-shot mounted-speargun helmet—that it was a silly looking thing made it no less deadly, and certainly didn't take the sting out of the small spear that had torn through the Mariner's shoulder. . . .

And there was one shot left on that helmet rig.

With his unwounded arm, the Mariner grabbed a harpoon from a cockpit scabbard, lifted it high, and jammed it straight down into the Berserker, and through the bastard, and his spine.

The Berserker dropped away, a moment of frothy red foam announcing his departure on the water's surface.

"Keep this course," he told the woman, and staggered off to try to remove the damn spear. On the stern hull, he collapsed, passing out, his blood trickling down into the water as the trimaran skimmed along.

The Deacon stood atop his pile of human rubble, looking through the scope at the very disappointing outcome of his well-crafted plan to ambush the trimaran. His second-in-command, the Nord, came climbing up, stairstepping up skulls and shoulders and knees, joining his fuming chief.

"I say," the Nord risked, "we load all the go-juice on one boat and just run the freak down."

The Deacon lowered his telescope and cast his one-eyed gaze at his most trusted adviser.

"Gullshit," he said. "If we can't catch him in ten boats, you want to send *one*? Tell me you're joking."

Shaking his head, he raised the telescope to his eye. Whoops—wrong eye. There . . .

"Besides," the Deacon said, adjusting the telescope, "there are other ways."

The Deacon had the trimaran in his sight—it was getting smaller, but he could see it. He could see the fish-man, apparently unconscious, on the stern hull. What was that splash of red on the man's shoulder?

Blood?

"I think we've wounded him," the Deacon said.

"Wounded him?"

The Deacon nodded, and smiled a most self-satisfied smile for a man who had just been outwitted by a woman, a child, and a fish-man.

"He's left us a trail of bread crumbs," the Deacon said.

"What?"

"Very old reference, from Land Days. Let 'em rip."

"Sir?"

"Unleash the tracker sharks," he said.

And very soon, the wire-mesh centerboard of an underwater cage opened as tracker sharks nosed out, circling the water faster and faster, as if the scent of the blood were simultaneously driving them mad, and mad with ecstasy.

Then they knifed away.

19

Leaving the wheel lashed and close-hauled as she'd seen him do so many times, Helen moved across the netting deck of the trimaran, even as the ship itself moved swiftly along the water. Emotions stormed in her—ebbing fear from the Smoker ambush, a sickly relief at being out of harm's way (momentarily, at least), but most of all, bubbling anger at the Mariner's betrayal. She felt sure her host had planned to sell her, and Enola, back at that hellish Slaver trading post.

The anger subsided somewhat when she realized he was unconscious, sagging over the side, blood trickling down the side of the hull from his speared shoulder. She hauled him up, onto the deck, and he came quickly awake, as if startled from a dream.

Pain seized his face, and he blinked and got on his haunches and started working at tugging the spear out.

"Can I help?" she asked, bending down.

"Get away," he snarled.

That did it.

She stood hovering over him, not caring how much pain the bastard was in. . . .

"You *lied* to us," she said. "You were going to *sell* us back there!"

"We both lied," he grunted, working at the spear.

"What . . . ?"

He stopped his efforts with the spear to look at her, dead on. "You said the markings on the child's back didn't mean anything. *You* lied."

"I . . . I *don't* know what they mean. . . ."

He gritted his teeth, tugging at the spear. Then, breathing hard, eyes closed, he said, "Those Smokers are after the girl. That's what that ambush was all about."

"You're *crazy*. . . ."

"I saw what I saw!" He jerked a thumb at the speared shoulder. "I got this from a Smoker who lost his life trying to grab her!"

The child, hearing this fuss, began moving tentatively toward them, across the netting deck. Her face tightened with concern as she neared the wounded Mariner.

"You're hurt," she said.

"Save your sympathy, Enola," Helen said crisply. "He was going to sell us."

And she reached out and snatched the crayon the girl was clutching and tossed the "drawstick" in the Mariner's face. He didn't flinch as it bounced off his cheek onto the hull.

Enola went after the crayon, but Helen stopped her with a shout: "Leave it!"

The child, head hanging, went off to be by herself.

"Why do they want her?" he asked. "What do the markings mean?"

Helen refused to dignify his questions with answers. Instead she looked down at him scathingly and said, "There's nothing human about you. They should have killed you the day you were born."

"They tried," he said, and with one swift motion, in a burst of blood, he yanked the spear from his shoulder, turning his face into a mask of agony that immediately fused into fury as he stood, filling his hand with a machete lying unsecured on the deck.

Blood streaming from the wounded shoulder, his good hand filled with the big, menacing blade, he pointed it threateningly at her, its point damn near touching her nose. "Now . . . what are the marks on the child's back?"

She didn't believe he'd use it . . . but she didn't exactly believe he wouldn't, either. . . .

Then she heard herself say, "People . . . people think it charts the way to Dryland."

He slumped, the machete lowering. "Dryland. Dryland's a myth."

How could he *say* that?

"It's not!" she blurted. "You said so yourself, you said you knew where it was, you said you were taking us there. . . ."

"I'm a liar, remember?"

Then he fell to his knees, and the machete clattered from his hand, onto the hull, and he flopped facedown, passing out from the pain.

When he came to, the pain had subsided somewhat, now more a dull throbbing. His shoulder was bandaged, and he was leaned against the mast, sitting up. Kneeling next to him, the woman offered him his water jug and he took it and gulped a drink.

"Why didn't you kill me?" he asked. "You could've."

"I need you alive," she said. "I can't captain this boat."

"You've learned a lot, quickly," he granted her, grudgingly, nodding about the boat. "But you're a fool, believing in something you've never seen."

Her eyes glittered and her smile was childlike. "But I *have* seen it."

"*You've* seen Dryland?"

"I've touched it." The fingers of one hand clutched at the air and turned into a trembling fist. "In these hands I've held and touched and savored dirt far richer and darker than what you traded back at the atoll."

He sat up straighter, interested in spite of himself. "Where?"

She was smiling a little, ready to share her secret. . . .

"It was in the basket," she said.

"Basket?"

"The basket we found Enola in."

198

So that was the ground her hope was built on . . . poor woman. Poor deluded woman. . . .

"There is no Dryland," he said softly. Almost gently.

"But . . ."

He clipped off each word: "It . . . doesn't . . . exist."

She was shaking her head, not wanting to hear this. "How can you be so sure?"

He nodded to the sea. "Because I've sailed farther than most have dreamed . . . and *I've* never seen it."

Still shaking her head, her eyes desperately trying to hold onto hope, she said, "But . . . the things on this boat . . ."

"*What* 'things'?"

Her voice charted the struggle between hope and despair she was waging inside. "These . . . these things no one in Waterworld has ever seen . . . shells in your hair . . . reflecting glass . . . if *not* Dryland, where *did* they come from?"

"So you want to see Dryland," he said. He laughed, but there was no humor in it. "You *really* want to see it?"

Her eyes were almost crazed. "Of course! What do you think—"

"Then I'll show it to you."

At the stern of the boat, a bell-shaped wire-cage salvage rig bobbed, half-submerged, in the water. She watched the Mariner, down in the water, attaching tethered weights, jury-rigging a large jellyfishlike membrane to a tube connected to a gas canister fastened to the rig.

She had helped him assemble the rounded cage—disturbingly invoking, in her mind, the Slaver cages—from wire sections he provided from below. She continued to be astounded by the almost endless array of tools and weapons he could magically provide from below deck, where they had been secreted in compartments and hidden cubbyholes.

But then she remembered what he'd said back at the atoll: he had survived, out here, fifteen lunars between atolls. . . .

She had helped him toss the wire salvage cage overboard, while the child looked on with wide eyes. The trimaran was back in trawler mode, its windmill sail churning, thrumming. The Mariner had ducked back under deck again, in the stern crawl space this time, emerging with a handful of tubes.

"What are those?" she asked.

"Flares," he said.

The word meant nothing to her, until he brought them one by one to fiery, spark-spitting life, pitching them underwater. *What was the point?* she thought. Surely the water would put the firesticks out. . . .

Now he was down in the water, treading there, the diving apparatus ready, calling up to her: "Get in!"

Enola, her enormous eyes taking all this activity in, said yearningly to Helen, "I want to go, too."

Helen called down to him: "What about the child?"

"There's only air for one," he yelled up. "Get in the water, now!"

She flashed a "sorry" look to the child, who nodded with wisdom that belied her years, then, trembling with anticipation, Helen splashed in beside the Mariner, bobbing up next to him.

The water was cold but refreshing, her body a sea of goose bumps.

"Get in the bell," the Mariner said.

And she dove below, steering herself up through and within the wire-mesh framework, finding the opening of the air bladder, surfacing inside of it. *What was he doing out there?* It began to balloon around her, sealed off below her, and suddenly she was encased in the bubblelike bladder . . . and there was air to breathe.

She could see him out there, needing no air, requiring no breathing apparatus other than those gills behind his ears; his hair streaming, his face fishlike as he swam in place, he mouthed the word: "Okay?"

She nodded, within her transparent cocoon, and gave him a thumbs-up sign.

Now he was cutting a tether, and the whole rig came dropping down, the weights dragging it further and further below the surface, down and down and down. . . .

The Mariner kept one hand locked in the wire mesh of the rig, riding along on the downward journey. Inside her transparent bubble, Helen looked out as jellyfish and other sea denizens swam across her line of vision, some of them gliding, others seeming to crawl, their colors putting the drab blues and browns and grays of Waterworld to shame. Strange as some of these creatures were, she must have looked right at home among them, in her bladder bubble.

The rig had descended to a depth where the sunlight no longer could filter down its rays, yet there were orbs of rose-colored light just below, beginning to light the world. Then, as the rig dropped deeper, she realized what the orbs were: the firesticks, the flares, still tumbling down slowly, charting a course for them, like glowing pink lanterns.

Still falling, the rig overtook the flares, and they entered a murky twilight. *What did this have to do with Dryland? Nowhere in Waterworld could be wetter!*

And then the cage rocked to a stop, a landing softened by their water-cushioned fall. Something solid! She looked under her feet, and the cage was resting on something dark, something hard.

She couldn't see anything, not even the Mariner—at some point, he had slipped away. *Where was he?* Her breathing was getting shorter, and she felt trapped within her bubble, the world closing in, condensation building up inside it, smudging her vision even further. . . .

She calmed herself. Fought the panic down, and rubbed the condensation away from the plastic, or whatever it was, rubbing a circle to look out of, and there he was: the Mariner.

It startled her momentarily, but his reassuring motion—his mouthing of the word: "Wait"—steadied her.

And before long, the flares caught up with them, tumbling down to bring an artificial rose-hued dawn that settled its light upon a vista that made her gasp.

It was the wondrously jagged underwater skyline of a centuries-old city, riddled with a gorgeous cancer of sea life, the massive tombstones of a culture swallowed by the sea.

And Helen—in her bubble, in her cage—was poised at the edge of a rooftop. Beyond her was the mind-boggling array of what were called "skyscrapers," only they no longer scraped the sky, but reached like square stone fingers into the ocean above. Below, a dizzying perspective of a city world far below had her reeling.

That was when the Mariner tugged the cage off the roof.

And now they tumbled down, plunging past crumbling window frames . . . tumbling for what seemed an eternity. How incredibly tall these structures had been! The atoll's windmill had seemed towering; here, it would have been a toy.

With a water-cushioned clang, the cage landed on bottom—"street" level—and here the flares revealed the most incredible, indelible images yet: seaweed danced before a huge building labeled "First National Bank"; moray eels swam in and out of the glassless windows of a "Municipal Bus Lines" vehicle; street lamps stood, draped with kelp; vehicles—"cars," the magazines called them, or "automobiles"—sat rusted and encrusted; in the window of what must have been a store—"Nordstrom"—a figure of a woman, a sort of statue, naked but smooth and unfinished, wore a necklace of glittering glasslike stones mingled with barnacles; and, finally, everywhere, long lead boxes, swaying in the current . . . were they coffins?

Into this fabulous, and fabulously mournful, tableau entered the Mariner, as he scooped some mud off the ocean floor, cupping both hands full of it, showing her, displaying for her . . .

. . . his dirt.

And then it melted away in the water, the current gradually taking the mud away in streaming streaks of brown, breaking it up, scattering it into the sea, cleansing the Mariner's hands.

And within Helen's breast, something died.

On the deck, Enola kept watch at the depth gauge at the stern of the boat. Before he'd disappeared underwater, the Mariner had sternly warned her: "Don't touch anything."

And she hadn't.

She had just watched as the gauge's needle charted Helen's descent: twenty . . . thirty . . . forty . . . so very deep . . . seventy . . . eighty . . . ninety. . . .

How far down could people go? she wondered. But the Mariner wasn't exactly a "people"—she hoped Helen would be all right, that the Mariner wouldn't take her so deep she would get sick or even die or something.

Finally the gauge held at one hundred and ten meters. And then it stayed there a long, long time.

Just as Enola was starting to get worried, it began to reverse itself: one hundred . . . ninety . . . eighty. . . .

She sighed, smiled to herself, relieved that her friends were coming back home, and she looked toward the water, wondering when she'd be able to see the cage. She hadn't noticed how long it took them to disappear from sight, under the water, when they went down, 'cause she'd been so taken with studying the silly gauge. . . .

And now she could see something down under there, something blue, something blurry . . . not the cage, but something else, something alive—dolphins?

No. . . .

Sharks!

She reared back, terrified for a moment, then sighed in relief, happy to be safe here on the boat, where those horrible creatures couldn't do her any harm. . . .

The Mariner helped the woman onto the stern, and both caught their breath, the salvage cage bobbling on the surface, the collapsed air bladder a floating membrane within.

"I . . . didn't know," she said, shaking, and shaken. "All this time . . . I didn't know there were . . . *cities* down there."

"Nobody knows," he told her. "But me. And now you."

That was when he saw them, the Smoker boats, in the water, ringing the trimaran. No sign of the child. No Smokers on deck. But the rusted go-juice Smoker boats were everywhere, surrounding them. . . .

Now she saw them, too, and clutched his arm.

"Can you get us out of here?" she whispered.

A commanding voice from below deck bellowed a response: "I'd say there are two chances of that."

And a Smoker—but not just any Smoker, some kind of grand commanding chief of a Smoker, a one-eyed, bald-headed, grinning madman of a Smoker in tattered battle dress—stepped from the cabin.

"No way," the Smoker chieftain said, with his awful smile, "and no how."

20

From behind the Smoker chieftain, out of the recess of the main hull cabin, emerged two more Smokers— one of them the blond, cruel-featured trader from the atoll, the one who'd been a spy.

The Nord.

On the deck, unsecured, lay the Mariner's speargun. The Smoker chieftain and his two men wore gloating grins, and their eyes were on the Mariner and the woman. They apparently hadn't spotted the unattended weapon. . . .

The Mariner lunged for it.

But a powerful veined hand yanked it from the deck, and then the Mariner was on his knees, looking up at the angular, tauntingly smiling features of the Nord.

Who nudged the tip of the speargun under the Mariner's chin, forcing his head back.

"Shoulda bought me that drink, Dirt Man," the Nord said.

And he yanked the Mariner to his feet and shoved him back over by the woman.

Smokers began filling the decks of the encircling boats, their bushy, moronic faces watching, spell-bound, as their leader stalked the ship.

The Smoker chieftain—who wasn't really that physically large, but presented an imposing figure nonetheless—was lighting up a smokestick. His bald head was scorched red by the sun. He moved closer to the Mariner and Helen, his bearing a cocky swagger.

"Proper introductions, first," he said. "I'm the *Deacon*. . . ."

It was a name the Mariner was all too familiar with. A name all Waterworld knew and, for the most part, feared. But the Mariner kept his face impassive. He would not give this arrogant vandal the satisfaction of recognition.

"Maybe you've seen me before," the Deacon said, "and just don't recall the face. . . ."

And the Smoker chieftain pulled back the off-kilter eyepatch goggles to reveal the hideous charred hole where an eye had been, poking his face close to the Mariner's, staring at him like a demented cyclops.

"That may be because I didn't always look like this."

The Mariner kept his expression impassive.

The Deacon backed off, readjusted his goggle patch. "Now, I suspect she's somewhere close. . . ."

The Mariner knew who "she" was: the pirates had clearly come for the child. The woman was trembling.

Helen was no coward, whatever else he might think about her. Her fear was for the child, but he wished she wouldn't dart her eyes around the deck, giving away, one by one, possible hiding places.

Like the crossarm hatch, where Enola often went to be alone.

The Mariner could picture her there, scared out of her mind, huddled in the dark, hugging her box of crayons, each footstep on deck reverberating like thunder, voices echoing as if the trimaran were haunted by demon ghosts.

"We *could* tear the boat apart looking for her," the Deacon was saying, working out the possibilities.

Then the Smoker chieftain held out two open palms; it was a gesture so familiar, the Mariner knew at once it was a ritual.

A deadly ritual: the Nord and the Smoker guard each filled one palm with a handgun.

With a smile that threatened to burst his cheeks, the Deacon positioned himself between the Mariner and the woman and lifted both his arms, so that one handgun barrel rested against the Mariner's temple and the other against Helen's.

"But I'd rather someone just tell me," the Deacon said casually. "I'd hate to have to destroy such an unusual craft. Put a lot of work into this tub, didn't you, fish-man?"

The Mariner said nothing; the cold circle of steel against his temple pressed harder.

"Here's how we play the game," the Deacon said, loving it. "First one that tells me where the kid is, lives. The runner-up . . . well, actually there are no runner-ups in this game."

Gun at her temple or not, the woman was turning her head to drill a distrustful stare at the Mariner; he drilled her one right back. He didn't trust her any more than she did him. . . .

"Personally," the Deacon whispered to the woman seductively, "I'd much rather dispatch Sperm of the Devil, here."

The withering expression Helen cast upon the Deacon almost made the Mariner smile. It didn't make the Deacon smile.

"But I don't think you're going to tell me, are you?" the Deacon said, as if she'd let him down.

Then he shrugged and cast his one-eyed countenance the Mariner's way, putting a little nudge into the gun barrel in the temple.

"So, c'mon, fishy," the Smoker chieftain said. "Whaddya say?"

The Mariner said nothing.

With a sweep of one hand, the Nord pulled back the Mariner's hair, exposing the gills.

"She's not even your *kind*!" the Deacon shouted. "Not that you *have* a kind."

The Mariner said nothing.

"She's just deadweight—all women are." The Deacon leaned closer; he had terrible smokestick breath.

210

"Just say the word and she's outa your life—such as it is."

Helen said quickly, "If you tell, he'll still kill us both."

The backhand slap the Deacon gave her rang across the ship, echoed over the water like a gunshot.

"Let's not get ahead of ourselves," the Deacon said gently. Then he again leaned close to the Mariner and almost whispered: "If you don't tell me . . . I swear to Poseidon I'll torch your boat."

This foul-breathed threat should have enraged the Mariner. Instead, a peaceful calm settled upon him, like a comforting blanket. The wretched one-eyed Smoker chieftain had put things in sudden focus for him: there were humans in Waterworld who deserved worse than slaughter; but there were others who were worthy of life.

Looking past the Deacon's gun barrel, he trained his eyes on Helen, and her eyes stared back at him, hard at first; but she apparently recognized his change in attitude, and her eyes reflected a growing tranquility.

In their shared silence, the Mariner and the woman forged a new bond, no less strong for being unspoken.

Perhaps the Deacon sensed this, too, or perhaps he just realized he wasn't going to get an answer out of either one of them. In any case, he drew back, taking the gun barrels away from their temples. But this wasn't respite.

The Deacon swung a fist into the Mariner's jaw,

thrusting him back, hard, against the mast, and he slid down, slamming his butt into the deck.

"Damn," the Deacon said.

The Mariner was slipping a hand behind the mast, as he sat there, pretending to be more jolted than he in fact was; he soon found what he was searching for: the loop of the wrist lanyard. . . .

Still brandishing a gun in either hand, the Deacon turned to his blond second-in-command. "Refresh my memory. What happens when *neither* talks?"

The Nord seemed genuinely perplexed. Then he shrugged, saying, "Never happened before."

The loop was widening. . . .

Frustrated, the Deacon swept a look around the trimaran, his eye flashing with thought.

"All right," he said, and he raised one of the guns. "If they won't tell us where the kid is, we'll just do it now. Kill *both* of them. . . ."

And he fired the gun upward, twice, exploding the air.

The Mariner winced, knowing what the result would be.

The child came scrambling up out of the crossarm cavity, bursting topside, screaming, "No! No!"

Her distressed expression turned joyful as she saw the Mariner and Helen still alive, but then immediately melted back into gloom.

"Oh, so gullible, these children," the Deacon said. "But I do dearly love the innocent little brats. Bring her here."

The Smoker guard grabbed the child as if she were an object, not a person, and carried her to the Deacon, dumping her unceremoniously before him.

The Smoker chieftain bent over, tugging down the child's tunic to reveal the tattoo. He cackled, then hauled her up, a hand under either of her arms, and held her out, backward, for his Smokers to see.

" 'Take and ye shall receive!' " the Deacon shouted. "So ends your daily sermonette. . . ."

And, from the boats, the Smokers began to cheer as the Deacon stood triumphantly on the deck.

Another Smoker was emerging from the main hull cabin. "Look!" he called.

The Mariner, widening the lanyard loop, felt suddenly sick: the man had his *National Geographic*s.

But he didn't have them for long: the Deacon grabbed them and began leafing through the magazines, his eye staring widely, his mouth dropped open, as if drool would soon follow.

"Look at all that land," the Deacon said, his voice hushed as he moved through picture after picture. "I can't even begin to . . . magnificent! Just *look* at all this square footage!"

The Smoker guard came over to the Mariner and yanked him to his feet, but the Mariner maintained his grip on the wrist lanyard, behind him. The Smoker stood nearby, keeping an eye on the prisoner, but not much of an eye: his attention was on the Deacon, as the Smoker chieftain drank in the potent pictures of Land Days.

Finally, reluctantly, the Deacon returned his focus to Enola, though the precious magazines were tucked tight in one hand.

"Take off the tunic," he said, "and lay her out so we can get a look at those markings. . . ."

Several more Smokers had boarded, and they followed these instructions. The Nord and another Smoker joined the Deacon. They looked down at Enola's back as if it were a meal they were about to partake of.

"That mean anything to you?" the Deacon, indicating the markings, asked the Nord.

"No."

"I can't cipher it, either. . . . We'll do it back on the *'Deez.*" The Deacon gestured to Enola, with a waggle of his magazines. "We got what we came for."

The Nord glanced toward the Mariner and Helen. "What about them?"

"Do 'em both."

"And the boat?"

"Torch it."

The Nord frowned. "It's a hell of a boat, Deacon. . . ."

"It's contaminated. Unclean. Fishy. Besides, I promised I'd do it, and I always keep my promises. Now, *do* it!"

In one swift motion, the Mariner looped the enlarged wrist landyard over the Smoker guard's neck and kicked a lever, sending a counterweight plummeting . . .

. . . and the Smoker guard rocketing upward, up the mast, caught in a wrong-way gallows.

The Mariner grabbed Helen by the wrist and yanked her along as he ran to the bow and dove over the side, the Nord's gunfire blasting the air they had just vacated, then drilling the water as they plunged down.

21

His hand was gripping her wrist, guiding her, and she followed his lead, under the water, and suddenly they were surfacing inside a recession in the main hull, a wet well that she hadn't known was there.

He bobbed, patiently waiting for her to grab in deep lungfuls of air; her heart was racing.

"Enola's up there," she whispered.

"I know. Nothing we can do right now." He gave her a steely-eyed look. "We have to go under."

"Under?"

"Way under. And *stay* under."

She felt dizzy. "How? I can't breathe under there like you. . . ."

He touched her face, a surprisingly tender gesture. "I'll breathe for us both."

The raiders must have heard Helen and the Mariner talking, because suddenly bullets were triggering down blindly alongside the central hull. He nodded to her, and she followed his lead, ducked under the waterline.

They swam deep, deeper, as bullets chased them down, not catching them, the bullets water-slowed, sinking harmlessly around them like little lead weights. But then her air, bubbling away in increasingly smaller trails, began to give out, and she fought panic.

I'm drowning, she thought. *Heaven help me, I'm drowning!*

The Mariner stopped, treading underwater, and drew Helen to him.

It was as if he were kissing her, but it was a kiss of life as he shared air with her. Then he held her shoulders as they swayed together underwater, and his fish-buggy eyes sought to reassure her.

Calmed, she allowed him to loop an arm around her waist, and they went swimming away, together, deep under the water, kicking in tandem, like a fish school of two, pausing now and then for the Mariner to share his air with her in survival kisses.

It was dark down there, and cold, but after a while she felt warm, she felt close to this creature . . . this man. . . .

Perhaps an hour later, they surfaced far away from the trimaran. It was only a dot, barely visible on the horizon. But they could see the telltale trail of smoke curling like an awful question mark into the sky. They could see, too, the Smoker boats pulling away, in triumph.

As they treaded water on the surface, Helen shuddered to think of Enola's fate. Had they killed the child and stripped the skin from her back to make a more portable map? Or was she merely in the ruthless grasp of that insane one-eyed Smoker chieftain?

"We have to go back," Helen said. "I have to *know* . . ."

The Mariner nodded, bobbing next to her. "We can start now . . . we'll be there by sunset."

And they were. They traveled the last leg of their homeward journey underwater again, the Mariner bestowing air kisses upon her, and when they surfaced, cautiously, not knowing whether a Smoker guard had been left behind, they viewed the smoldering hulk of the once-proud trimaran, floating in the sea like a charred corpse.

"Enola . . ." Helen gasped.

"My boat," the Mariner said.

They swam to the wreck and climbed aboard. Helen fell to her knees, as if struck a blow, crawling along what was left of the main hull. No sign of the girl.

Then she saw it: the box of crayons, its contents a swirl of melted colors on the scorched hull.

She looked up and watched the Mariner as he walked with slumped shoulders, a dejected ghost haunting the ruins of his own house. He paused to finger charred bits of this and that; stood shaking his head, wearily, at the twisted wreck of his water purifying gizmo.

"Check below deck," she said. "See if they left her . . ." She couldn't make herself say "body." ". . . see if she's down there."

He nodded and went.

She sat, and as a breeze stirred the seared remnants of the trimaran, she could almost hear the song Enola used to sing: *There is a girl that lives in the wind, in the wind, in the wind.* . . .

He came up from below, shaking his head no. "They either took her," he said, "or dumped her overboard."

He had something in his hand: the bottle the drifter had traded him for half an hour of Helen's favors. The ancient yellowed pages were still within.

"They missed this," he said, crouching down beside her. "Maybe we can barter it for some hydro."

"With who? That seagull?"

"We're lucky they left anything behind."

"Lucky?" Her laugh was harsh and damn near hysterical. "*Lucky?*"

"We have to go on."

"I can't go on," she said, and tears trailed wetly down her cheeks. "Not without her . . . or any hope of Dryland."

He was staring at her. How could a face be so blank, so unreadable? Was that disapproval or support in those eyes? Who knew? Who in hell knew?

"I . . . I don't even want to live," she said, "if there's nothing left . . . if there's no hope."

"There's us," he said, and now she understood. It was *affection* in those hard eyes! How wonderful that expression might have seemed to her, before this boat had been burned to a chunk of charred driftwood, before those savages had stolen away the sweet child who represented to Helen, both literally and symbolically, the hope of a better tomorrow.

She reached out for the bottle in his hands, with its brittle precious pages; she could see children running, in one of the pictures. On land. Ground. Earth. She showed him.

"This is what the ancients had," she reminded him.

He gestured to the sea, and to his ruined boat. "And this is what they did to it."

She thought about that for a moment, then nodded. "You're right . . . you're right. . . ."

He gestured contemptuously to the gills behind his ears. "And it's also why I am what *I* am. . . ."

Standing, gathering determination around himself like a protective cloak, he strode over to the twisted water purifying system and began to examine it, searching for parts that could be salvaged.

The drift of the wrecked ship soothed her into ironic contemplation, a kind of calm despair.

"It's funny," she offered. "I always thought Dryland floated. Drifted with the wind. I figured that was why it was so hard to find. . . ."

He stood, giving up on his gizmo—for the moment, at least—and ambled over to her. "Why did you believe in it so much, when others didn't? When they even *fought* you over it?"

She gestured to her feet. "Because people aren't made for the sea . . . we've got *hands* and *feet*. We're supposed to walk . . . on something *solid*."

Her fingers drifted across the melted blur of crayon colors on the hull. And she began to weep.

"I miss the sound of her . . . her singing," she said. "Do you?"

He looked away. "I miss my boat."

For some reason, this didn't strike her as a cold thing for him to say so much as a *sad* thing. . . .

"You know," Helen said, "you're so much better at being alone than I am."

He crouched beside her. His expression was both distant and intimate.

"I was born on an atoll," he told her quietly. It was a whisper, really, that almost got lost in the whisper of wind. "People wanted to kill me. I was a freak."

She touched his arm.

He lowered his gaze. "My mother taught me to read, but she died young. Some, when they're beaten down, get stronger . . ."

He was talking about himself, she knew.

". . . others, gentle ones like her, just break into pieces."

"What about your father?"

He smiled. She had never seen a smile smaller, or more bitter.

"My father kept me alive out of the kindness of his heart," he said. "Used me to dive after fish. Kept me on a lead line."

". . . what?"

"He knew if he didn't, I'd never come back. So I stole his boat, after I killed him."

The wind seemed suddenly colder.

"I've been on one boat or another," he said, "ever since."

She stroked his face, moving the hair from his eyes. "How old were you?"

"That child's age," he said. "Maybe a little older."

"Enola knew what it was like to be different," she said. "I think that's why she liked you."

He said nothing.

She brushed his hair back again, gently. "After we escaped from the atoll . . . when I offered myself to you . . . why didn't you take me, when you could?"

"Because . . . you didn't want me."

She leaned forward and, very tenderly, kissed him on the mouth. He backed away, as if burned.

"No . . . no," she said, gently, very gently. "It's okay. What we did before . . . we started wrong. *I* started wrong. Let's try again. I want to try again. . . ."

She gave him another kiss, but he didn't respond, didn't kiss her back. His face was a stony mask. But there was something else there, something in his eyes . . . was he frightened?

"Have you . . . ever been with a woman?"

He looked away.

"You've never been with a woman, have you?" she asked.

His shrug was a nonresponse.

"It's been a long time since I've been with a man," she admitted. "Maybe I've forgotten how. . . ."

She moved closer to him, guided his arms around her. He seemed very young, suddenly; a child. . . .

"You were kind, to teach Enola to swim," she said. "Let's teach each other, now. . . ."

Sunset was turning the sea crimson and gold; it was as if the ocean had caught fire, and the trimaran—still trailing tendrils of smoke—was like a stray ember. There they lay together, teaching each other, loving each other, rekindling hope in each other's arms.

By the following afternoon, they had constructed a raft from the rubble of the ship. She could tell it was difficult for him—it must have been like picking through the bones of a loved one.

But they constructed the raft (or, mostly, he did), and set out to sea, bobbing, resting, their eyes closed as they waited for the wind to decide which way to take them.

"*Helen . . .*" a voice called, echoing over the water.

Was she dreaming?

Her eyes fluttered open and she looked into the puzzled gaze of the Mariner.

"*Is that you . . . ?*"

Their eyes searched the sea, but then, seeing nothing, they shrugged at each other. Who was talking to them? The Great Provider? Or Poseidon, maybe?

"*No, no, no . . . out here!*"

And then drifting into view, just above them and to the right, an impossible apparition popping into view, was the cigar-shaped dirigible with its quiltwork balloon, and sitting in his chair, controlling it all . . . Old Gregor.

Joy leaped in her chest, and she sprang to her feet, making the raft sway. "Gregor!"

"Smart thinking," the old man said conversationally, as if the last time they'd seen each other was over breakfast, "burning your boat . . . never would have seen you if not for the smoke. Who's that with you?"

The Mariner had risen to his feet, as well, sizing up their hovering visitor.

"Why, it's Ichthyus Sapien!" Gregor said, working his controls, delight lighting up his white-bearded countenance. "Is that really *you*?"

The Mariner said nothing, but Helen cried, "What're you *doing* here?"

"Looking for survivors from the atoll attack," he said. "The rest of us are on the eastern banks." He was moving in closer, his smile as big as the dirigible. "This is a miracle, a bona fide *miracle*! Here, grab hold . . . I'll lower some lines and pull you on. . . ."

Soon they were climbing up into the dirigible seats that had been designed, once upon a time, for Helen and Enola.

And this finally prompted the absentminded inventor to ask: "Oh, dear—the child! Where is Enola?"

"Smokers took her," Helen said morosely. Then she brightened, indicating the Mariner. "They'd have *me*, too, if it hadn't been for him."

The Mariner, looking a little nervous to be sitting in

a boat that rode the sky not the sea, was looking wistfully toward his ruined trimaran.

"Very human of you," Gregor said.

And they sailed away.

In the sky.

22

In the distance, dots along the horizon gradually revealed themselves as a ragtag cluster of boats, rafted together, with gangways between them. The survivors of the Smoker raid on Oasis had banded together, rebuilding, beginning a new atoll.

Helen, turning in her seat in the dirigible, hair mussed by the wind created by the ride, felt a stirring of pride at the resiliency of her fellow Atollers. But at the same time, she knew this wasn't the way. The atoll life was doomed. Their efforts, their hopes for tomorrow, were misplaced. . . .

Then she caught the Mariner's expression, as he sat gripping the arms of his armchair seat, the bottle with the two precious magazine pages wedged between his legs.

It was as if he were afraid of this sky-sailing; but she knew he'd gotten used to being up in the dirigible hours ago. This was something else.

"Are you all right?" Helen asked him.

"This is wrong."

"What?"

"I should've stayed with the raft."

Then she understood.

"They won't try to harm you," she said.

He shot a skeptical look at her.

She reached around and touched his arm. "They'll be grateful . . . they'll welcome you, just like Gregor did. . . ."

The wind was ruffling his hair; she could see the gills behind his ears.

"Last time," he said, "they welcomed me into their organo barge."

"I'll tell them what you did . . . how you saved my life. . . ."

He was shaking his head no. "I don't want to stay. I just want a boat." He nodded toward the bottle with the brittle pages. "I'll give them my pages for anything that floats."

"Is that what you want?"

"It's what I want."

She searched his face, but it didn't tell her anything. "Will you take me with you?"

Now he looked at her, eyes narrowed. "Is that what *you* want?"

"I want to go after Enola."

"In *one* boat?"

Now she shook her head no. "I want to talk them into untying all those boats and going after the Smokers . . . going after Enola. . . ."

He looked at her a long time, then he sighed, laughed humorlessly. "They won't do it."

Stubbornly, she said, "They may."

"And the child may already be dead."

"I know. But I have to try."

He shrugged. "They won't do it."

And the balloon dipped, as Old Gregor guided it toward the ramshackle array of boats, the pitiful armada she hoped to launch in pursuit of the Smokers, Enola, and (the hope was back, in full sway) Dryland. . . .

Dusk turned the fishing trawlers of New Oasis into starkly abstract silhouettes against the copper sky. Dories dotted the water, ashimmer with gold.

On the deck of a beat-up trawler, the Mariner sat by himself, eating a bowl of mush provided by an Atoller woman who had given him a suspicious look even less appetizing than this cold turd of a meal.

Within the trawler, a meeting was being held. His fate was being decided. Once again, he had not been invited to his own trial.

Helen had assured him this was *not* a trial. No one had made any attempt to restrain or chain him; and the voice of authority, in New Oasis, belonged not to a stodgy Elder . . . no Elders had survived the massacre . . . but to an old friend of the Mariner's — the broad-shouldered, burned-brown lawman who carried over his title from the old Oasis into the new one: the Enforcer.

"I'll see to it you aren't harmed," the Enforcer had assured him.

The Mariner believed the man, and now he waited while Helen—whose face he occasionally caught in the window of the trawler, gazing out at him— pleaded his case.

In the meantime, he decided that this trawler would do as well as any here, and began removing Atoller belongings, tossing them onto the dock. He didn't want their raggedy things. Just the boat.

Just the boat.

She stood at the window, staring out at the lonely figure of the Mariner, with his bowl of mush and blank expression, while behind her the Atollers bickered and railed.

Some things never changed.

"It's not *safe* to leave him unchained out there!" an Atoller man was shouting.

A woman said, almost tearfully, "He's right! We have *children* here!"

She turned away from the window and faced the group, some sitting at tables, others standing; fear was in damn near every face. An exception was Old Gregor, sitting on a bench in front, his smile comforting, his nods quietly cheering her on.

"You needn't bother figuring out what to do about him," she said. "He's leaving."

"How?" another Atoller man said.

"On one of *our* boats?" demanded another.

She shrugged. "You can give him one . . . or he'll just take one. Your choice."

The brawny figure of the Enforcer moved through the group like a parent among small children. "He's earned that much. And he's free to leave."

There were murmurings, but not very loud ones: the Enforcer's word was law here.

But Helen knew that the man within that powerful frame was not cruel; that he was, in fact, fair—as his next words demonstrated.

"We have a decision to make," the Enforcer said. "Helen has asked that we unlash our boats and set out for the child."

"She's among *Smokers*," someone said.

"Let's hear her out," the Enforcer said, and he gestured to Helen, took a seat on a bench by a table, and said, "Helen—please speak."

She positioned herself in the middle of the room; she proudly held her head high, but she was trembling. She knew how important her little speech was—to her, to Enola, to tomorrow.

"The world wasn't created in the Great Deluge," Helen said, as eyes around the room went immediately wide at this heresy. "The land was not washed away—it was *covered* by it."

A woman from the back chimed out shrilly, "The Elders say—"

"They say nothing," Helen clipped her off. "They're dead. All of them. I'm alive, and I'm here before you

231

to say that I have *seen* it with my own eyes. There's *land* right under our keel . . . there are cities down there, dead ones, but they were once alive."

The murmurings were louder now, and the Enforcer silenced them: "Quiet! Helen . . . go on. . . ."

She did. "If there's land down there, that means there could be land *above* water, too—somewhere on the horizon."

Now there were derisive laughs. A voice called out: "Where, then?"

Another voice scoffed, "What heading? How far?"

Helen, frustrated, was momentarily at a loss for words.

Old Gregor sprang up with a youthful vigor belying his years.

"My friends," he said, in a booming voice, "listen to me. You *know* me—you *trust* me, I hope. I'm convinced Enola carries the way to Dryland on her back. I haven't yet solved the puzzle . . . but I know *this*: without her, I never will."

Another Atoller stood. "Do we have to listen to this nonsense? Dryland's a hoax—we decided that *years* ago, and the sooner you two accept that fact, the better off we'll *all* be."

Heads were nodding, and murmuring turned to muttering, which the Enforcer, standing, silenced, to take the vote.

But Helen knew, even before the show of hands, what the outcome would be.

On deck, the Mariner had been preparing the trawler to get under way, stripping all the belongings of the Atollers off. In his mind he had begun redesigning the boat; he needed better sails, and it would take months of salvage work down in the dead cities to gather the necessary barter to . . .

She was standing beside him.

Her face was long. "They're not going after her."

"What did you expect?"

She sighed, shook her head. "You have to understand, they're afraid . . . they're only human . . ."

"I wouldn't know about that."

"Sorry."

He shrugged, kept at his work. "I don't understand people, human or otherwise, who won't go after their own kind."

Her hand settled on his shoulder, fingers gentle as flower petals. "Will you go after her?"

"No."

Her hand fell away. Dusk was blending into night. There were no street lamps in New Oasis. Perhaps the old inventor would build them a new windmill for the Smokers to come and burn down.

"You say you don't understand people who won't go after their own kind," she said, not accusingly, really. "But then you say *you* won't go, either . . ."

"She's not my kind."

His words made her wince. "I thought you and Enola . . ."

"You thought what?"

From her expression, you'd have thought he'd slapped her.

"I need six Gs of hydro," he told her. "They can have my pages . . ."

"You'll get it," she said, businesslike. "I'll see to it. There're still some decent people here."

He continued his work, pausing to say, "This coil of rope—it goes with the boat, right?"

She didn't answer. Instead she said, "Enola said you were her friend."

And now it was as if she had slapped him. The sensation puzzled him. He felt a sickness in his stomach, too, from these words—or was it just the mush?

He shrugged it off and went back to coiling the rope.

Helen's voice trembled as she said, quietly, "What do I tell her when I see her again?"

What was there to say to that? Hadn't he told the woman the child was probably dead? And if she wasn't, among those barbarians she would have been better off dead. He turned his back to her, went on about his business, doing his best to get this sorry tub shipshape.

He didn't see her step off the trawler, onto the deck.

Later that night, on the dock, with Old Gregor beside her, slipping an arm around her, she stood with folded arms and stern expression, watching the Mariner at the tiller of the trawler as it blended into the night and disappeared.

"Don't blame him," Old Gregor said gently. "Survival is all he knows."

"Survival isn't living," she said.

"No. But it's a start. That's why someday, there'll be many more like him, a whole race of them, a species." The old inventor's chuckle was sorrowful. "And, I dare say, so very few of us. . . ."

23

Enola was cold, and she was afraid. Inside a cell in an area she heard the Smokers call "the brig," she was chained by her ankle to a bare metal bunk in a bare metal cell, huddled next to it on the bare metal floor.

Hope burned inside her, and she wasn't as afraid as she was cold, but she still couldn't keep from crying. She missed Helen. She missed the Mariner. She thought of his wonderful boat and saw again, in her mind's eye, the trimaran on fire, flames licking the sails, turning them black.

And she cried.

Outside the cell, the leader—the one-eyed man called the Deacon—was announced by the sound of that awful go-juice land boat of his; they had brought Enola to the brig in it. Now it was back, bringing the Deacon with it.

She could hear him out there talking to the mean blond man called the Nord.

"What's the latest?" the Deacon asked.

"Not a word," the Nord said. "She just sits there and leaks outa her eyes."

Outside the cell, where she couldn't see, something awful was being prepared for her. The diseased-looking Doc, his gas canister cocktail-maker cart wheeling behind him, feeding the tubes up his nose, had a puffer fish in one hand and a hypodermic needle in the other. The hypo had been plunged into the puffer fish, and the Doc was withdrawing from it a bilelike fluid.

"A little shiver from the liver," said the Doc cheerfully. "Quite toxic—she'll give up all her secrets with this."

"Yeah," the Deacon said, "or it'll kill her." He waved at the Doc to move aside. "I'll try talking to her, first. You know how good I am with kids."

"Oh, yes," the Doc agreed, scurrying back a few steps.

She had heard—but not understood—this conversation, and as the door to the little cell was unlocked, and swung open, the Deacon—with the mean blond Nord following him—stepped in and greeted her with a smile that looked like an awful wound in his face.

"Such a sweet child," he said.

The Nord smirked.

And then the Deacon's expression darkened with mock sympathy. "What's the meaning of this? Take these chains off the child! Are we barbarians here?"

A very hairy Smoker guard lumbered in and removed the chain from her ankle.

"There," the Deacon said. "Isn't that better?"

Enola said nothing.

"Sit up on the bunk, now, with me. Take my hand."

Reluctantly, she took his hand; it was surprisingly soft, as it guided her next to him on the metal bunk.

"Isn't that better?" he said again, with another awful smile. He dug out a square object from a pocket of his grandly tattered uniform. It was a little paper package of smokesticks. He took one out, lighted it, then held out the package to her. "Cigarette?"

She shook her head no.

"Well, then . . . what about this?"

And he showed her an object that had a similar shape . . .

Her crayon.

A Smoker had pried it from her fingers, on the trimaran, and she'd thought it was long gone. How dearly she wanted it back! She could decorate these horrible bare walls. . . .

But she kept her face stony blank. She gazed at him, eyes big and unblinking, thinking about how the Mariner would behave if he were this crazy man's prisoner.

"It's yours," the Deacon said, and he took a deep draw on his smokestick, "if you can help me with this one problem."

She said nothing.

"In fact, I believe I have a whole box of these . . . crayons, they're called . . . in my storeroom. Would you like them?"

She said nothing.

"I should explain," the Deacon said reasonably. "You see, I got this congregation. I mentioned I was a man of God, didn't I? Well, I am, and I got this congregation, good congregation. Large congregation. Getting larger all the time, in fact." He shook his head. "In fact, there's just not enough space on the ol' *'Deez* for all these people."

"Why don't you make less people?" she asked.

He blinked. "Pardon?"

"At the atoll," she explained, "a baby gets born only when there's room. That way, there's food and hydro for everybody. The baby, too."

His expression seemed glazed, his awful smile frozen. Then he patted her on the head and said, "Well, isn't that a quaint suggestion . . . but, darlin', it just doesn't apply here. You see, we are the Church of Eternal Growth. Too many people ain't the problem."

"They aren't?"

"No, no, no. It's not that there's too many people, dear—it's that there's not enough room."

"Oh."

He patted his knees, and his smile tightened. "Now . . . I'm told the tattoo on your back is actually a map of some kind . . ."

She nodded. "It's the way to Dryland, Gregor says."

He beamed at her. "Now we're getting somewhere! Uh . . . by any chance, could you, uh . . . tell me how to *read* this map?"

She shook her head no.

"Setback," the Deacon muttered. He thought for a moment, then said, "Well, did your friends ever say anything about it? Your mommy, or that big pet fish of yours?"

"Helen isn't my mommy," Enola said crisply, "and you shouldn't make fun of my friend. He wouldn't like it."

The Deacon blinked again. He had a funny expression on his face—sort of like he thought what she said was funny, and sort of like he was angry because she said it.

There was a nasty edge in his voice now. "Girl, I don't give a flying shit *what* he'd like. That animal took my eye out. If I ever see him again, I'm going to cut open his head and eat his brain—raw. You think he'd like *that*?"

She didn't show him she was afraid. She just quietly, matter-of-factly said, "You can't kill him."

The mean blond man stepped forward; he looked very angry. "I'll shut her mouth—"

But the Deacon raised his hand, and the Nord stopped.

Very softly, he asked Enola, "I can't kill him? Why not?"

241

She shrugged. "'Cause he's fast, and he's strong, like a big wind. And he's even meaner than you are."

The Deacon frowned. "There's not a man alive who can make that claim."

She shrugged again. "He's not a man."

That awful smile was back, but Enola knew it didn't have anything to do with feeling happy. There was hatred in that smile—he was almost glowing with hate. His breath, when he leaned in, was very bad. He must have smoked a lot of smokesticks. . . .

"You're right about your friend," the Deacon told her. "He's a big, nasty animal and he makes me shiver. But he ain't here, and he ain't coming. So no one is going to save you."

She swallowed, but kept her face impassive. It was hard, with that smelly, hot bad breath in her face.

"No one is gonna save you," he repeated. "Get it?"

She scooted away from the awful face and worse breath. "He *will* come . . . and save me. . . ."

He leaned closer. "Well, then, you better tell me what I want to know, or he can save what's left of you in a goddamn *jar!*"

She just looked at him. Glared at him.

Suddenly he stood, and he seemed very calm. Composed. He patted her gently on the head.

"I'm glad we had the chance to have this little talk," he said. "Food for thought. Guard!"

The hairy Smoker lumbered back in.

"Chain the brat," the Deacon said.

Then he stormed from the room, the Nord on his heels. The guard was refastening the chain as she huddled against the wall, whispering to herself.

"He'll come and find me," she said. Nodding. Nodding. "He'll take me away . . . he'll find me. . . ."

The door clanged shut.

24

The ramshackle trawler looked grand beside the burnt-out shell of the Mariner's once-proud three-hulled boat. On the deck of the trawler were tools, weapons, and other hidden treasures from within the cubbyholes of the trimaran. The Mariner had been on a salvage job on his own ship.

Right now, he was in the charred husk of his cabin, sitting on the scorched bunk looking at a chart the scavengers had missed in their haste to destroy his home. He'd found a writingstick, too—one of Enola's crayons that had hidden from the heat in a cubbyhole.

He made a dot on the chart and wrote, in what he did not realize was a childish scrawl, the word DENVER. That was the drowned city he and Helen had visited, not so long ago. On this chart were other dots, labeled with the names of other long-dead cities: SEATTLE, RIO, FLINT. . . .

But in many cases, the cities were marked only with

dots. Cities destroyed in that ancient cataclysm weren't always easily identifiable.

For years now, however, he had been keeping track of the cities down there, to better understand his world. And his world was *more* than Waterworld—it was that undersea kingdom below. . . .

But today, in the main hull cabin of his lonely roasted wreck of a ship, something nagged him as he studied his homemade map.

He went back to his cubbyholes and found—praise Poseidon!—this ancient, weathered map of the Land Days world. As he had many times before, he checked it against his homemade chart, and he frowned.

But then he smiled.

The addition of "Denver" had suddenly brought everything into focus—or at least, explained why things had been *out* of focus. . . .

Placing the homemade map on the grandly printed one—his chart paper was thin enough to see through to the old world map underneath—he turned his map upside down and . . .

. . . all his labeled, dotted cities lined up with the cities so labeled below. Denver with Denver, Rio with Rio, and on and on.

Now he could identify the unlabeled dots; now he could . . .

And something else clicked.

There was a pattern, here, that he had never seen before. . . .

"Crabs of hell," he muttered. "Here's the answer."

Numb from the knowledge, he absently turned over his homemade chart, planning to roll it up and place it among the things he'd salvaged, when he noticed Enola's drawings there, sketched-out memories of their days at sea together. . . .

The trimaran in sailing mode.

Helen with her hair blowing.

The Mariner tossing Enola in the drink. (This made him smile.)

The whalephin, leaping from the water.

He and Enola swimming. (This one took the smile away.)

He traced the simple yet eloquent lines of artwork with a gentle fingertip. If there had been anyone there to see him, they would have seen the Mariner's face at its most tender, its most childlike, its most serene, its most human.

And then they would have seen it harden, settling into resolve, and when he stepped onto the deck, his eyes were looking out, not at any one thing, not at his ruined ship or the pitiful trawler or even the horizon.

He was looking at what he had decided to do, and the wind rushed up, ruffling his hair, exposing his gills, as if in agreement, urging him on.

The shotgun blast tore a hole in the night, startling Helen awake. She instinctively reached for Enola—who of course wasn't there—and then sprang from her cot in the cabin of the leaky old scow where she and Old Gregor had been given shelter.

Gregor was awake, too; she could hear him up on the deck where he'd been sleeping, stirring noisily. She could hear others, in the atoll, clambering onto their boats. And soon she, like they, was looking out into an eerily beautiful moonlit night, the water a glistening textured ivory, fouled by the presence of a pair of oil-leaking jetskis straddled by Smokers.

One was plump, the other skinny; both were hairy and unkempt, which seemed to be the official Smoker condition. They both were grinning, too, idiotically, bobbing on their thrumming, idling machines. The skinny one's smoke-belching jetski had a trail of oil behind it like a black ribbon stretching to the horizon.

The fatter one had fired the shot, from a smoking shotgun he held in one hand, tilted skyward, as if he were aiming it at the moon.

Just a boat over from Helen's scow, on the deck of a trawler to one side of the entry to the small lagoon of New Oasis—no gates yet, not hardly—stood the darkly tanned, heavily muscled Enforcer.

There were frightened murmurings from the decks of the other lashed-together boats, and this made the atoll's lawman frown.

"Everyone stay quiet!" the Enforcer called.

The two jetskis chugged noisily as the Smokers floated there, looking at each other, laughing, like a couple of naughty children.

"What do you want?" the Enforcer demanded of them.

"All *kinds* of things," the fat one said. "But we'll settle for everything you got. Ain't that right, Bone?"

Bone, the skinny one, giggled his reply: "Right, Chester!"

Chester, the plump Smoker, was the brains of this outfit. He holstered his shotgun in a scabbard alongside the jetski. "We're waiting," he said, crossing his powerful arms.

"Why don't you come on up," the Enforcer snarled, "and *see* what you get?"

Chester snorted a laugh, floating, bobbing. "Doesn't work that way. You don't wanna cooperate, fine. We'll go back and get our friends, and *then* we'll 'come on up' . . . we're part of a religious group, y'know."

"Religious," Bone giggled.

"We believe in sharing," Chester affirmed.

"You've destroyed our home!" an Atoller male yelled out. "Why can't you just let us be?"

Chester shrugged. "I don't know. Even religious folk have character flaws. Ain't that right, Bone?"

And Chester looked toward Bone, and so did Helen, only suddenly Bone wasn't there.

Just his jetski—floating, bobbing. Unattended. A small, abandoned, ghostly, go-juice–guzzling galleon on the oil-fouled ivory sea.

Chester's expression was surprisingly thoughtful, Helen thought. Puzzled, the chubby Smoker reached for his shotgun in its scabbard . . .

. . . and the Mariner flew from the water in a splash of rage, from right beside the jetski, landing

249

smack on top of his plump prey, tackling him, dragging him over backward, into the water, down under the water, where the splashing was ferocious, limbs flashing out from under, then disappearing, a leg, an arm, a hand with a raised blade, and then, in the moonlight, as blood spilled below, a billowing out on the surface, more black than red.

Swimming gracefully from waters that still churned from the aftermath of the struggle, the Mariner stroked to the nearest boat—the scow—and allowed several Atollers . . . who seemed very glad to see this "mute-o," suddenly . . . to ease him onto the deck. He got to his feet, the bloody knife clutched in his teeth. He removed the blade, sheathed it, and went to Helen.

His face looked savage.

But very human.

"You came back," she said, her face risking a smile.

"I'm going after the child," he said simply.

The Mariner's shabby trawler was docked alongside the scow, which now seemed to be Helen's home. At a makeshift dock—the beginnings of Atoller civilization, here in New Oasis—the Mariner, with the plump Smoker's jetski tied up nearby, was filling a few ancient glass bottles—labeled "Coke" and "Coca Cola"—with oil. Then he would stuff rags in them.

Old Gregor was helping him. "You know," the old man said, "as hideous freaks go, you're not so bad."

The Mariner just looked at him.

"That was a joke," the old man explained. "It was meant to be friendly."

"I know what the picture was."

Gregor frowned. "What picture?"

The Mariner said nothing, just stuffed another rag into another Coke bottle.

"Oh!" Gregor said suddenly. "The one I showed you! In the organo barge cage! Yes."

The Mariner nodded.

Gregor was trembling with excitement. "Is it a map? I always *thought* it was, with longitude and latitude, but—"

"It is a map," the Mariner said. "But it's upside down."

"Upside . . . ?"

"Down," the Mariner completed. Another oil-filled bottle, another rag. . . .

"The world . . ." The old man's brow was knit in deepest thought. "Could the poles have . . . reversed?"

"You're the scientist."

"How could you *know* these things?"

The Mariner nodded toward the sea. "I've been mapping the cities, below."

"What a wonderful idea!" the old man said. "And you're sure Enola's map is upside down? Oh. Oh. Oh, *my*! This is wonderful!"

"Hand me that rag."

The old man leaned close to the Mariner, his

expression, his tone, conspiratorial. "Is that why you're going after Enola? So you can find Dryland?"

"I don't care about that," the Mariner said.

Gregor nodded. The old man seemed to make an effort to calm himself, saying, "No, of course not. It's the child you care about . . . not that you'd ever admit it."

The Mariner glared at him.

"But what you've told me," Gregor said, overwhelmed, his voice hushed, "it's worth so much. I . . . I don't know what to say. . . ."

"Good," the Mariner said.

Gregor laughed; it was a rich laugh, and the Mariner had to work at it, a little, not to smile. The old boy was glowing as Helen approached.

She was not glowing.

She had a resolute expression as she said, "I'm going with you."

The Mariner took a moment before he replied. "It's easiest if I go alone."

Several Atollers were approaching. They seemed to be a small, self-appointed committee. The Mariner, Gregor, and Helen tabled their conversation, for the moment.

The Atoller man in the lead said, "This is ludicrous, going after the Smokers. It's dangerous. Why make trouble?"

The Mariner said nothing, stuffing another rag in another oil-filled Coke bottle.

"You don't even know which direction they came from," the Atoller said.

The Mariner withdrew from his pocket the little round "lighter" stick called a Bic. He flicked a flame to life, then ignited the strip of cloth in the latest bottle he'd filled. He chucked the flame-streaking bottle, almost casually, lobbing it over at the still bobbing, unattended jetski that had belonged to the late Smoker named Bone.

The bottle smashed, the jetski ignited, exploding into a fireball that made the nighttime momentarily day, the Atollers on the dock yelping in surprise, covering their eyes at the harshness of the blast.

Then they were all watching as the trail of oil behind the jetski caught fire and flames went streaking, shooting, all the way back to the horizon. Lighting the Mariner's way. . . .

He looked at Helen—hard. "If she's alive, I'll bring her back to you."

Then he loaded the bottle bombs onto the jetski and mounted it, turning it around, heading off in the direction the flame trail indicated.

As she stood watching him getting smaller and smaller, her heart pounding with hope, Helen could only wince at the remarks of the Atollers around her.

One woman was saying, "We're wasting valuable time, here. Those Smokers will be back. We need to get moving. . . ."

A man said, "She's right. That freak will only make them more vengeful."

Another atoll man touched her shoulder. "Forget about that mute-o. . . ."

There was just enough sexual suggestiveness in his tone—and in his bad, raw-fishy breath—to enrage her.

She brushed the hand off as if it were seagull droppings. Then she slapped him. Hard. The sound echoed across their tiny lagoon.

Standing among them, she said, "So, what . . . run away again? We've barely started over, and you're ready to start *again*? Create *another* atoll . . . *New* New Oasis? Sooner or later you have to realize that a place like this can *never* be our home. We can't *live* like this anymore!"

She pushed through them, and came face to face with the Enforcer and Old Gregor. The Enforcer was frowning, but Gregor had a wicked, secret grin.

"The others may be cowards," the Enforcer said, "but they're right. He's on a suicide run."

"I'm going after him."

"It's suicide for you, too."

She shook her head, helplessly. "I don't care. I can't . . . can't run away again, and I can't just stay behind, waiting."

Gregor leaned close, beaming. *What was this old fool so damn happy about?*

Then he whispered in her ear: "Oh, but my dear . . . we're *not* going to stay behind. . . ."

25

Dawn was as fiery as the line of fire the Mariner chased as he drove the Smoker jetski; he only hoped its go-juice supply would hold out, carving through these choppy swells. He kept his eyes locked dead ahead, glued to the horizon, waiting for something to show itself, reveal itself, waiting to find out just what foul secret place the Smokers skulked off to, after their vicious atoll raids. . . .

The Mariner, hunkered over the jetski, with a sense of purpose as single-minded as a shark with blood in its snout, whispered, "I'm coming, Enola. I'm coming for you. . . ."

No one heard these words but the wind—and the Mariner himself.

Or did the child, locked away in some dank cell, hear them, too, by way of a tingling on the back of her neck?

They had dragged her here, from the cold cell, to this enormous, ugly room. Well, not all of it was ugly— Enola liked the glitter of the glass pieces that hung from the fancy lantern in the ceiling. But most of the drawings—"paintings" was the word Old Gregor had taught her for fancy color drawings like these—were hideous, and the floor was covered in awful orange cloth.

She was where the mean blond one, the one they called "the Nord," had dumped her: on the floor, on the awful shaggy cloth floor covering, next to a big, soft-looking chair covered in cold, crackly plastic.

The Nord was watching her, guarding her, and that awful doctor, who dragged those big canisters on wheels behind him, tubes stuck up his nose, was there, too. Yesterday the Doc had stuck a needle in her arm, and it had made her terribly sick. She'd burned up through the night, had a worse fever than that time she had what Helen (who'd nursed her through it) called the "flu."

She still felt sweaty and sick to her stomach, and her arm was sore and bruised from where the Doc stuck the needle in. Sometimes she made sick sounds that she couldn't control, whimpers, groans.

"Shut up," the Nord said. "If you're not answering a question, shut up."

"He's coming," Enola said quietly. "He'll ride the wind. He'll come and save me. . . ."

"Shut up!" the Nord said.

"Afraid she can't help herself," the Doc said. "She's

not entirely in control of her faculties, after receiving my 'treatment.'"

"Well, you said she'd spill her guts for us," the Nord snapped accusingly, "and all we got was babbling! No answers!"

The Doc shrugged and smiled weakly. "I'm afraid in Waterworld, medicine is something of an inexact science. . . ."

From another room that connected to this one, the Smoker chieftain swept in. The Deacon had changed into an elaborate patchwork robe with flowing vestments, very colorful, purple here, yellow there, black, gold, each patch a precious fragment of the past. None of it went together very well, but it was impressive, Enola thought, in an awful way.

"How do I look?" the Deacon said, eyes aglitter; or, anyway, eye. "Be brutal, now. . . ."

"Like a king," the Doc said.

"A warrior king," the Nord added.

"Bless you both," the Deacon said, beaming. "I feel like a samurai pope!"

The two men seemed as confused by this as Enola; neither "samurai" nor "pope" meant a thing to her. But they obviously meant a lot to the Deacon, who was gliding around his quarters, twirling before his two cronies like a girl with a new tunic.

"In fact," the Deacon said generously, "bless *every*-one! Even our little friend, here . . . and how *is* our little guest?"

The Doc moved nearer to the cowering Enola. "Still

mumbling about her fishy friend. Delusional. Unfortunate side effect of my treatment . . ."

The Deacon was frowning, his giddy goodwill ebbing.

"The men are assembling," the Nord told him. "Getting restless, I imagine."

The Deacon nodded toward Enola. "Well, this oughta keep 'em happy." To the Nord he pointedly said, "You know your cue?"

"Oh, yes."

The Deacon squatted next to Enola. "When this is over, my dear . . . I'm gonna introduce you to the Lord."

And he rose and went out, in a sweep of colorful patchwork robe, leaving the Doc, the Nord, and Enola behind. The doctor was adjusting gauges on his canisters, while the Nord was smiling toward Enola. It wasn't a very pleasant smile.

What did they have in mind for her? she wondered.

And who was "the Lord"?

Whoever he was, she was pretty sure she didn't want to meet him.

The fiery dawn had given way to a foggy morning, which slowed him, the path of flames seeming shorter, now, getting eaten up in the mist. But that path the late Bone had unwittingly provided him with was less important, now: voices and clatter and vague shapes were emerging from the distance. He guided the jetski toward the sounds.

Then there it was, knifing through the fog, rising before him like a great, grotesque sea beast! Crabs of hell, what *was* this thing?

A ship!

Poseidon save him, the biggest ship he—or anyone in Waterworld—had ever seen, an ancient vessel taller than ten of Old Gregor's windmills, the bow of the beast rising high, curving out over the Mariner's head as he approached, a steel monster encrusted with barnacles and deeply rust pitted.

He cut his engine and jumped from the bobbing jetski onto a shelf of barnacles at the ship's base, where water lapped at the rusty waterline as if licking a wound. He began to climb, finding rusted-out holes that provided purchase as he went.

It took forever to get to the top, the curve of the ship so severe he eventually was climbing damn near upside down. An engine purred, way above, like an insect buzzing. . . .

What was it? This ship was stationary, more or less. What engine *was* that, droning up there? He shrugged it off, kept scaling the rusty slope. Finally reaching the top, fingers clutching the steel lip, he peeked over.

And every Smoker in Waterworld rushed at him, charging him, screaming bloody murder.

Confused, scared witless, he ducked back down, wondering how the hell his secret assault could have been discovered, wondering if he'd be dead in the next instant. . . .

But the next instant turned into another instant, and

another, and while the screaming continued, no Smokers with murderous intent (or any intent, for that matter) were yanking him aboard.

He was still just hanging there, and their screams were continuing, as was the purring engine noise, which was getting louder, too. . . .

Then he noticed a rusted-out hole in the bow that allowed him to peek through without sticking his head up over the edge; like a peek hole, through it he could now see Smokers—perhaps a hundred of them, or even more—fanning out to either side of the deck, in two ungainly groups, pulling a thick, heavy rope between them, tight, as if they were playing a big, bizarre game of what the ancients had called tug-of-war.

And they didn't seem to have seen the Mariner's head pop up over the side of their ship. They had been busy, distracted, by their mission. . . .

And what that mission was soon became clear to the Mariner, as that purring engine sound built into a roar, above and behind him.

The Mariner, still hanging there, looked up and saw, half-invisible as it emerged from the fog, the same battered seaplane that he and his trimaran had battled, not so long ago. Clutching rust holes, he clung to the bow, making himself small, as the plane swooped down, thundering in, right over the Mariner, and down onto the deck, slamming into, rattling the world.

Through his peek hole, the Mariner watched as the plane's pylons were snagged by the rope, the Smokers grunting and groaning and yelling as they strained to slow the airship, the rope sliding burningly through their hands as they were moved, in a mass, with the still-moving plane.

Then, a few yards from the bridge of the ship, the plane—and its Smoker landing crew—finally came to a screeching stop, the men tumbling and bumping into each other, but whooping with glee now.

Another successful Smoker landing.

The sound of another engine, a go-juice boat engine, caught his attention below. He looked down at the bobbing jetski, where he'd left it, and saw a small two-Smoker patrol boat pull up beside it.

He peeked through his rust-hole again, saw Smokers spooling a hose down a long shaft, dragging the hose toward the now-silent seaplane, a spurt of oil shooting out prematurely, splashing the deck. Then the nozzle was stuck into the plane's go-juice tank.

Too much activity there; too many Smokers on deck. And only *two* Smokers below him, in jackets and goggles, one of them with a harpoon rifle in hand, checking out the empty jetski, leaning over the side of their boat, not looking up.

Better odds.

When they finally looked up, the two Smokers saw—much too late, of course—the Mariner dropping down like a stone between them, grabbing onto them in a double headlock, taking them right over the side of their boat and into the water with him, and a splash.

Once underwater, still holding the men, he pulled them down deeper, deeper, their air bubbles trailing desperately away; but they were powerful brutes, and one of them squirmed out of his grasp, the one with the harpoon rifle, managing to trigger it as he did, firing at the Mariner, who twisted out of its path, allowing the second Smoker to get the shaft, blood streaming blackly from his instantly dead body.

The Smoker with the harpoon rifle was out of harpoons—and air. He frantically swam toward the surface, air bubbles exploding from him, then diminishing to nothing, as the Mariner caught him by the ankle, holding him down, a few yards from the surface. The Smoker clawed wildly at the water, staring up at a watery window he could neither open nor reach, occasionally looking down with wide, frenzied eyes, searching for pity in the Mariner's face.

A useless search.

Not long after, the Mariner emerged from the water, alone, and mounted the jetski . . . wearing the Smoker's goggles and jacket.

Smitty was the Smoker in charge of the launching room, a good-sized chamber right at water level. Short ramps led in and out of the giant rust hole in the side of the ship, with two feet of water standing in the chamber, allowing Smokers to pilot jetskis in and out of the *'Deez*. A number of the vehicles—in various states of repair—lined the metal walls. Two pain-in-the-ass Smokers—Truan and Djeng—had dropped by to hound him about getting their jetskis back up and running; the vehicles had been out of commission since the Oasis raid.

Didn't they know he was a busy man?

"I'll get to it, I'll get to it," Smitty told them. "I'm the one who's gotta make sure these things are safe enough to ride. You wanna perish in some terrible accident, you lamebrain morons?"

The noise of an approaching jetski summoned him to the rusted-out opening of the chamber; he plodded through the two-foot puddle and straddled the entrance, legs apart, arms akimbo, squinting out into the fog.

"Horse?" Smitty called. "That *you*? Throttle down on that sucker, for crab's sake! Bring it in slow!"

But there was, instead, a sudden revving of the jetski engine.

"I said *slow*, damn it! You're gonna—"

And those were Smitty's last words, as the jetski came flying into the chamber, slamming right into the Smoker's chest, caving it in, killing him.

The Mariner, his jetski brought to a convenient and sudden stop by a now-deceased Smoker, found himself in the ship's jetski launching chamber, with two surprised-looking Smokers approaching him, splashing through the shallow water covering the floor. He just sat there quietly, waiting for them to make a move, his hand hovering over the scabbard that held the late Chester's shotgun. . . .

"You killed Smitty!" one of the Smokers said.

But the other one was . . . laughing.

"Nice landing, dumbshit!" the second Smoker called out to the Mariner.

The other one was shaking his head. "That Smitty, man, always gettin' in the way."

"Yeah!" the second one said. "Looks like he perished in a terrible accident!"

"Yeah!" the first one said. "What a lamebrain!"

And, arms slung around each other's shoulders, the two Smokers exited the chamber, into the ship, their laughter echoing off steel walls.

Surprised but relieved—thinking what a rare, strange, and stupid breed these Smokers were—the Mariner eased off the jetski, taking Chester's shotgun with him, slinging it over his back on its strap, leaving the vehicle and his dead Smoker landing pad behind.

The Mariner stepped cautiously through the roughly sawed out doorway that led into the bowels of the ship. Suddenly a voice boomed above his head, making the Mariner whirl, knife whipped from its sheath.

"*Here he is!*" the voice resounded, and it was coming from a small cloth-faced box fastened at head level on the steel wall! What kind of box was this, that could speak?

And it continued on: "*Rise up, brothers and sisters! Turn your eyes and open your hearts to your humble benefactor, your spiritual shepherd and dictator for life—the Deacon of the 'Deez!*"

264

Was this box somehow relaying a voice from elsewhere on the ship?

Whatever it was, wherever it was coming from, this was nothing he wanted to hear. He slapped the box, as if it were an offending face, and smashed it right off the wall. It clattered onto the floor in pieces.

He sheathed his knife and pressed on, moving deeper into the recesses of the ship, hoping his Smoker goggles and jacket would pave the way.

Truan and Djeng, the Smokers who had witnessed Smitty's "terrible accident," returned to the launching chamber shortly thereafter with a replacement Smoker, who would take the deceased Smitty's place as master of the launching area.

But something just outside the entrance, close enough that the fog couldn't conceal it, had caught their eyes. Standing in the very spot where Smitty had stood and unwittingly waited to be killed, Truan looked out at an empty, bobbing patrol boat . . . and two floating Smoker corpses.

"We've got an intruder," Djeng said.

"Shit," Truan said. "And he was right in front of us . . ."

"Don't tell the Deacon," Djeng said.

"What, and get killed?"

Above them came the roar of the Smoker crowd, cheering the Deacon's entrance. Truan considered the consequences for all of them if the Deacon's big night was spoiled by sabotage. And what if this had been the work of that fish-man? The *'Deez* was rife with rumors of the child captive's murmurings of the demon who would come to save her. . . .

"Spread the word," Truan said. "Find him."

"Bag and tag?" Djeng asked.

"Bag and tag," Truan affirmed.

26

From the bridge of the *'Deez,* the mass of Smokers on deck below made a throng whose behavior was as unruly as their personal grooming habits. Yelling, jostling each other, this was a mob on edge—joyful at the prospect of reaching Dryland, a notion fueled by the rumors of a girl with a map on her back (and scuttlebutt had it the girl was a captive on this ship, this very moment!); but also restless, tense, tired of empty promises and hopeful hearsay, as even these dimwits knew that supplies on the *'Deez* were growing short. The only ammo they had was courtesy of melting down their own walls, and atolls were getting scarcer than magazines.

Still, as their leader climbed the metal stairway to the bridge of the *'Deez,* they erupted in wild, enthusiastic cheers that rose up to meet their smiling leader as surely as the smell of their collective (and considerable) body odor. His colorful finery seemed to ignite them further, gasoline splashed on their fiery enthusiasm.

The Deacon, smiling modestly, waved at them—first as a greeting, then encouraging them to silence.

Standing before a microphone, backed up by the Doc and his Smoker council, his words booming out not only here on deck but through every corridor and compartment, the Deacon began to preach.

"Children of the Provider," he addressed them, head high, "citizens of this ship of good faith, pilgrims of goodness . . . hear me speak. I . . . have . . . had . . . a . . . *vision*!"

But from among the wide-eyed, adoring crowd came a dissenting voice, a voice that indicated just how thin was the line between their joy and their despair.

"We're *tired* of visions!" the dissenter called. "What about the *land* you promised?"

And other voices chimed in: "Yeah!" "Yes!" "What about it?!"

The Deacon was not alarmed by this discord; his Smokers were children, simple souls, and he knew very well how to control them.

Undaunted, seemingly ignoring them, he continued in his commanding voice: "A vision so great, so magnificent, that as it came to me . . ." And he lowered his voice to a dramatic whisper. ". . . I wept."

There was a collective gasp from his sentimental Smokers.

"Yes, my children," the Deacon continued, his voice building, "I wept! Because in this splenditudinous figment of wonder I saw . . . can you guess? . . . do you know . . . ?"

Every childish eye was open wide; so was every brutish mouth.

". . . I saw the *land* . . ."

"*Land!*" the dissenter cried. Completely won over.

And the crowd exploded into cheers, the deck rocking with glee, with hope, with faith.

The Deacon, smiling mildly to himself, waited for them to compose themselves. He was in no hurry.

In the Deacon's quarters, Enola huddled on the floor, waiting for rescue. She felt better. Her arm was still sore from getting stuck by that needle, but at least her stomach wasn't so upset. And her mind was clear.

He would come for her. She knew he would come for her.

The mean blond one, the Nord, was rustling around in a cabinet that had a lot of bottles in it. He grinned and lifted one of them—labeled "Gin"—and stole several gulps. Then he frowned, looking at the low-ered liquid level in the clear bottle, and filled it back up from a hydro jug.

"Shouldn't be doing that," she told him. Needling him, just a little.

He whirled, long blond hair swinging; it was as if he'd forgotten she was there. Maybe he didn't expect her to have any spark left in her.

"You'll get in trouble," she chided.

"Oh, I forgot," he said. "You're not afraid. Your pet freak is coming to rescue you."

"That's right," she said, scooching up straighter. She was still on the ugly shaggy orange floor covering, next to the plastic-covered chair. "Only he's not a freak. And he could beat you up, anytime."

He smiled, mildly amused. "Beat me up?"

"Anytime," she affirmed.

"Is that a fact."

The voice of the Deacon had been coming from a small box mounted on the wall; but for the last few minutes, nothing had come out of the box but cheering. This seemed to make the Nord nervous. He was pacing.

She needled him some more.

"He's killed dozens of people, you know," she said.

"Is that right."

"*Now the Provider told me this personally*," the Deacon's voice said.

"And he doesn't show mercy or anything, on anybody," she said. "He even kills little girls."

"*We need to go there*," the Deacon was saying, "*and settle it. Build on it . . .*"

"Kills little girls, does he?" the Nord said, and smiled big at her. "Well, I'm glad to hear we have something in common . . ."

Enola swallowed. Maybe needling him wasn't such a good idea. . . .

•   •   •

The Mariner moved along a catwalk. It was obvious to him that some sort of alarm had been sounded, that his presence aboard the ship was known. Smoker patrols were rushing down corridors, climbing ladders, drawing weapons. They were organized groups, and even in his Smoker jacket and goggles, he might not blend in easily.

He decided to stay out of their way, keep to the shadows, keep scaling the floors of the ship. All the while those little talking boxes, some positioned high on walls, were emanating the sound of the Smoker leader's voice, as if cheering the search parties on.

But he had decided, from the crowd sounds that would follow the Deacon's pronouncements, that most of the Smokers were gathered in one place, listening to their leader speak. And that place, logically, would be the deck.

". . . *we're gonna mechanize, modernize, and otherwise monopolize that whole big pile of dirt!*" the Deacon was assuring his congregation, courtesy of a cloth-covered box just above the Mariner's head.

Footsteps on the metal walkway announced company.

Just past the rail, a heavy, hanging chain beckoned him. He leaned out—it stretched up at least two walkway levels—and then grabbed hold and started to climb.

On the bridge, the Deacon was railing at the air with a fist, hanging on to the microphone stand with his other hand, his robes of office swaying with his emphatic gestures, underscoring his commanding, amplified voice as it shook the deck below.

"If there's a river," he cried, "we'll *dam* it! If there's a tree that's standing, we'll *ram* it! Because, my children, I'm talking *progress*!"

"Progress!" the Smoker chorus chanted in overlapping semiunison.

In the Deacon's nearby quarters, the Nord's nerves were on edge, listening for his cue. Back at the liquor cabinet, he was risking several more swigs of gin. The chief would never miss it, once the Nord had added a few more dollops of hydro.

"We shall suck and savor all the sweet flavor," the Deacon's voice said, distorting the ancient speaker box, *"of Dryland!"*

"Come on, come on," the Nord muttered impatiently. "Get on with it . . ."

"Getting nervous, aren't you?" the child's voice chimed.

He turned and glared at the kid. "I don't *get* nervous."

But out there, the Smokers were pounding the deck with feet and fists, chanting, *"Dryland . . . Dryland . . . Dryland . . ."*

It was enough to drive the sanest man as mad as a sunbaked, thirst-crazed Berserker.

"Your face is all red," the kid was saying. Her eyes were huge, looking up at him accusingly from where she cowered by the chair on the floor. "Helen says that anyone with a face that red has had too much sun . . . or too much happy juice."

"I don't give a shit what Helen says."

"Well, I don't think you've had too much *sun.* . . ."

"That's it . . ." He slammed the gin bottle down on the liquor cabinet counter, and started toward her. "I'm gonna rip your little—"

The cabin door opened, and the Doc stepped in, trailing his wheeled cart of gas goodies. This halted the Nord.

"Almost time," the Doc said. "Something wrong?"

"No," the Nord said. "We were just talking about her friend."

"The fish-man?"

"Actually," the Nord said, "about the woman. Says her name is Helen. Wouldn't mind an afternoon with *her.*"

"What's your *other* friend's name, dear?" the Doc asked.

"He doesn't have a name," she said.

"Really," the Doc said.

"That's right. You know why?"

"Why don't you tell me, dear."

"It's so death can't find him."

The Doc glanced at the Nord; it was a ghastly look, even for the Doc.

"He doesn't have a home, either," the child said, starting in babbling again. Hadn't that damn medicine worn off yet? "And he doesn't have people to care for

him, or to care *for*, either. He's not afraid of anything . . . men, least of all. And he can hear hundreds of miles underwater, and he can *see* hundreds of
miles underwater, too. . . ."

"Shut up," the Nord said, fingering the hilt of the
blade on his belt.

But the kid didn't stop; maybe she couldn't. "He
can hide in the shadow of a noon sun. He can come up
right behind you, and you won't even know it till right
before he makes you dead."

The Nord hurled the knife and it whizzed past the
child's cheek, thunking into the arm of the chair,
quivering there, beside her face.

The Doc seemed shocked. "Oh, dear," he said.

But the kid barely blinked.

"Give it a rest," the Nord advised her. He advanced
toward the child, and she shrank back, plastering
herself to the chair, making its plastic crinkle.

"He'll come back for me," she said. "He will. Wait
and see . . ."

"Yeah?" The Nord bent down and she cowered,
covering her face with a tiny protective hand.

But he reached past her to yank the knife from the
chair.

And with his face very close to hers, the Nord said,
"Well, I hope he does come for you. Gives me
something to look forward to."

The child's eyes were unblinking and clear and hard
as she said, with sudden adult power, "I'll remember
you said that."

● ● ●

Truan, leading the search for the intruder, spotted a Smoker climbing a chain, advancing toward an upper-level walkway.

"You, there!" he called up. "Identify yourself!"

But the Smoker either didn't hear him, or ignored him, and kept on clambering up the chain.

Truan frowned in thought. One of the floating corpses had been minus a vest and goggles. The intruder—who was possibly the fish-man—was very likely disguised as one of their own. . . .

Moving quickly, Truan rustled up some Smokers to check out the chain-climber, and—gathering ladders, heading upstairs—they scurried off, to cut the man off.

Only now, when Truan looked back up, there was only a dangling chain, empty, taunting him.

On an upper walkway, a Smoker was dropping to the floor, dead, his neck broken by powerful hands that had gripped him from behind. One of those powerful hands was removing, from a limp Smoker hand, a pistol.

The Mariner slipped the pistol into the pocket of the jacket and headed down a dark corridor. Footsteps echoed toward him, proclaiming more company. He looked above him, saw metal rafters, and jumped, hoisting himself up.

Right beside his head was another of those cloth-covered boxes, emitting the Deacon's nonsense: "*Look at us! We are the reason for creation!*"

Below him, at a jog, came a Smoker, a furry-faced bruiser whose eyes popped fish-eye open when the Mariner—hanging from the rafters by his legs—dropped in his path and grabbed him in a choke hold.

Pulling himself up with his legs, the Mariner also pulled the Smoker up and off the floor, a good two feet off the floor, the man's legs shaking spasmodically.

"*Dryland's not just our destination, but our destiny!*"

The attack had been so sudden, the Smoker could do little about it; even his arms were slack, as they tried to paw up after the drop-down assailant.

"*For are we not men?*" the Deacon's voice asked from the box.

The Smoker seemed to nod in agreement, but it was just one last twitch before he went flaccid and died.

"*And though I am first among men,*" the Deacon was saying, "*I fell to my knees . . .*"

The Smoker corpse, released from its choke hold above, fell to its knees.

"*'Show me the way,' I beseeched the Great Provider. 'How shall I find this place?'*"

The Mariner dropped to the floor, beside the corpse, which had flopped on its face. He got himself a few more weapons, off the body, before trotting on.

"*And the Great Provider said to me, 'A child shall lead you!'*"

•   •   •

In the Deacon's quarters, the Nord grabbed the child. She drew in a quick, terrified breath.

"Lucky you," the Nord told her, hauling her bodily toward the door. "That's your cue. . . ."

27

The Deacon, caressing the microphone stand with one hand, gesturing grandly with the other, looked out on the throng of wide-eyed rabble on the deck of the 'Deez below him, and said, "Behold—the instrument of our salvation!"

And he gestured toward the Nord, coming up the steps onto the bridge, dragging the child with him by one hand—she wasn't resisting; she was obliging enough. Only it wasn't the Nord that the Deacon had crowned instrument of their salvation, but the child.

The child who would lead them.

Holding her up like a trophy, the Nord displayed the girl to the teeming riffraff below, confirming the rumors of a captive child, and they went wild, cheering, whooping, screaming.

"Look at all those people. . . ." the child said, to no one in particular.

"They're not people, girl," the Deacon whispered, as he tugged her tunic down over her shoulders.

"They're my loyal congregation . . . and thanks to you, I own their souls again. . . ."

And the Deacon bade his blond second-in-command to display the markings on the girl's back to the cheering crowd; their cheers caught in their throat—they were stunned into awestruck silence.

"She is our guide in the wild," the Deacon intoned into his microphone. "She is our beacon in the darkness! And she has shown me the *path*!"

The Smokers below bellowed their approval, their delight, their almost orgasmic exhilaration. The Deacon nodded to the Nord to put the girl down.

"Good pilgrims all," the Deacon told them, and they quieted to hear his wisdom, "our destiny is at hand, for *this* is the day of our ascension! And before the holy moment is upon us, let us sacrifice one to the Great Provider. . . ."

The Deacon held out his hand and one of his advisers filled it with a bottle labeled "Jack Daniels." The eyes below were riveted on the Deacon as he shattered the precious bottle on the railing, spraying the child with glass shards and happy juice.

"This is the moment we've been waiting for!" the Deacon called, both hands grabbing the sky, eyes gazing upward. "*Get this tub of shit up to* speed!"

Down on the deck, Smokers yelled hallelujah and began firing their pistols into the air, the rounds blurring into one thunderous roar, and flare guns sent comets streaking up into the overcast sky. And then the deck began to empty, as the Deacon's flock ran to take their stations. . . .

Within the *'Deez*, it began raining Smokers, as the creatures began cascading down poles, coming down ladders, sliding down ropes and chains, scattering here, scattering there. The Smoker leading the intruder search, Truan, having just discovered two Smoker corpses with their necks snapped, almost got trampled.

Outside, cables began to stretch from the looming ship's bow to tugboats whose engines whined and groaned and bitched and moaned, but finally cranked over, props churning water, straining under the sheer tonnage of their burden—the biggest scow in Waterworld.

And the tugs weren't enough, the vast ship remaining motionless until through rusted-out holes from stem to stern, just above the waterline, oars extended, grabbing water.

In the lower level of the *'Deez* sat the ship's willing galley slaves, Smokers everywhere, manning, sharing, the massive oars—with the smallest and loudest of the Smokers sitting at their head, shouting at them through a conical device: "And stah—*rohhhke!*"

And stah-rohke they did, one vast human dynamo, mighty morons in perfect unison . . .

. . . as, for the first time in centuries, the *Valdez* left port.

On the bridge, the Deacon kept triumphant watch; Smokers were still streaming off deck.

Oozing satisfaction, he told the Doc, "We're moving."

The Doc frowned, puzzled. "In what direction?"

And the Deacon shrugged grandly. "I haven't the foggiest damn idea."

The Doc's frown deepened, and he snorted through his tubes. "Wha . . . ?"

"Don't worry," the Deacon said, patting his personal physician on one bony shoulder. "They'll row for a month and not figure out I'm faking it."

"But . . . ?"

"Get serious!" the Deacon said. "I'm not telling those animals we haven't figured out the map yet. But I gotta keep 'em busy till I do. Don't look at me that way! I promised 'em results, and they'll *get* results, if I have to cut that map off that damn kid's back."

The child heard this threat, but didn't react. She stood quietly beside the Nord, who held onto the chain still attached to her ankle. She was damp with happy juice, but had not been cut by the flying glass of the broken bottle.

The Deacon, glancing down at the nearly empty deck, frowned. "Who is *that*?"

One Smoker, in goggles and jacket, remained. He stood just below them and stared up, as if not aware the speech was over.

"Who *is* that?" the Deacon demanded of the Nord. Then he yelled down at the straggler Smoker. "Why aren't you *rowing*?"

The Smoker took off his goggles, and the Nord gasped, "Crabs of hell—it's him!"

The child stepped forward, beaming. "It *is* him." Then, looking from the Deacon to the Nord, she said, almost sympathetically, "Boy, are you guys in a lot of trouble. . . ."

She rushed to the railing and began to wave hello, enthusiastically; so the Deacon whacked her in the head, discouraging her, as the Nord grabbed her, pulling her back.

"I'll be damned," the Deacon said, leaning over the railing, staring down at the fish-man. "The gentleman guppy. . . ."

"All I want is the girl," the fish-man said.

The Nord whispered harshly to the Deacon: "Cut her throat. Right in front of him. Let the blood flow down on deck, at his feet. *That's* what they both deserve. . . ."

That made the Deacon smile; what a lovely notion! No wonder he kept the Nord around.

But then reality set in, and he told his second-in-command, almost sadly, "We just can't. Not till we find out where Dryland is."

"You said it yourself," the Nord said, exasperated. "Kill her and *skin* her, and you'll have your damn map!"

The child was whimpering; she was holding onto the Doc's stained off-white trousers. Apparently the Doc was as close to a sympathetic figure as she could find.

"No, no, no," the Deacon said. "She's become a symbol to my congregation. You don't butcher a religious artifact, I'm afraid." He patted the Nord's shoulder. "I did like it in *theory*, though."

From below came the fish-man's demand: "Well? Give me the girl! Copy the map off her back, first—I don't care! But just set us adrift and we'll call it even."

"Even, he says," the Deacon said softly, to himself more than anyone. Then he called down to the fish-man: "I always thought you were stupid, my fine fishy friend. But I underestimated you—you're a complete imbecile! You could give my Smokers idiocy lessons. . . ."

"I want the girl. That's all."

The Deacon leaned over the railing and the veins in his face popped as he practically screamed: "And what on this screwed-up Waterworld of ours makes you think I'm gonna give her to you?"

The fish-man pulled a flare from the Smoker jacket and popped it alight. He held the glowing stick in front of him—and right over the shaft where, not long ago, a hose had been used to refuel the seaplane.

The refueling shaft connected to the ship's oil supply, overseen by the Deacon's human depth gauge. They might have been running low on fuel, but there were still three refueler loads down there.

More than enough to blow the *'Deez* and everyone on it to burned bloody rubble.

"You know where this leads," the fish-man said,

holding the spark-fizzing flare right over the opening. "I drop it, and you burn."

From behind the Deacon came the doctor's pitiful voice: "We *all* burn. . . ."

The Deacon merely smiled down at the fish-man. "Let's not do anything . . . *rash*, here. I mean, are you sure she's worth all this trouble?"

The child was openly frightened now. She was moving back into the shadows. "He'll do it," she was saying. "He'll *do* it. . . ."

"I mean, do you *really* want this kid?" the Deacon asked him, reasonably enough. "After all, she *never* shuts up!"

"I've noticed," the fish-man granted.

"So what is it, the map? You had her long enough to copy it a hundred times!"

"She's my friend."

The Deacon threw his hands in the air. "Well, Provider preserve us while a tear rolls down my saintly cheek! You're gonna *die* for this little friend of yours? And kill *her*, too, doing it?"

The fish-man shrugged. "If it comes to that."

The Nord was clutching the railing, glaring down at the man who held out the glowing flare over the hole. "He's bluffing . . ."

"He's not bluffing," the child's voice chimed. "He *never* bluffs."

"Shut up!" the Deacon said, raising a hand to slap the child, only she was out of range. Then he returned to the railing, and he spoke down in that reasonable tone again. "I don't think you're gonna drop that torch down that hole, my friend."

"And why is that?"

"Because you may be stupid," the Deacon said, "but you're not crazy."

The fish-man locked eyes with the Deacon. A tiny grin appeared on the man's face, and that grin told the Deacon that he surely was, as the child had indicated, in a lot of trouble. . . .

"You shoulda smiled when you said that," the fish-man said.

And he opened his hand, the flare tumbled out, and down, into the shaft, on its way to the oil.

28

The Deacon's anguished cry—"*Noooooooo!*"—was an unnecessary alarm bell: his Smoker advisers were already scrambling through a doorway off the bridge. His eyes caught the child—plastered to the wall—but she was no longer a priority.

Survival was.

The Nord had not flown, nor had a pair of the Deacon's most trusted guards; but they were standing there, stupidly, frozen by what they'd just witnessed.

"Don't just stand there!" the Deacon shouted. "*Kill* him!"

Down on the deck, the Mariner was taking off running, and the Nord—the pair of Smokers trailing him—stormed down the bridge steps after him.

The Deacon's mind was whirling; where can you take cover on a ship about to explode?

And his eyes landed on the spot where the child had been plastered to the wall, but she was gone. Probably slipped through that same doorway his trusted advisers had flown through. . . .

Meanwhile, tumbling down the calibrated shaft, bouncing off its sides with metallic thunks, traveled the glowing, fiery flare, rickety-rattling down its long, deep path, where it finally splashed into the lake of oil, where on his raft, the Deacon's human depth gauge sat, biding his time.

The depth gauge looked toward the sound of the splash and saw a wall of flame grow before him; then more flames raced across the iridescent blackness toward him, a sudden death on its way to embrace him.

He smiled, having just enough time to cherish his deliverance.

"Provider be thanked," he said.

And a storm of flame exploded around him, burning him to a glowing human ember, ending his suffering as it sparked new suffering, igniting a larger explosion that sent a fireball shattering through a rotten bulkhead. Rumbling, roaring explosions began in the bowels of the ship, and began working their way up, as fire and destruction shook the *'Deez*.

The ship's volunteer galley slaves were already working up a sweat at their massive oars. One was about to turn to the other to ask, "Is it getting hot in here? Or is it just me?" when the floor ruptured beneath them, and flames rose and swallowed them, followed by more flames spewing through the oar holes in the hull. It was as if hell had burst. . . .

And, yes, it was hot in there.

The Deacon was fleeing down a corridor, the floor beneath him shaking. He could hear distant explosions, but each one seemed closer. His whole ship was shuddering with repeated blasts.

He almost bumped into his faithful pilot, his eyes wild, his battered pilot's cap on crooked, his breath heaving.

The Deacon caught him by the arm. "Now, where are *you* off to?"

"Deacon, this tub is exploding! We gotta get outa here!"

"We? I take it you're issuing an invitation . . ."

The pilot nodded frantically. "There's room for two . . ."

The Deacon nodded, said, "And only two," and withdrew a pistol from under his flowing robes and shot the pilot point-blank. An explosion below seemed to echo the gunshot as the pilot dropped, open-eyed, openmouthed, to the metal floor.

The Deacon kicked the corpse aside and moved on.

His floating castle was doomed, and his idiot army was dying. But he already had a new plan: the Deacon was nothing if not resourceful, and he had an unceasing belief in the possibility of a better tomorrow. That was how he had raised himself up from among the rabble of the pirate gangs of Waterworld.

He had a way out—he was one of only two men on the ship who could pilot the scout seaplane; and the other was dead.

But before he made his way back to the deck, and the refueled seaplane, he needed to find something he had carelessly misplaced.

His map. His human map. . . .

Truan, his search party diminished to a pair of Smokers, his mission in tatters, one floor down from the deck of the ship, moved down a corridor, gun in hand, the floor beneath him quavering from explosions.

"That fish freak did this!" he shouted to the two men following him. "What I'd give for a *shot* at that bastard!"

And then, as if the Great Provider had answered Truan, a figure dropped through a hatchway roughly sawed in the deck above, and landed hard on the floor, just as Truan and his pair of Smokers rounded the corridor corner.

The figure wore a Smoker patrol vest, but he was no Smoker: it was the intruder.

The fish-man.

And suddenly Truan had more than just one shot at the bastard—he unloaded his pistol in a wild barrage that pinged and zinged at the metal floor and walls.

But the shots weren't enough, because none of them struck their target.

Truan was calming himself to aim better when the

intruder swung around a shotgun and blasted Truan, sending the insides of him outside, some on the walls, some spraying the Smokers behind him; and then another shotgun blast rocked the two Smokers back, spraying the walls with their own insides.

The Mariner, seeing the Nord and the pair of Smokers coming down the metal stairs from the bridge to pursue him onto the deck, had ducked down the rough-sawn hatchway. After blowing away the trio of Smokers, he ran on, cutting from the corridor down a walkway.

He needed to stay just below deck; his goal was to get back up there, up onto the bridge, where he could search for the child. She wasn't down below—there was nothing down there but fire and continuing explosions.

Smoke was seeping up through rust holes in the floor. He rounded a corner, stopping short at a yawning hole that suddenly ended the corridor—and all the corridors below it. Several Smokers on the other side of the hole were trying to leap it, and were hurtling themselves down, screaming, into flames licking up.

Reluctantly, he backtracked, and took stairs down to a walkway that was already taking him deeper into the recesses of the dying ship than he cared to hazard. Enola was up there—and, crabs of hell, here he was, forced to go *down*. . . .

As the Mariner jogged along a walkway, a Smoker from above, clutching on to one strand of a dangling pulley chain, swung himself onto the landing, right in the Mariner's path.

The Mariner thrust the shotgun up and pointed it in the ugly face like a pistol, and squeezed the trigger. . . .

The click of the gun reminded him that he'd used both barrels, back there.

Amused, relieved, the Smoker grinned. There were holes in the grin, and the Mariner put in some new ones, slamming the nose of the barrel into the man's face and shoving him back, over the railing, where a pain-racked scream started loud, then gradually diminished, as the body fell into the hell below.

Footsteps clattered behind him, and the Mariner whirled, slamming the butt of the shotgun into another Smoker face, sending the bones of his nose on a fatal ride into little-used brain matter. The Smoker fell dead, and as another flock of the barbarians came rushing down the walkway toward him, firing handguns, sending bullets whinging and whanging around him, the Mariner tossed the empty shotgun toward them, in hopes of tripping at least one of them up, and yanked a pistol from under his vest, returning fire.

The pulley chain dangled nearby.

Well, it had worked before. . . .

He leapt for one strand of it, clung to it, the pulley taking him down as the shots whizzed by his head. Then a shotgun blast—which if it had hit him would no doubt have cut him in two—instead blasted a chain link apart.

His lifeline went limp and went twirling downward as he leapt to the other strand of pulley chain, and it took him down. But he knew the ride was temporary, because before long the snapped strand would work through the pulley wheel and drop him to hell and gone.

He swung on it, trying to maneuver himself over a wider walkway two floors below where he could drop with relative safety; but just as he swung over the walkway, the bright yellow eyes of a rumbling beast came bearing down upon him.

The Nord, with a pair of Smokers tagging along, had dropped through the hatchway in pursuit of the fish-man and ran toward the sound of shotgun blasts, arriving too late: the fish-man was gone, and Truan and two other Smokers lay like so much bloody debris.

He followed the logical path the fish-man would have taken, and wound up at the same gaping hole where the corridor now came to a new, abrupt end. Gunfire below indicated the fish-man may have gone down, in order to work his way back up to search for the child. . . .

Then the Nord had an idea (a capacity that separated him from your run-of-the-mill Smoker).

He gathered his two men and headed down to where his master's chariot sat awaiting a man with initiative.

I've always wanted to drive that monster, he thought, and grinned.

And soon, gathering enough stray Smokers to get behind it and push, he was popping the clutch, savoring the roar of the engine lurching to life, and rumbling off to go fishing for fish-man, by Deacon-mobile.

The Mariner had seen land boats before, but only dead ones—rusty, seaweed-draped relics in the dead cities he explored.

This land boat—with the crazily smiling Nord hunkered over its wheel, behind his curved glass windscreen window—was very much alive, its engine thundering, and the Mariner, on his pulley chain, was unintentionally swinging directly into its path.

Then the pulley chain ran out, catching up with its bullet-severed self, and swung the Mariner up and just over the nose of the massive land boat, the beast missing him by inches. Then the now-slack chain deposited the Mariner in an unceremonious pile on the metal floor, even as the car spun around, ready to make another pass at him.

Its metal wheels threw brilliant sparks in all directions as the great machine with the Nord at its wheel came bearing down ominously on him. A Smoker in the seat beside the Nord was standing on that seat, aiming a rifle at the Mariner.

The Mariner, on his feet now, raised his pistol and fired first, the bullet piercing the glass windscreen as well as the Smoker's chest. The Smoker's bloody body flopped onto the Nord, who was already struggling to see through the spiderwebbed windscreen, and the land boat weaved and careened.

The Mariner rolled out of its path as the vehicle slammed into a metal support beam, the Nord's head bouncing hard off the wheel.

The Mariner took off running.

He did not see the Nord crawl from the land boat, face streaming with blood; but he did hear the man's scream of rage echoing through the metal walls.

Perhaps he should have taken time to kill the bastard, but there was no time for second thoughts, barely time for first thoughts, as the Mariner scrambled up a stairway and began working his way through the maze of corridors, trying to find his way back to the bridge.

The ship was starting to shake, to tip. The few Smokers he encountered offered him no battle: they were too busy running, screaming, finding rust holes big enough to jump ship from, joining countless other Smokers who were escaping in boats or on jetskis or just swimming, or drowning, down there.

So he didn't take the time to kill any of them.

There was nothing left of this fight but the goal— the girl.

Then, there she was! Or, damn it, rather there *they* were: fifty yards away, on an open stairway, the Deacon dragging the child after him, up the steps. The Mariner didn't call out. Neither the Deacon nor the child had spotted him; he still had surprise on his side. . . .

But as he ran for them, *he* got surprised: an

explosion—just a small one, just enough to send him flying—sent him flying. He landed heavily. He got to his feet, somehow, just as a Smoker, encased in flames head to toe, went twisting, dancing, screaming by.

Well, he thought, *at least I'm not on fire. . . .*

But in a way he was, as he ran after the girl and her captor.

Enola, too, had been doing her best to find her way through the maze of dark, smoky corridors, when she'd turned a corner and walked smack into the open arms of the Deacon himself.

Now the Smoker chieftain was dragging her, taking her back out onto the bridge of the ship.

"See that?" he said, pointing to a plane on the deck, where his Smokers were running around in utter panic, jumping ship, dodging fires. "That's your salvation."

"Your ship is blowing up," Enola said. "Was that your big vision?"

He knelt beside her, slipped an arm around her. His breath was terrible from smokesticks. "Got me a new vision, darlin'. A pilgrimage for two. Me . . . you . . . and a bungalow in Dryland."

". . . What?" She didn't understand. He was a grown-up. . . .

"Oh, I know you're a little young for me," he said, standing back up, his hand clutching hers so tight she thought she'd cry. "But I'm willing to overlook it.

Nothing improper—husband and wife, with the Provider's blessing."

"You're a screwball."

"Maybe so . . . but you're gonna be seein' a *lot* of me. . . ."

And he dragged her down the steps, from the bridge onto the deck, moving through the fiery chaos toward the waiting plane.

29

The Mariner bolted onto the bridge, leaning against the harpoon gun mounted there, eyes slowly scanning the pandemonium on the deck below, as Smokers avoided the gaping steel-toothed, flame-belching holes blown here and there in the deck, trying to find their way to some sort of safety or means of escape. Many were just leaping the-hell-with-it overboard.

But amidst the frenzy was the Deacon, at the seaplane, calmly—if roughly—positioning Enola in the rear of the plane, in the gunner's seat. *Could that one-eyed bastard pilot that thing?*

Apparently the Deacon at least thought he could, because now he was getting into the cockpit and thrumming the engine alive.

But, damn! The seaplane was a million miles away, at the other end of the deck! How could the Mariner get there in time to stop him?

Then he blinked: he was *leaning* against the answer!

And what he needed was gathered for him in a supply box beside the harpoon gun station: from this, he grabbed a harpoon shaft, tied heavy line to the end of it, and loaded up the big weapon.

He was just about to aim the weapon down toward the deck when he heard a voice behind him: "You shoulda bought me that drink, Dirt Man."

The Mariner turned and there he was: the Nord, long blond hair dripping with blood, his face streaked scarlet and smudged with soot, his eyes glittering maniacally, his grin as self-satisfied as it was deranged.

And in the hand of one outstretched and amazingly steady arm was a pistol.

In half an eye blink, the Mariner swung the huge harpoon gun around and discharged a weapon that could have easily slain a whalephin.

And yet the Nord's gun blasted away, firing again and again . . .

. . . but it was only the reflexive action, the convulsive twitching, of a hand no longer in communication with a dead man's brain. The harpoon had slammed through the Nord's forearm, on through his chest, pinning him to the bulkhead like a wriggling fly with a mean child's pin through it.

"Nothing's free in Waterworld," the Mariner advised the wide-eyed dead man, as he placed a foot on the Nord's chest for leverage and yanked the harpoon free.

Down on the deck, the seaplane was wheeling

300

around for takeoff. The Mariner's eyes—not ordinary eyes—focused on the deck down near the bow. What could he use? *What could he use?* Then he smiled.

The Mariner loaded up the harpoon and fired it across the length of the ship. Line trailing after it, it thwacked into the deck, catching purchase a few yards from the bow, near the seaplane's launching ramp. The harpoon, and its line, stretched way out ahead of the plane, which was making its way down the runway of the deck toward that ramp, just beginning to pick up speed.

The Mariner yanked the harpoon line taut and tied it off on the rail of the bridge. From the open supply box by the harpoon station, he took an iron bar, thinking *This will have to do*, and he climbed over the rail, slipping the iron bar over the line, then holding onto either side of the bar.

And he jumped.

Sliding down the stretched line, streaking over the deck, the Mariner did his best to outrace the seaplane, its tails up, trying to take off.

The Deacon, at the controls, was cursing at the sight of the Mariner as the seaplane headed for the curved launch ramp, building speed, building speed, building speed. . . .

But then the plane began slowing down, as if its wheels were caught in mud. The Mariner grinned as he coasted along his line: *the scalding deck was melting the rubber of the plane tires!*

The Mariner, ahead of the plane by a nose now, let go and landed nimbly on the deck, where he gathered up the pile of old tailhook cable he'd spotted from the bridge. Working fast, handling the heavy steel cable as easily as if it were featherweight, the Mariner looped the free end around a stanchion, yanking it taut, so that it stretched out like a leg hoping to trip up an unwary walker.

The plane's landing gear slammed into the cable, shearing off both wheels with a pain-inducing metallic screeching scream, sending the seaplane skidding on its belly up the launching ramp, where it teetered . . .

. . . and fell, upside down, off the end of the ramp, crashing into the bow—not a devastating crash, just a damaging one, landing on its side, snapping a wing, engine crushed, permanently grounding the plane.

From behind the stanchion where he'd crouched, the Mariner emerged on the run. The go-juice in that plane could turn it into a fireball in moments; he had to get the child out of there. And if she'd been badly injured in the crash, or killed, he'd face a lifetime of sleepless nights . . . even though he knew death for the child was preferable to life with that Smoker madman . . .

. . . who was slumped over the wheel, bloody, unconscious, perhaps dead. What was more important was the cargo in back: the child, groggy, frightened, *but alive*, and as the Mariner pulled her out of the wreckage, her dark, lovely, soot-smudged face blos-

302

somed into a dazzling smile. Lifting her out in his arms, he deposited her on the deck.

"Can you walk?" he asked her.

"I can *run!*" she said, smiling.

But he knew there was nothing to smile about. The ship was coming apart around them, deck heaving, explosions below deck—not that *far* below deck— rocking the ship. He took her hand and was looking toward the bridge, trying to formulate his next plan, when he heard the awful voice.

"If I can't have Dryland," the Deacon said, "you think I'm gonna let some walking catfish have it?"

The Smoker commander had a flare gun in one hand, pointed right at the Mariner, and at the child whose hand the Mariner held. Burnt, his clothes in tatters, his face streaked with red, the Deacon rose from the rubble of the plane, keeping his aim steady.

"We all die together, friend," the Deacon said. "That's the deal. You'll join my congregation in hell. . . ."

The Mariner was thinking *Maybe I can jump him before he fires that thing* when somebody beat them both to the punch, as a bottle filled with oil, stuffed with a fiery rag, came hurtling from the sky like a bizarre hailstone and slammed into the deck almost at the Deacon's feet, exploding in a small but very satisfying manner, tossing the Deacon on his ass, his flare shot streaking off harmlessly wild as he went sprawling backward.

Astounded and relieved, the Mariner and the child looked up to the sky, to see what god had dropped this gift.

And there, sailing above the deck of the *'Deez* like a lovely apparition, was Old Gregor's balloon!

But this was a fortified version, a new, bigger, battle-ready basket with metal sheeting protecting both the basket and the underside of the balloon itself. Over the bullet-proof armor plating peeked three welcome familiar faces: Gregor, Helen, and the atoll Enforcer, who had another bottle bomb in hand, ready to light it.

Normally the Mariner liked solving his own problems, but he decided to make an exception this time. . . .

"Enola!" Helen called. It was a greeting, and an affirmation, as the woman dropped a line over the side.

Before they could grab hold, a massive blast erupted, a flower of fire blooming up midway through the deck, cutting the ship in two, making it jackknife, its two ends rising up as if to meet each other.

And suddenly, the half of the deck the Mariner, Enola, and the Deacon (who had gotten dazedly to his feet, after the bottle bomb smoke cleared) found themselves on had turned into a gigantic slide, all three of them slipping, tumbling down toward the edge of the torn-apart deck, and an endless fall into the water.

The Mariner grabbed the dangling line. "Enola!"

The child, skidding by, latched onto his waist.

And the Deacon completed the chain, grabbing on to Enola's leg.

"I'm gonna rip your cute little *lungs* out," the Deacon yelled at her.

"You talk too much," she shouted, and reared back her free foot and slammed her heel into the Deacon's left eye, his bad eye, his goggle-covered eye, the lens shattering, the Deacon howling.

And letting go.

He went sliding down the deck and dropped off the edge, and it took a long time before he splashed.

With Enola clutching his waist, the Mariner climbed the dangling rope, leaving the deck behind; bullets were whizzing around them, bullets pinging off the metal siding of the armored balloon they were heading for. A Smoker, riding the bridge of the ship as it began its inevitable voyage to the bottom of the sea, was firing up at the climbing figures, and the balloon they climbed toward.

The Enforcer dropped a bottle bomb down, onto the deck, and the Smoker stopped firing, and did what every good Smoker should do, in the Mariner's view: he lay there, a dead flaming moron, smoking.

The Mariner, with Helen's help, half climbed, half got pulled, into the basket, bringing Enola along with him, to the safety of the armor-plated nest.

• • •

It took more than a plane crash, a few explosions, and a long drop into the drink to kill the Deacon. Drawing power from how pissed-off he was, the Deacon swam away from his burning ship, and when he got a safe distance away, began treading water.

And swearing. "Crabs of hell," he muttered, splashing. "I'll tear that fish-man's head off and shit down . . ."

A motor roared up, water splashed him, as a Smoker on a jetski pulled up next to him.

"Your Deaconship!" the loyal Smoker shouted, extending a hand as his jetski idled. "Climb on back!"

"Thank you!" the Deacon said, accepting the hand, getting on back. "These things burn more go-juice with two aboard, don't they?"

"Yes, sir!"

The Deacon jerked the Smoker's pistol from his belt and shot him in the back of the head.

"That's what I thought," the Deacon said, pushing the corpse off the jetski with another splash. "But thanks for the ride, just the same . . . I really mean it. . . ."

A shadow crossed him, and he looked up, and there the damn thing was: the balloon! He swung the pistol up and started blasting away, shouting every obscenity he knew and coining a few new ones. . . .

When the bullets rose up to them, zinging against the metal plating, everyone within the armor-plated basket ducked reflexively.

"Don't worry," Gregor said. "We can't be harmed."

That was when a bullet severed a line, throwing the balloon off kilter, the basket tipping suddenly, throwing the child off balance.

"Noooo!" Helen cried, reaching out for the girl, as was the Mariner; but it was too late.

Enola had slipped over the side, and she plummeted helplessly, eyes wide, not even venturing a scream before she plopped into the water, and the sound was less a splash than a gulp, as if the sea had swallowed her.

And below, the Deacon—astride his idling jetski—grinned at the sky, waving his pistol in triumph. "Hole in one!" he cried. "Hole in one!"

He paused, waiting to see if the child would surface—and she did, sputtering, flailing at the water.

Then he gunned the engine, even as he waved other Smokers on jetskis to join him. His troops were greatly reduced, but a trio of Smokers, each from various vantage points around the sinking hulk of his ship, came angling toward him; they too gunned their engines, this hardy handful of Smoker survivors, eager to join their chieftain on his rebuilding mission.

The Deacon drew a machete from a scabbard on the jetski and carved at the air with it, laughing at the sport of it; he'd lop her head off, and drag the map of her corpse along with him.

Seeing their leader pull a weapon, the Smokers—coming from their various angles, converging on the child, who was treading water now—filled their hands with their bulky patchwork pistols.

From four directions, the trio of Smokers and their glorious lord closed in on the tiny, bobbing target.

Above, the Mariner was reeling in the bullet-snapped line, but not to repair it: he was leaving such efforts to the Enforcer, who was doing his best to keep the floating basket from breaking apart. And Old Gregor was restraining a nearly hysterical Helen, who wanted to dive in after the child, which was not a good plan.

But the Mariner had a good plan—anyway, a better one than Helen. As he pulled the line quickly in, he relished the flexible consistency of it—it wasn't rope, but something very precious in Waterworld: rubber.

In seconds that seemed like minutes, he had reeled it in and had reached its bullet-severed tip; then he bent and tied the end of the line around his ankles.

"What are you—" the Enforcer began.

But the woman knew. Helen knew. She smiled tightly and nodded, and he nodded, too, affirming their bond, and in as graceful a swan dive as Waterworld had ever seen, he plunged from the basket and into the sky, the rubber line trailing after him like an eel in close pursuit.

The child, treading water skillfully, was staring in terror at the jetskis closing in on her, howling closer.

The Mariner yelled, "Enola!"

And she glanced up as he dipped down and caught her by the arms, and he had just a split second to give the Deacon one last hard look before the rubber line recoiled, snapping the Mariner and his precious catch back into the sky.

Right before he collided with the other three jetskis, the Deacon had a final vision: his own death.

He raised his arms, shaking a protest at the sky, but it didn't last long. Not as long as the explosion, and the orange and red and blue fireball that cannoned into the sky, narrowly missing the hovering balloon, into the basket of which the Mariner and Enola were being hauled in over the side by the Enforcer and Helen, respectively.

Helen wrapped the child in her arms and held her very close; joyous tears rolled down the woman's cheeks as she hugged Enola, and as she gazed with a look of profound thanks at the one who had saved the child.

And who himself felt an odd surge of emotion, as he witnessed this reunion between virtual mother and daughter.

Enola turned to look back at the Mariner. "I was swimming!"

He nodded, smiled. "I noticed."

Then they watched as, below, the stern of the broken ship gurgled beneath the surface. Soon nothing was left of the Deacon's once-grand empire except floating debris, some of it mechanical, some of it human, none of it functioning.

And before long, stars bright overhead, leading the

309

way, the balloon sailed, but not toward New Oasis. Everyone was asleep—Helen and Enola secure in each other's arms; Gregor flat on his back, snoring; the Enforcer curled up like a big baby, dreaming peacefully. Everyone was asleep but the Mariner, that is.

He was steering.

He had set a course, based upon a certain map. . . .

30

Several days later, food supplies running low, but buoyed by increasingly pleasant weather, the little group in the armor-plated balloon drifted into heavy cloud cover. The Mariner, steering, guided the air boat down, and as the balloon emerged from the clouds, a tropical mirage displayed itself before them.

Only it was not a mirage.

It was an island . . . not an atoll . . . but land, dry land.

Dryland.

The island was mostly a mountain, but it wasn't a stony, lifeless peak, not at all. This mist-hazed wonder glimmered with green, all shades of green, more shades of green than he ever knew existed—seaweed wasn't like *this*!

And there was a beach, a glowing white sand beach, and trees lined the beach, so many trees, so many kinds of trees, more trees than any picture in any magazine or book he'd ever seen. . . .

And yet there was, to the Mariner, something unsettling about the paradise they'd found, unfolding before him. The others—Gregor, Enola, Helen, even the hard-bitten Enforcer (and never mind how tired they were from the journey, and no matter how haggard they might have looked or felt)—were mesmerized.

No whoops of joy. No "land ho!" as sailors were said to say, in the ancient land days. No tears. Not even smiles.

These were the faces of sailors come home from the sea.

But the sailor who'd brought them here, even as he drank in the splendor of the shimmering vista before him, knew that his home *was* the sea. . . .

Water cascaded over rocks into a pool. It was magnificent; the Mariner's mind reeled, but his feet felt unsure on this . . . this . . . *earth*.

Old Gregor knelt at the pool, scooping up water in his cupped hands, feeling it stream through his fingers as he tasted it.

"Fresh!" he shouted, over the music of the falling water. "All of this—*fresh*!"

From a ways up the mountainside, the Enforcer called down: "I've found something!"

And with Helen in the lead, Enola trailing after, they moved up the hillside, through vegetation, under the shade of trees whose leaves extended like great green knife blades. But green wasn't the only color—

there were leaves of red, and orange, so bright it was like staring at the sun.

Gregor looked back at the Mariner, who was bringing up the rear. "Have you noticed?" the old man asked, gesturing to the ground. "It doesn't *move*!"

"I've noticed," the Mariner said, his every step tentative. He tried to fight down a wave of nausea.

Then, as they were moving into a clearing, a thundering shook the ground, and the Mariner—startled—leaned on a tree to keep his balance. And then—crabs of hell!—a herd of four-legged beasts, with wild eyes and flowing manes and torsos rippling with muscle and veins, galloped by, creating a cloud . . . a cloud of *earth*!

Such a sight.

"Horses!" Helen shouted, joyfully.

The Mariner let out a breath, slowly, and pushed off the tree and began walking again, head spinning.

"Look there!" Helen called.

Off to one side was a gathering of structures, yellow-brown dwellings that were formed from . . . what? Dried-out leaves?

"Huts," Helen identified them. "This is what was known as a 'village'. . . ."

And moving quickly, excitedly, she headed for the huts, Enola on her heels. But as the woman and child stood taking in the marvel of this place, it was Gregor and the Enforcer who first entered the central hut.

Then Helen and Enola followed after them.

313

But the Mariner had no interest. Something else had caught his eye, something half hidden in the weeds.

A boat. Barely more than a canoe, but with outrigger fittings.

The feeling of unease abating, he headed toward it, walking, then damn near running. . . .

Helen, with Enola at her side, entered the thatched hut, curious to see what Old Gregor and the Enforcer had found.

But what they had found was death: a pair of skeletons, entwined as if lovers had died in each other's arms, the bones disease-blackened. On a simple table nearby were many objects, but one arrested Helen's attention: a paper with a map on it . . . identical to the markings on Enola's back.

"They . . . they must have known they were dying," Gregor said, his tone hushed, respectful.

"We should put them under the dirt," the Enforcer said. "I have heard that that was their way, the land people."

"It was," Helen affirmed. She was watching the child taking in this terrible yet peaceful tableau.

Enola did not cry. She merely walked to the table, where Helen thought the girl would examine the map; but instead Enola popped open a small carved-wood box.

And when the lid opened, something within the box made a wonderful sound: music.

The tune the box played was a familiar one.

It was Enola's song, the song she sang to the wind.

"I'm home," the child said, quietly.

Helen looked toward Gregor; his eyes, like her eyes, were brimming with tears. He nodded to Helen, as if to say, *We're all home.*

Then Helen frowned; someone was missing.

"Where's the Mariner?" she asked.

"Who?" Gregor replied.

"That's what we call him," Enola explained.

But Helen was already rushing from the hut.

She found him, where she knew she would, where she feared she would, on the beach. He was pushing a small boat across the sand, toward the blue of the sea.

"I don't understand," she said.

Mildly surprised, he turned and gazed at her expressionlessly. "What don't you understand?"

"You brought us here. You belong here as much as any of us." She shrugged. "Maybe more. . . ."

But he said nothing; he began pushing the little boat across the sand again.

She followed, but didn't help him. "What are you looking for? What do you think you can *find* out there?"

He stopped, looked at her, then out at the glistening water. "Gregor once said that there might be others like me, somewhere."

"Oh . . ."

He bestowed a smile on her. "If I run across others like you . . . others with hope, and courage . . .

315

I'll tell them about this place. And how one woman found it."

She held back the tears. "We found it together."

He nodded. "Yes, we did."

She didn't know what else to say. "Don't go until we can help you. You might as well stock up on hydro, and supplies. How often is it you run into a place like this?"

"Once in a lifetime," he said.

Parading onto the beach with various supplies they'd gathered came Helen, Gregor, and the Enforcer. The Mariner had lived alone for longer than he could remember; he was surprised by the feeling of warmth these people spawned in him.

But Enola was not helping. She was sitting on a log, staring out to sea, her expression morose. It was as close to pouting as he had ever seen her come.

He padded across the sand to her and said, "For the first time in your life, you have nothing to say?"

She said nothing, didn't look at him.

"Sing that song of yours," he said.

"You hate that song."

"I like it when you sing it."

She still didn't look up at him, so he knelt down beside her, closer.

"Enola . . ." He touched her arm. ". . . I have to go now."

Now she looked at him, and the big blue eyes were clouded with tears. "But—you came *back* for me!"

"Of course I did," he said. "You're my friend."

And she threw herself in his arms, and the tears flowed.

"Why . . . why are you . . . *leaving* us?"

He patted her back. "Because I don't belong here." He eased her away, looked at her hard, but gently. With his head, he gestured toward the sea. "I belong out there."

"You belong *here*."

"No," he said softly. "It's too . . . strange, here. It doesn't move under my feet."

The child's voice was nearly desperate. "Helen says it's just land sickness. It'll go away soon!"

The emotion that passed through him, in a wave, was worse than the nausea. How strange! How terrible! How wonderful. . . .

"For me . . . it's more than that," he said.

The child's lower lip trembled. "I . . . I can't change your mind, can I?"

"No."

She stood and revealed something she'd had tucked behind her back. It was a small wooden box with odd, lovely carvings. She popped open the lid and music played. A tune.

Her tune.

"Take this gift," she said. "And think of me."

Then she kissed him and ran away, in tears, toward the village.

The Mariner made his way to the little boat, where Helen was waiting. Gregor and the Enforcer walked

317

up; the old inventor was lugging a sack over his shoulder.

"What have you got there?" Gregor asked, nodding toward the music box.

"It's mine," the Mariner said, sounding more defensive than he'd meant to. "Enola gave it to me. . . ."

"I'm sure she did," Gregor said, his kindly face wrinkling into a smile as he laid a gentle hand on the Mariner's shoulder. "I have something for you, too."

The old man swung the sack around from his shoulder and it plopped heavily on the sand, at the Mariner's feet.

"It's dirt," Gregor said, and then loaded it into the boat. "Don't trade it all in one place . . . or maybe I should encourage you to barter it freely. That way you'll sooner have a reason to come back and visit us."

The Enforcer stepped forward and extended his hand, awkwardly. "It's all I have to offer, drifter."

"It's enough," the Mariner said, and the two shook hands, eyes locking, in the bond of warriors who have survived battles together.

Gregor nodded to the Enforcer—implying that Helen and the Mariner might want some privacy— and the two men walked off the beach, toward the village.

The Mariner continued packing the supplies his friends had so generously gathered, while Helen stood, watching.

"Is it that easy for you?" she asked.

"What?"

"To just drift away?"

He swallowed, loaded up a clay villager's jug, filled with clear hydro. "I never said it was easy."

"I . . . I have something for you, too. Something you may need on your journey. . . ."

These gifts were making him uneasy.

"I'd feel better," he said, "if I had something to offer as barter. . . ."

"No. This is free."

"There's nothing free in—"

She said, "Let this be a first."

His eyes locked on hers.

"It's a name," she said.

And she gave it to him.

"I . . . I have something for you," he said.

"I said I didn't need barter. . . ."

"It's free. It's a gift."

And very gently, very tenderly, he kissed her.

From the mountaintop where they'd moved through trees to a clearing near a cliff edge, they watched him, Helen and Enola, hand in hand, watching as in the distance his boat made its way across the shimmer of blue, into the mist, the boat becoming smaller and smaller, swallowed by the endless expanse of ocean.

Even after he'd disappeared, the woman and child stood, watching, holding hands.

"That name," Enola said. "Where'd you get it from?"

"An old, old story, about a great warrior who returned from battle."

"An old story?"

"Yes."

"Tell me, Helen. Tell me the story."

And Helen did, and when she had finished, she and the child moved away from the cliff's edge, almost tripping over something, the remnants of a banner someone had once stuck in the ground, in ancient times, most likely. Next to it they could see, half hidden by dirt, a very old plaque that read: *On this spot in 1953, Hillary and Norgay first set foot on the summit of Everest.*

Then Helen took Enola's hand, and they moved into the trees, and down the mountainside, toward the village. As they went, Enola sang, but her song had changed.

"There is a boy," she sang, "lives in the wind, in the wind . . ."

EPILOGUE

. . . There is a boy, lives in the wind, his mother is the moon.

What is that, my children? What was the story Helen told the girl?

Well, the great warrior had just set sail when the water god cursed him. For ten years the warrior drifted on the seas, unable to find his way home.

Yes, it is a sad story . . . but it has a happy ending.

At last, the gods took pity on him. They called up a warm wind that blew him home—to his family. And you know what? He never left them, or his home, again.

His name?

Ulysses.

Yes, that *was the name Helen gave the Mariner.*

Did he ever return?

Oh, but my children—old Enola tires of all this talk, and that's another *story. . . .*

ABOUT THE AUTHOR

MAX ALLAN COLLINS has earned an unprecedented six Private Eye Writers of America Shamus nominations for his *Nathan Heller* historical thrillers, winning twice (*True Detective*, 1983, and *Stolen Away*, 1991). The new *Heller*, *Blood and Thunder*, is an August 1995 Dutton hardcover.

A Mystery Writers of America Edgar nominee in both fiction and nonfiction categories, Collins has been hailed as "the renaissance man of mystery fiction." His credits include four suspense novel series, film criticism, short fiction, songwriting, trading card sets, graphic novels, and occasional movie tie-in novels.

He scripted the internationally syndicated comic strip *Dick Tracy* from 1977–1993, is cocreator (with artist Terry Beatty) of the comic book feature *Ms. Tree*, and has written both the *Batman* comic book and newspaper strip. His most recent comics project is

Mike Danger for Tekno-Comix, cocreated with best-selling mystery writer Mickey Spillane.

In 1994, he wrote, directed, and executive-produced *Mommy,* a suspense film starring Patty McCormack and Jason Miller. He is also the screenwriter of *The Expert,* a 1995 HBO World Premiere film.

Collins lives in Muscatine, Iowa, with his wife, writer Barbara Collins, and their son, Nathan.